CW00659954

IRON ORACLE

MERRY RAVENELL

9 SWORDS

Iron Oracle

Copyright © 2018 by Merry Ravenell

All rights reserved.

Iron Oracle is a work of fiction. Names, characters, places, and incidents are either the product of the author's imagination or are used fictitiously. Any resemblance to actual persons, living or dead, events, or locales is entirely coincidental.

No part of this book may be reproduced in any form or by any electronic or mechanical means, including information storage and retrieval systems, without written permission from the author, except for the use of brief quotations in a book review.

For E, V, T, & S

BEFORE

My fingernails dug more red marks into his flesh, pulling up layers of skin.

His grip tightened, his tongue hot and rough against mine. The scratching, raw pain in his flesh coursed through the Bond, transmuting to pleasure as it reached me.

He was dark, hot, storming Tides. The Bond wrapped us up and smothered both of us, together.

And I wasn't afraid.

Beads of blood welled up from his skin afterwards.

"Buttercup," he pressed his index finger to one of the freshest gashes, pulled up a fingertip and the blood created a shallow stain between the ridges of his fingerprint, "you almost are cruel with those claws."

"Should I restrain myself?"

"You should try harder." His voice was husky. He pulled me back down into the blankets, lips seeking mine.

It was too easy to want him.

Now my reserve had no excuse, my hesitation pointless. I should have cast it all off and embraced everything between us, but...

"Old habits die hard," he whispered.

We had taken the vows, I knew his secrets, it was possible I knew more about him than he knew about himself, yet, I couldn't quite let go of the ledge I dangled from.

He didn't care. "You'll trust me one day, buttercup."

One day.

He was the Moon's Dark Comet, and served Her anger.

I was an Oracle, and the Balance-Keeper, the point on which light and dark turned.

Complete trust and faith were for fools.

WEED WHACKING

My first official act as Luna would be an execution. Gardenia waited in the basement.

Gabel went with me, but only to observe. The discipline of she-wolves was my concern now, and one Gabel was very glad to hand over to me. He didn't know what to do with a female who needed rough handling. It seemed unfathomable to him that females could behave just as badly as males.

Hix didn't care about handling anyone roughly, so he'd shackled Gardenia in the basement. She slumped against the concrete wall. Shackles held her hands above her head. She trembled on her knees from the burning agony of the silver bars inset on the skin-side of the leather shackles.

The leather was as much a torment as the silver. The silver prevented shifting, but (in theory) you could still chew through the shackles. The moment the silver components were (unavoidably) ingested made things so much worse.

It also provided a way for a wolf to kill themselves. A dignified option given to those who didn't need to be kept around for questioning or spectacle, but for whom death was still a certainty.

Hix had given Gardenia the option of ending her life herself, at her choosing. How appropriately Hix.

Gardenia had apparently not realized the severity of her situation.

Her skin was translucent and blue-tinged, her eyes haloed in purple darkness, bruises forming on tender flesh as the silver poison caused tiny capillaries and blood vessels to rupture.

What a damn waste.

She could have been so much more. Even now she was still full of fight, and wouldn't quit, even with silver eating away at her cardiovascular system and poisoning her brain.

Her gaze moved to Gabel, then back to me.

"This is the end," I told her.

She looked at Gabel again. This time she didn't look away.

Gabel said nothing.

Gardenia believed she could have had Gabel. She believed she had been denied.

"It's over," I repeated.

She tore her gaze away from Gabel. She hissed like a pit viper.

In a weird way, I admired her. Flint had been right about the courage of females: a male would have broken by now and probably gobbled down that silver (or at least been begging for forgiveness), but not Gardenia. I understood. I'd fought the Bond and punished my body just to punish Gabel. It hadn't mattered how much it'd hurt. It had mattered that it *had* hurt, and it had been a pain of my own choosing, and no one else's.

But I hadn't been willing to die for any of it. Death was the ultimate price for a failed grasp at power, and I wouldn't have accepted failure. I also hadn't intended to succeed.

Gardenia? She had failed.

She could have amassed her own power and prestige without trying to siphon it off a male. I had even offered her prestige on a platter if she'd played along with the decoy story. Not good enough for her.

"I gave you every chance," I told her. "You had the chance to help this pack by playing along with the story that you were a decoy to tease out traitors. You chose to chase power with the maw between your legs."

She hissed. "Fuck you, Luna. I know how Gabel touched me, and how his cock felt inside me."

Did she think I'd eventually believe this story? "He never touched you. He *used* you, and if you had any quality, you'd have realized he was never going to touch you, and you were just his pawn."

"That's hilarious coming from you considering he used you worst of all. Have you forgiven him now that you have him?" She giggled to herself.

I couldn't forgive Gabel for what he'd done. I may have taken the vows, but everything that had happened in the beginning still sat uneasily within me. "I will never forgive him."

She curled her lips at me. "And I'll make sure you think about it all the damn time."

"Good luck with that. You won't be here. You're a rabid bitch and too dangerous to let live."

Her eyes narrowed, and the blue tinge under them deepened as her pulse increased and her blood pressure shot up, causing the leaky vessels to deteriorate faster. "You can't execute me. I'm pregnant."

A smack of shock and horror hit me. The last thing I wanted to deal with was Platinum's little pup-spawn. She'd make a lot of noise about it having been sired by Gabel, or Hix, or Flint, or whatever other male's name seemed most advantageous at the time.

Then I composed myself. I was Luna now, and this was IronMoon, so I needed to set the tone on this sort of nonsense. "So what? You think I want your little pup-spawn around?"

"You wouldn't execute a pregnant female." She managed to toss her head even though the motion rattled her shackles.

No, I probably wouldn't, but she wasn't pregnant. "How stupid do you think I am? You aren't pregnant. All that silver would have caused a miscarriage."

Silver attacked our brains and cardiovascular systems. Placentas dissolved, and the bleeding began within hours, but the pup was usually dead before then. The silver passed through the cord from the mother. Very occasionally an older, larger pup close to term could survive if the exposure was small, and the pup was delivered promptly.

Gardenia hadn't gotten a fatal dose of silver from the shackles, but she was bruising. If there had been a pregnancy it should have been smeared everywhere by now.

She scowled at me and hissed a third time.

I turned and walked to the large, floor-to-ceiling cabinets lining the wall under the stairs. One contained cleaning supplies. The others contained implements that caused a shudder to go through my system.

The Moon saw none of this. Oh, She was aware of what transpired down here in this bleach-white hell, but She didn't care.

I chose a leather collar, thick and sturdy, with large silver plates sewn all along on the inside. Many of the things in the cabinets had some horrific arcane purpose, but this item was straightforward. Unlike restraint collars with small plates, or the spiked collars Gabel had used on the runners, this one's leather was fully lined with silver plates.

Gabel watched Gardenia without sympathy or even

moving, seeming not to breathe. Sensing my gaze, he turned his head towards me, ocean eyes calm.

The stiff leather of the collar pressed into my palms. I could just have Gabel do it with swift, practiced claws. He expected me to ask him.

This was between the bitch and I, and I was the Luna of IronMoon.

I'd prove to myself I could do this.

"I'll never grovel to you," Gardenia spat at me.

"Didn't I tell you we're past that now? You seem to think it's just another punishment for you to endure, another pack going to throw you out, and you'll go somewhere else, like you always have."

She snarled, lips curling with a feral grin. "There are opportunities out there."

I stepped over the shallow lip into the basin of the holding pen. She tugged against her shackles, the silver burning into her wrists and she hissed as her skin burned. I told her, "This isn't your punishment. This is your execution."

Her blue eyes widened in horror. She yanked at the chains again. "You—you—"

I sprang forward and smashed my knee into her face. Her head snapped back and bashed into the concrete wall. Blood splattered me and the white wall from her broken nose, and she slumped, dazed, against her chains. I hooked the collar around the back of her neck, and quickly slid the end through the buckle, tightening it to a snug, gagging squeeze as she clawed out of her fog. Blood gushed out of her mouth and nose, staining my hands and wrists, splattering my dress further.

The silver plates met the soft skin of her neck and sizzled. She jerked and thrashed, then gagged once.

I stepped out of her reach.

Her hands tried to claw at the collar but the shackles only allowed enough slack for her fingertips to scratch at the leather.

I forced myself to watch her flailing. "This is how you die. Alone. No one knowing. No one caring. No announcement. No decree. No public reckoning. No spectacle. Just this collar and nothing else. I'll tell Cook in private once you're dead."

She screeched, "You can't do this!"

For Gardenia there couldn't be a worse punishment than dying alone and powerless, robbed of even the ability to scream obscenities and lies as she died. Alone, forgotten, the pack not asking nor caring... that was punishment for any wolf. Even her. Especially her.

She screeched again, fingertips scratching at the latigo, tears bubbling out of her eyes, and the bruising spreading in a blue spiderweb as the stress collapsed more of her blood vessels.

In her weakened state the larger silver plates of the collar would cause fatal bleeding soon. She'd be in a fog within half an hour, and dead within a day at most. She wouldn't be aware for most of it. Some might say she deserved to suffer horribly, but suffering would have given her a leather strap to bite down on, a chain to throw herself again. Simply being stopped, without an audience was the real punishment for her.

"He'll never love you. He'll always think of me," she gasped.

The cold, cruel resolve within me didn't hesitate or second guess or even pay her any mind.

Gabel turned and went to the steps.

I gave Gardenia one last, distant look.

So this was how it ended for her: trying to scratch at the collar, her gaze pleading with Gabel's back to turn around, acknowledge her, stop me.

I followed Gabel up the stairs, and didn't look back.

"Buttercup." Gabel came into my workroom. "What are you doing here?"

I looked up from my place slumped against the wall by the windows. "Sitting."

He crouched down next to me, elbows on his knees.

I had done it, without hesitation, feeling, or remorse. My hands hadn't even had the decency to shake. I had a sore spot on my knee from where I had broken her nose, and I didn't care. She was probably down there right now, the Hounds on their way for her, and I didn't care.

I cared that I didn't care.

Gabel said, "You didn't flinch when it counted, buttercup."

I hated Gardenia. She was ruin encased in flesh, and I was still crying. "Don't tell me it gets easier, Gabel."

"I've never found it difficult, so I won't say that. You did what had to be done."

"It's that it had to be done at all! That stupid bloodsucker!"

"Is that what's upsetting you?"

"I don't know. Maybe it's that I didn't hesitate."

"This is a good thing."

"And we still have her mess to deal with," I said bitterly, and I looked away from him.

"She's gone now," Gabel pointed out.

Yes, yes she was. Her memory would linger for a few years, a weapon too powerful for our enemies to resist. Gabel of Iron-Moon, the wolf who killed those who broke promises, had himself engaged in some unthinkable discretion with Gardenia.

It would have been better if he actually had. Because then it'd be the truth. Simple. Clean. Easy to understand. No one would ever believe the truth. The truth was worse.

He swore to me he'd never touched her. I could imagine how he might have lured her with looks, the force of his presence, the sound of his voice, whatever words he'd used to convince Gardenia there was something, *something* there, all the while his goal being to goad me into a jealous rage.

Just to prove to me he could. Just to feel the Bond punish him so he could refuse to obey.

"You should have just fucked her," I said.

Gabel asked, "Would it make you feel better if you thought I'd done it out of lust?"

"Lust beats petty malevolence. That petty malevolence will haunt me, us, and this pack for the rest of our lives. The truth is so much worse than the lie everyone half-believes."

Gabel cocked his head to the side. "It's a little late to hate me, buttercup. But you can be aggravated as long as you like. You are Luna now. You have won."

A stupid, pointless fight I hadn't been able to prevent from going to this final conclusion. "No comment on how I should just be able to deal with it, Gabel?"

"You did deal with it."

"And it was a stupid reason to spill blood."

"Stupid is one of the best reasons. There is too much stupid."

"Then I should cut off your balls for causing it."

"Check and mate, buttercup. But I learned the error of my ways. She kept right on with her doomed ambitions."

Good point.

Gabel shifted on the balls of his feet. "Gardenia no longer merits thought, not that she ever merited much at all. But what does merit thought is I have not heard from MarchMoon about their dead Alpha yet."

THIS WON'T GO WELL

At our mating, Gabel had given the MarchMoon Beta two days to re-affirm loyalty or deliver a writ of war. It was now several days later.

"I will have to tell Hix to get ready," Gabel said matter-of-factly. "If they think silence will confuse the issue, they're wrong."

"It's probably just cowardice," I muttered. The March-Moon weren't going to declare loyalty, and they weren't going to declare war. "Did they surrender outright before?"

"No, had to bloody them up. More than a little. It was a good fight."

I thought back to the SpringHide Alpha, who had gasped *it's not supposed to be like this* as Gabel killed him, and the SaltPaw who had simply run away. Marcus of MarchMoon had been the MeatTaker. He'd struck his deal with Aaron of IceMaw.

Aaron claimed he could smell my lure-scent. That I smelled of the night-blooming cereus.

I had never revealed to Gabel the details of the MeatTaker vision, and the MarchMoon's disloyalty. I hadn't needed to in the end. MarchMoon had tried to abduct me when I'd gone to GleamingFang to recruit Ana.

I still hadn't told Gabel Aaron was the one pulling Marcus' strings, not that I needed to. Gabel had decided there were two prime suspects to be pulling strings: Gabel's absent father, Magnes of SableFur, or Aaron of IceMaw. Hell, they probably were *both* pulling strings.

"Reinforcements are too far away," I mused.

"Neither Aaron nor Magnes will show their hand by sending reinforcements to MarchMoon, just like neither of them helped SpringHide or Shadowless," Gabel said. "March-Moon is expendable. It's too deep into IronMoon to be useful as more than an outpost for spies. They will let it go. March-Moon has not realized this yet."

I did not want to deal with more bloodshed. I knew I would have to. The IronMoon crown would always be soaked in blood.

Gabel misread my quiet. "Buttercup, I promised I would keep our den safe."

An impossible promise to keep. He would keep it as best he could, which would be better than most.

He rose out of his crouch and looked at my wrapped lumps of obsidian. "How long?"

"Six weeks, then they have to be carved. Spring."

"But you still have the blue stone. You could use that, yes?"

"The tourmaline?" I gasped. It was wrapped in silk and on the shelf, my body still bruised and aching from the last time I had touched it. "I can't control it! Even meditating over it is dangerous."

"You think the same thing will happen again? That it will drag you to the Place Beyond the Tides?" He cocked a brow.

"I don't even know what happened the first time." I shuddered. The memories of being dragged through that glowing blue water, where I could neither breathe nor scream, bubbled up from the surface of my memory and washed over my brain.

"I researched it. It's a rare stone, but not extremely so, and hardly considered precious. Don't you think if it was dangerous you'd have been told?"

"Maybe not. Maybe we weren't told about powerful but dangerous things. Temptation. Anita warned me against using the Balance rune too."

He frowned. "I find that foolish logic. Like humans who believe if they do not tell their children about sex, they will not have sex. Plenty of babies to show for that idea."

"Please, Gabel, I don't want to touch it again." My brain tumbled around as if it were back there, and the Moon's Eye opened and closed, and those endless dark stairs.

Creases on his face formed, deepened a bit. "I'm only asking if you still have it. I was here in this room when you woke, remember? But if the need were great enough, would I have to ask?"

"If you think the MarchMoon are worth it, think again."

"Of course they are not. I didn't want you to waste yourself on that petitioner wolf months ago, I would not ask you to waste yourself on them again for my sake. I will simply deal with them myself. Where is the stone?"

I got to my feet, and reluctantly pointed to the shelf. "I was thinking of putting it out in the yard as a demented garden gnome."

"May I?"

There was no reason he couldn't touch it. I figured I'd have it carved into some kind of statue. It would probably be very beautiful decorating the koi pond. Eventually. Where it had taken me still quivered under my awareness, ready to leap out and scare the shit out of me all over again.

He flipped back the silk and cradled the tourmaline in his large hands.

It seemed to clutch light within its sea-and-blue depths.

I turned away.

"I could look at it for hours," Gabel said.

"Bad idea. I know what happens if you gaze at it for ten minutes."

"If it's of no further use to you, may I have it?"

"What would a male want with it?"

"It reminds me of you."

"Now you are talking crazy."

He chuckled. "It reminds me of you. Let me have it for my office."

"Keep it if you like, but be careful with the thing." I didn't trust it. The way it held light, the shifting blues and greens... no. No trust at all.

"I enjoy dangerous things, but you know that."

"There is no escape or rescue from where it took me. Haven't you learned not to toy with the Moon?"

"I am male, buttercup, and the Moon grants us nothing but bone and claw for use on this earth. I'm sure this thing is harmless to the likes of me." He tossed the silk back onto the shelf, but tucked the blue stone under his arm. "It's lovely. Perhaps it would make a beautiful crown for you."

The MarchMoon's silence didn't break before dusk. Gabel told Hix to choose a team and go south.

"Be wary of an ambush," Gabel warned him. It was a long trip to MarchMoon, and plenty of time for the MarchMoon to make sure a careless IronMoon party would meet with an... accident.

Arms folded across his chest, Hix grunted and nodded once. His shirt obscured the gash still healing on his torso. He and Gabel were still scabbed and raw from earlier injuries. Hopefully the First Beta was as hale as he claimed to be.

As if he sensed my worry, Hix gave me a stern look. Well, couldn't he just pass for a grouchy school marm.

Gabel went on, "Bring them to heel. No abuse of females or pups. No pillaging. They are IronMoon. They are just..."

"Naughty." I supplied the word Gabel was looking for.

"They are more than naughty," Gabel growled.

"They are also IronMoon."

Gabel's face twitched, but he told Hix, "Go as far as needed with the males. Kill them all if you have to. Gianna will have to decide what to do with the females and pups."

My mouth dried up. Not even a Luna for a week. First Platinum's execution, now this. It was my place, and what I had agreed to, but...

Hix grunted again.

I wanted to tell him to be careful, but he wouldn't appreciate it. He'd be as careful as the MarchMoon allowed. I wished he and Gabel would value their flesh a bit more.

"Buttercup," Gabel whispered against my neck as Hix left to prepare, "should I be jealous?"

"Of what?"

"That you worry after our First Beta so." He nipped my skin.

I sighed.

"I think you are a little too fond of him."

"Does victory leave you bored?"

He chuckled. "I just wanted you to admit you notice he's alive."

"I'd certainly notice if he were dead. Dead things smell and decompose. I also wouldn't have a training partner."

The Bond shone like the twinkle of stars, laughing and quivering with amusement. Gabel turned me around. "You know I don't approve of you training."

"In case you haven't noticed, I need it. Or do you think kneeing Gardenia's face so effectively was something I know by instinct?"

"And what about pups?" he asked. "We might not know until it is too late."

"Then what's the line?" I retorted, frustrated. I needed to be have some physical skills. I was a Luna. Every Luna, unless she was very old or infirm, needed to be able to do a little bit on her own, and recent events had unfolded like they had because I could at least handle myself for thirty seconds in a fight.

Gabel's concern was also valid.

"I know Flint crossed it," Gabel said.

"Oh, come on, that wasn't typical," I scoffed. "Hix barely hits me. I hurt my knuckles worse punching him than he ever does to me. He hates sparring with me. Maybe if you watched, you'd see that—"

"You clearly have no idea how difficult it is for a male to watch that sort of thing," Gabel growled.

"It's just training."

"It is another male leaving marks. It doesn't matter, buttercup. It's instinct."

"Well, you're smart. Get over it, Gabel. I'm in a lot more danger day to day being Luna of IronMoon than unknowingly having a pup in my belly while I spar."

He grumbled, "How can you even negotiate the safety of unborn pups."

"How many times have I needed to use my teeth and claws since getting here?" I retorted. He was right, but so was I. Six months of instruction wasn't going to make me a warrior, but it did make me more than a soft, squishy target.

"We'll figure this out a little later. There has to be a middle ground."

"We'll make one if there isn't."

Before midnight, Hix left with his team. He had a breakfast date with the MarchMoon.

WE STILL HADN'T HEARD from him by dinner the next day, and I told Gabel, "He hasn't called."

"Are you always so nervous when a warrior goes to do his job?" Gabel asked with annoyance.

"Yes." Before it had been my father, and that had been frightening enough. Now the weight of the entire pack pressed on me, and the awful question of what would happen if things went badly. A lot of eyes would turn towards us for leadership and a solution, and I, frankly, wouldn't have either.

I hadn't been trained to rule.

Gabel sighed tolerantly. "Buttercup."

"You aren't nervous?"

"These things either take no time, or a good deal of time. I guess the MarchMoon put up a fight."

He meant full-scale rebellion. Gabel's lack of concern grated, but he did have more experience with this than I did. Still, Aaron's threat about Gabel not knowing how to hold on to what he had echoed in my head. Gabel could conquer, but could he hold on to what he won?

Gabel's phone rang a few hours before dawn.

The MarchMoon had been half-ready for them, but in the oddest way possible. The IronMoon hadn't found themselves trying to suppress a full-scale revolt. MarchMoon itself had been in revolt.

Part of the pack refused to fight and wanted nothing to do with Marcus' betrayal. The other half were loyal to Marcus. Chaos tore everything apart while Hix had tried to figure out who was the enemy and who wasn't. At first Hix had thought it was a clever trick, and he'd be double-crossed, but realized soon enough MarchMoon was in genuine splinters.

"A pack divided at least two ways," he told Gabel. The best he'd been able to figure out was to fight those who attacked, and leave everyone else alone, except that *had* resulted in some back-stabbing. The IronMoon forces had overwhelmed everyone, and rounded up any runners, and only now did he feel like he had the situation corralled.

"We are still going through houses now," he added. "But it seems the guilty expected us. The pack is in tatters and shock. You are needed here, Alpha. It is not my place to make sense of this."

ACCUSATIONS, STATED AND IMPLIED

We arrived in the early afternoon at the center of MarchMoon: a single story farmhouse in the middle of a cleared field. It had once been a working farm, but now the fields were thick and overgrown under the blanket of snow.

The house had taken damage, with broken windows, the front door splintered, a hole in the siding. Blood on the snow, the mud, the house timbers.

Hix greeted us. A new gash split his cheek, and his skin had a faint pallor. He moved stiffly around his mid-section and I belatedly remembered the wolf still had stitches in his belly from the revolt in IronMoon.

Hix glared at me, then at Gabel. "She shouldn't be here, Alpha. Your enemies will catch word your Luna comes to battlefields. You are fully capable of punishing females."

"Do not tell me what *I* should do, First Beta," Gabel growled.

Hix stood his ground. "She should not be here. She needs to be safe. This is not safe."

Gabel snarled at Hix. Hix looked down and placed his

hands behind his back, shifting his weight between his feet, but smelled of resentment and anger.

"Show us where they are," Gabel commanded.

Hix took us around the back of the house where a group of three dozen or so MarchMoon waited. About half of them were prisoners, bloody and roughed up and bound, a mix of males and females.

"The females of rank," Hix explained. "A mix of loyal, confused, and rebellious. The rabid ones are tied up."

One of the bound ones spat in his direction and growled a challenge at him. Hix gave her a tolerant look, clearly unimpressed at her absurdity.

"Come on, big boy," she growled at him. "Big IronMoon Beta afraid of a little female?"

"I tied you up for your safety," Hix replied.

She snapped her teeth. She snarled, squirming like a snake in her silver-laced bonds. Just enough silver twisted in the rope to prevent her from shifting, but from the snarling, it seemed she might be able to generate enough fury to overcome the silver.

"Keep an eye on that one," I told Hix. "Enraged females can overpower silver."

"Really." Hix looked at the female with newfound respect. "I would like to see that."

"Keep picking a fight with her and maybe she will," I said dryly. "Who is the highest ranked female here?"

"That old matron. Marcus was a bachelor."

"And the pups?" I asked.

"Elsewhere. Safe," Hix assured me. "I'll fetch them if you wish, Luna, but I didn't see any reason that they should witness this."

"There's none, I just wanted to make sure they were safe." It would also make the females less frantic. My first concern would have been for my babies, and to hell with any wolf who tried to tell me different.

Gabel selected the male with the most prestige. With Hix having killed his MarchMoon counterparts the next in line seemed to be this older male about my father's age.

The male snarled at Gabel.

Gabel kneed him in the kidneys. The male crumbled into the snow, chuffing and coughing.

Gabel said, "If you're going to stage a rebellion, best to have the whole pack on board with it, mutt."

The wolf wrestled himself upright and snarled at Gabel. "Fuck you."

"This explains why we didn't get a writ of war, my Luna." Gabel kicked the male away from him. The wolf howled in pain and tumbled into the snow. "The rebels didn't want their own pack to stop them. Traitorous from both ends."

The wolf shuddered on the snow but still managed to spit at Gabel.

Gabel snarled and grabbed the wolf by his shoulder, his left hand extending and darkening with oily fur. Bones in the wolf's shoulder creaked and blood spurted around Gabel's claws. The wolf shrieked in sudden, startled pain.

Gabel slashed his claws across the wolf's throat.

Blood exploded outwards in a thin horizontal curtain. Gabel released the body, and the wolf fell forward into the snow, gurgling and his blood steaming, congealing in the icy cold.

I licked my lips and swallowed the nauseated lump in my throat. The bound female scooted back a bit and re-evaluated her situation.

Gabel's partially-shifted claws melted into something more human. His eyes swept the males again, identifying the next male of prestige with the instinct males had for such things, and approached him. He bent down and shoved his face in the male's face, weighing him, then pulled back in disgust. "This one knows nothing I care about. Just takes orders."

"Perhaps you should not have killed that one?" I nodded to the dead one.

"He spit at you, buttercup." Gabel stepped over the dead body, his bare feet stained red from the blood.

I was not having a good first week as Luna. "He spit in my general direction."

Gabel cricked his neck in response. "Intolerable insolence. These males have nothing of value. That leaves the females, my Luna. Will you question them, or shall they just be killed to save us time?"

I resisted the urge to bite my lip. This was what I'd signed on for when I'd agreed to take the vows, although I hadn't had so much of a choice in that either. Blood and bone were the reality of being an IronMoon.

I surveyed the females, looking for some sign or clue that some of them knew something useful. Gabel wouldn't force me to kill them, but that wouldn't be necessary. If there were enough loyal females, I could leave the traitors to their tender justice.

My attention fell on the old matron. Hix had brought her a little stool, so she didn't have to sit in the snow. He was a civilized sort of monster.

She stared up at me with an unimpressed, unwavering gaze. Reminded me of Anita, smug and oh so serene, like her age gave her immunity against respecting rank and prestige. Her pack was in tatters, her Alpha had betrayed his Lord, and now her pack and home were about to be razed, and she stared at me like somehow she was exempt from caring?

Deep inside a dark, angry part of me, I growled. "We know

Alpha Marcus had betrayed Lord-Alpha Gabel. Who is he working with? Who else is involved?"

Interrogation was not my strong suit.

She didn't reply.

"Why did he order my abduction in GleamingFang three weeks ago?" I pressed. "He wasn't going to bring me back here to MarchMoon. Gabel's Hunters would have found me within days and butchered you all. Where was I supposed to go? Was I going to be delivered to someone?"

The whole abduction attempt had been so half-assed that I believed it could have been Marcus' foolish idea, except I suspected it was Aaron, counting on Marcus to bungle it for reasons I couldn't fathom. Just to rattle Gabel? Prove he could? "How did Marcus know I had arrived in GleamingFang he had a team on me within hours?"

The old bat knew. Maybe not all of it, but there was information shifting around in her brain. She curled her lips in a tiny smile as if I were an insolent child and she didn't have humor me. I was just the little upstart Luna, and she wasn't impressed in the least. If she had hissed at me, spit at me, snarled, growled, refused, fine. But instead she acted like oh, wasn't I adorable, silly little girl.

She looked around at her cowering, bloody, and in some cases, dead, packmates and then back to me. "I'm not telling you anything, deary. What are you going to do to an old woman anyway?"

"An old wizened crone who has lost all her wisdom is useless," I growled, dark anger flowing forth from within me, seeping into my blood like a toxin. "I am your Luna, and you are a traitor. Your sagging skin isn't armor."

She chuckled at me. A delicate grandmotherly chuckle.

I smashed my fist into her face.

She fell backwards off her seat and tumbled in a heap into

the snow. Blood poured out of her nose. Her rheumy eyes rolled around a bit, up at the sky, at the world, orienting herself as everything shifted.

The dark toxin in my veins didn't let me flinch or look away. It pumped anger through my heart so I didn't waver for a moment.

She floundered on the ground. Blood steamed and froze on her face and shirt. I bent down, grabbed the stool and righted it. "First Beta, do help the old marm back to her seat."

Hix, playing the part of the gallant knight, gathered up the woman, murmuring deferences in Turkish, and half-helped, half-shoved her back onto her seat.

I waited while she pawed at her nose, remembering Gabel's patience dealing with the wolves he questioned. The defeat needed to be in her mind and in the minds of those who looked on, realizing further resistance would meet with increasing punishment. They had to see that she had done it to herself, and I only reacted with as much force as needed, and only when provoked.

Who am I to think these things?

The IronMoon Luna.

You have been watching Gabel do this too long.

I am the IronMoon Luna.

You are an Oracle.

The Moon is cruel and angry. Gabel is proof of that.

I decided to focus on what I wanted to know most, and what was most likely to lead to Aaron's name being mentioned. *I* knew who the MeatMan was, *I* knew who Marcus had been in bed with, but I needed to get someone else to say the name. "How did Marcus know about my arrival in GleamingFang?"

The crone seemed to consider the reality she might have to bow to me, which made her angry. Good. Anger didn't piss me off so much. Don't pat me on the head and tell me how adorable I am. I am your Luna, you are a traitor, and you need to realize that, you old bat.

She shifted a bit. I waited. Close now.

"I don't know," she finally said.

"You don't know? Are you sure?" I leaned forward, eying her, trying to catch her scent, weigh if she was telling the truth.

"I don't know," she muttered.

"Who ordered my abduction?" I asked.

"Alpha Marcus."

"Why?"

"Trophy hunting." She pulled her lips back over her blood-washed teeth.

"To bring me back here? You know what Gabel would have done to this pack. All of you dead in the most painful and horrible ways you can imagine, starting with the pups," I said. Someone needed to confess what had really been going on in Marcus' inner circle.

Unfortunately all those wolves might already be dead.

"I was going somewhere," I pressed. "Where? Because it wasn't here. Marcus wasn't that stupid."

She stared at me.

My brain made another connection. "In IronMoon there was a revolt. I was supposed to be kidnapped. Where was I going? Someone wanted me somewhere other than IronMoon. *Who?*"

She kept staring.

Time to take a risk. A huge one. "Aaron of IceMaw claims he can smell my lure-scent through my Mark. That's the name, isn't it? That's who Marcus was taking orders from, isn't it?"

"Oh yeah? How do you know that, *Oracle?*" the rabid she-bitch howled.

I had just explained it, but if she needed it spelled out for her, fine, so I didn't have to deal with accusations I'd violated some vow. "Aaron was at Anders' Solstice party and made it known on no uncertain terms that he wanted me for himself. He and Gabel came to blood. It's not hard to put all this together. Unless Marcus was a complete idiot and thought he could hold me captive right under Gabel's nose, in which case maybe this entire pack should be butchered for being stupid beyond redemption."

I pressed the matron with a few more questions. She had been aware of the objectives, but not the methods, and she didn't know the details. She also refused to admit that Aaron was involved at all. The more I pressed to try to get her to drop the name, the harder she fought back, with a sly, cruel smile in her eyes.

Marcus had kept the details of everything limited to his most trusted, highest-ranking wolves. They were all inconveniently dead.

Good job, Gabel.

This rabid she-bitch. The one who had called out my being an Oracle. I sidestepped over to her. She snapped at me. Hix was right that she didn't seem to be a MarchMoon, but that didn't mean she hadn't been some kind of acquisition or couch-surfer.

There had been something else in her tone when she addressed me as *Oracle* that nagged me. An accusation. If I was hearing that right it meant she knew about the petitioner wolf, and the MeatMan vision, and she'd tried to trick me into incriminating myself.

I liked her right away. Smart, fierce, tough, and clever. "Hix, I think she's your type."

"What?! No!" the she-bitch snapped.

"You could probably tame her." I needed an excuse to study the she-wolf without looking like I was aware of her veiled accusation. Who had the Petitioner Wolf been to her?

Brother? Lover? Thrall? Not mate. No chance of that. Speaking of which—where was the Petitioner Wolf? Was he dead?

Hix came forward, pulled the she-wolf up by her arms and pressed his face to her neck. The wolf shrieked and flailed, but bound and burning with silver could only sort of thump on him, which wasn't going to stop Hix.

He dropped her back into the snow. "Not my type, Luna. Perhaps Eroth's type."

"Eroth has more than he can handle already, but Ana might enjoy the competition." Eroth was Ana's favorite (but not only) toy, and Eroth was more than willing to follow her around like an obedient puppy. That was the extent of things: Ana used him, Eroth delighted in being used. Ana would probably get some perverse amusement from having to share her toys.

The she-wolf growled and curled into the snow. The other MarchMoon females looked on like her antics were normal. Perhaps she'd come to MarchMoon as a potential mate but it hadn't worked out, and she couldn't go home, so she'd remained, gnawing away at prestige.

She should have come farther north. IronMoon would have welcomed her. There was a stripe of quality that ran through her, even with her jaws latched onto my ankle.

"I don't trust her," Gabel muttered under his breath. "A spy, perhaps."

"For who?" I whispered back. "These wolves know her. She's been here a while."

"It doesn't mean she isn't a spy," Gabel murmured.

Well, true.

Gabel told some of the IronMoon warriors to sniff her to see if she was a match for them, which caused her to screech

and claw and snarl, and from the reactions of the March-
Moon, they felt no pity and weren't surprised.

"Who is your birthpack?" Gabel asked her.

She tossed her matted, stringy braid over her shoulder and
declared, proudly, "EmeraldPelt."

EmeraldPelt lived beyond SableFur's western border. The
Luna was one of Luna Adrianna of SableFur's sisters,
although I couldn't remember if she was older or younger, or
what her name was.

"Why did you come to MarchMoon? You're far, far from
home," Gabel prodded.

She growled in response.

Gabel dismissed her. "Search the house. We won't find
anything but we are here, so the attempt must be made."

A SIMPLE PEN

The exterior of the house was battered, but the interior was splinters, tatters, shards, and not much else.

"They cleaned this out." Gabel tossed a box of shredded documents aside.

"We did give him two days warning." I nudged some folders with a toe. Frost clung to surfaces. I picked up a wad of shreds and sort of eyeballed them as best I could. "This just looks like utility bills and bank statements."

"Marcus liked paper." Gabel kicked aside more shreds. "Even I've heard of thumb drives. Unless someone made off with those."

"What's there to make off with? This isn't some human cover-up, and if they were involved with human criminals, like we care."

"I care, but your point is well taken. It's not what we're after." Gabel tossed his coat onto the remains of a chair.

"What are you doing?"

His fingers stopped at the third button of his shirt. "Taking my clothes off?"

"Why?"

"So I can use my nose?" Gabel pulled off his shirt, started on his belt, stepped out of his shoes.

"I'm cold just looking at you." I shivered at the way the frosty air hit my own skin. Gabel pulled off his socks, belt, and his jeans. Then went the boxers. "Damn, Gabel."

He looked down at himself. "It's cold, buttercup. No male is impressive in cold."

"Leave it to you to make it about your cock," I sighed.

Gabel chuckled as he melted into wolf-form. The frost clung to the oily patina on his leathery skin. He crunched across the debris, nose to the ground and sniffing everything with care. Spittle dripped from his lips, steaming in the air, and I swear it had an audible hiss like acid.

Gabel's claws scratched on something. He sneezed dust out of his snout and a low growl summoned me.

A piece of something seemed squished between two other clumps of debris. I plucked it from its place. An ordinary pen. Gabel sniffed it carefully for a few long moments. His ears slicked back, and another growl rumbled in his throat. He shifted back into his human form.

"The SpringHide Alpha."

I frowned. He said it like it was an accusation. "So? Spring-Hide was the pack next door. Their Alpha having been down here doesn't mean anything. It'd be more interesting if he'd never been here."

"Exactly. He wasn't here. His scent is just on that pen." Gabel shrugged his shirt back over his shoulders.

"Okay, then Marcus went to SpringHide and pocketed the pen. We know Marcus was a traitor, and the SpringHide Alpha expected something other than what he got. I'm not even sure what you're looking for."

Gabel plucked the pen from my hands and twitched it at

mc, then put it into the pocket of his shirt. "I'm looking for who the SpringHide Alpha was expecting. Do I have a SableFur infestation, or an IceMaw infestation, or both?"

"I don't see how that pen brings you any closer to teasing it out." My knuckles ached in the cold. I looked at my hand. I had punched an old woman in the face. I shook my hand, but the lingering ache didn't get better, and the punishing cold cracked sharp pains through the joints.

Gabel's attention was elsewhere, searching the ruined walls for clues.

Hugging myself didn't help chase away the cold. "The SpringHide are dead. That pen doesn't matter."

"Everything matters."

"Gabel, dammit—" My voice cracked, but I didn't quite understand why.

"Everything, buttercup. Everything matters."

Anyone eavesdropping would think I was trying to keep Gabel somewhat contained, or that I didn't have faith in him, or I was weak. I was, in a way. I didn't want Gabel going off rampaging across the countryside on instinct. By the Moon, that was stupid.

But how accurate was a comet's impact anyway?

...how much was left of a comet when it impacted a celestial body...?

Not much.

Was there going to be anything left of me that I recognized when Gabel was done?

"So what are we going to do about the surviving MarchMoon? It's winter, their leadership is dead, this place is in ruins," I said once we got back into daylight. Gabel was already off and running towards his next kill, but his attention needed to remain here a few more minutes.

Gabel shrugged. "There is no MarchMoon. They are Iron-Moon now."

I stopped walking. "And I get no say in this?"

"Did you want one?"

"Yes! This territory is a long way from our den. How do you intend to administer it?"

"The SableFur manage."

"The SableFur have been SableFur for generations. They *want* to be SableFur." The SableFur were proud to call themselves that. A network of highly placed wolves acted as advisors and regional overseers for Alpha Magnes and Luna Adrianna. Even if a rebellion brewed, it'd just be a coup, not an attempt to splinter the pack.

Gabel raised a brow. "There is always a first generation."

I gripped his sleeve. "If you're going to do things the way SableFur does, than who are you going to have here as your proxy? IronMoon isn't flush with candidates for that job."

"Hix."

"He's the First Beta. We need him in IronMoon, not down here." That, and he clearly had some injuries that needed time and rest to heal.

"It will be good for me to have a set of eyes I trust here in the south," Gabel countered.

Hix being down here might be very disruptive to whatever the southern holdings were trying to put together (if anything), but not having him in IronMoon's heart would be a significant loss, and Eroth wasn't qualified for the job. First Betas were replacements for Alphas, but Second Betas weren't replacements for the First.

The old she-wolf's nose had stopped bleeding, but she was matted with blood and snot. The rabid one braided and re-braided a few strands of hair. The surviving males kept their gaze pinned at the snow.

"Hix," Gabel told him.

"Alpha."

"You will remain here," Gabel instructed. "The March-Moon are no more, this is IronMoon now. When you identify wolves who can be trusted to manage things return to Iron-Moon's heart. Until then I will need you to remain here and administrate this place."

Hix's dark eyes flew to me, then back to Gabel. His whole body stiffened and his spine jerked taunt. He almost protested but caught himself at the last moment. Gabel's tone left no room for misunderstanding.

"Deal with them fairly, but as harshly as they require," Gabel added.

Hix's posture didn't falter, but he wasn't pleased, and neither was I. He glanced one more time at me, waiting for me to countermand Gabel, then said, "As you wish, Alpha."

Gabel walked over to the elderly female. He hooked his finger under her chin, lifted her face so he could look at her. "Welcome to IronMoon. Obedience and loyalty are all that is expected. That is all I asked for, but it is not what I received. Remember that before you let another rebellion brew under your nose, Old Mother."

"I was born a MarchMoon, and I will die a MarchMoon." Her voice quavered.

"Then you have had ill-luck to live this long. I have cut off MarchMoon's head, and all that has survived is these withered squirming bits too timid to look at me, or too weak and broken to do anything but bare toothless gums. Welcome to Iron-Moon, Old Mother," Gabel said with a cruel smile.

The shred of fight still in her visibly fled, never to return.

"Come, buttercup. We have somewhere to be."

"SPRINGHIDE!" I exclaimed.

"We are within a few hours." Gabel's attention was elsewhere.

"Who cares about SpringHide? You need to focus on other things, not digging around in the cordial relations of neighboring Alphas. I know the concept of two Alphas being able to talk in a civil fashion is foreign to you, but it can happen," I snapped.

"Because we are here," Gabel growled, "and I want to find those damn SaltPaw."

"I don't care about SaltPaw and neither should you!"

He was far away, distant and remote, cold like the winter air. It was snowing, lightly, white flecks illuminated by the headlights.

We arrived at the eastern edge of the old SpringHide territory just before midnight. Gabel sent two of the wolves across the border into the old SaltPaw territory to scout for them.

"Gabel," I said in the darkness. Snow powdered the shoulders of his long coat.

"Buttercup."

"You know I shouldn't be here." I kept my voice low to match the night. "*We* shouldn't be here."

He looked at me as if he didn't understand what I was saying, or didn't care. Probably didn't care.

I tried again. "SaltPaw and SpringHide are just the rabbits that got away. They *aren't* important."

"Are you asking if you should start calling me Ahab?"

I didn't get the reference. "Ahab?"

"*Moby Dick*. The obsessed Captain chasing the whale that took his leg. Classic literature, buttercup."

"I'll put it on my reading list. Don't change the subject."

Gabel's attention moved to the trees. I smelled the ocean, the faint scent of salt when the breeze blew just right. The

SaltPaw were tiny and meaningless. No strategic value. Gabel had thought he'd devour them in one bite. That's all this was about. His pride.

I rubbed my sore knuckles again. I didn't want to be anywhere near Gabel's conquests, punching old women in the face, growling and snarling and menacing and trying to beat the truth out of wolves who may or may not know anything useful. This couldn't be leadership.

But was it conquest? Was it cementing a hold on territory? Was it all pieces of the same machine?

The King-Alphas of old were spoken of with a certain contempt. Admired for their greatness, but infamous for their brutality and constant fighting. Even the ones considered wise and fair rulers had also administered cruel justice, and there had rarely been any peace between the kingdoms. Any periods of stability had been flanked by periods of strife and bloodshed.

I hated that I had the stomach for this. It would have been easy to say Gabel had corrupted me, but I had seen worse in visions. The stomach for it had always been there.

There was no moon through the thick, snowing clouds, just an endless, murky dome of sky that reminded me of the Place Beyond The Tides.

Eventually the two scouting wolves returned, little balls of snow on their paws and in their ruffs. They returned to human form and quickly dressed before telling Gabel, "The SaltPaw are back, Alpha."

"Back?" I asked before Gabel could even form a word around his feral anger.

"Back, Luna. We scouted the houses, everyone seems accounted for."

Gabel snarled.

I grabbed his bicep. It was cold, it was late, it was snowing.

This had gone on long enough. He was tired, I was tired. What was he going to do? Go down there and slaughter all of SaltPaw for outsmarting him? We couldn't afford to linger here, and we weren't going to take the SaltPaw with the handful of wolves we had.

The SaltPaw weren't worth anything. Gabel had said as much before he had come down here the first time. They'd been something for the IronMoon to do. A notch on the belt. A box to tick.

"Buttercup," Gabel growled.

I growled back and yanked, dragging him back a few steps. "They aren't worth this!" I hissed. "You're just pissed because they outfoxed you and they're about to do it again. You think you aren't being played as an idiot? You *are*. This is how you play right into Aaron's hands!"

He growled at me, deep and threatening, for questioning him in front of the scouts.

"Don't growl at me like that," my voice rasped in the darkness. "I am your Luna and your Oracle and your mate and the mother of our pups and I will tell you when you're being foolish!"

He snapped his head to the side, spat out a half-bark, half-gasp of anger, and growled at the scouts to get back into the lead car.

I stayed on my side of the car, wary of his anger but unrepentant.

"Do not question me again in front of scouts," he finally growled at me.

"Don't go chasing whales and I won't have to," I retorted.

He growled, malevolent and eyes burning ocean-blue even in the faint winter-night light.

The anger and fury seared me, and I curled up against the door, glaring at him over my shoulder.

"I cannot look weak," he said.

Black, smoldering anger like lava and ash seeped under my skin, and it wasn't mine. I looked out the window, shuddering, and containing whimpers. His rage hurt, and I didn't want to fight the wall of his dark anger.

This shouldn't be happening. Weren't we past this by now?

My belly hurt. I wrapped my arms across myself and huddled up against the window, the cold burning into my skin.

A GLIMPSE

We didn't get back to IronMoon until the afternoon. Gabel and I had not said a word to each other since we had left SaltPaw, and I hadn't slept, and neither had he. He looked more haggard than he probably wanted me to tell him, with almost two days of scruff on his normally clean-shaven jaw that only drew out the circles under his eyes. I was sure I looked like roadkill. I felt like roadkill. Flat and well-jerked by summer sun.

The Bond punished us when we snarled at each other.

Flint greeted us on the front steps, gleaming with steaming sweat from training. Eroth and Ana flanked him, Ana thinking this whole greet-the-leaders when they returned silly. The Master of Arms noted each of us, then asked, "Where is First Beta Hix and the others?"

"Remaining in the south until the situation is stable," Gabel said, voice impatient and taunt.

"And the MarchMoon?"

"Dismantled. They are IronMoon now." The tightness of Gabel's voice increased.

Flint glanced at me for a cue. I twitched my head. Gabel

still seethed under that tired skin—he had not forgiven me for questioning him in front of the scouts.

Flint changed the subject. "Gardenia is dead, Luna. We have disposed of her body without ceremony."

"Is Cook still here?" I asked.

Flint nodded. "He understands she made her own end and had infinite chances at redemption."

"One chance too many," I muttered without thinking.

I was so tired. My brain shifted in a bed of sand.

Dragging myself up the stairs sapped the last of my energy. Forget the shower, forget food, I just wanted to sleep. I wearily stripped off my clothes, and even that was too much effort. I collapsed onto the bed with bra, panties, shirt and one sock still on.

"I will wake you for dinner," Gabel said.

"Where are you going?" I mumbled.

"The pack will talk if I am not present."

"Most of the pack isn't here," I reminded him. "Come to bed, Gabel."

"No. I am fine."

"You are not fine. You are exhausted and being unreasonable about SaltPaw. Come here."

"No."

I groaned. Demands wouldn't work. Gabel was flinging himself against his chains. He'd probably go obsess over the defiant SaltPaw, and he was exhausted, and that combination wouldn't end well. I tried a different tactic. "I won't sleep well if I know you're prowling around. It'll worry me."

Gabel caved as if I had sliced a blade across the back of each hamstring. "Only if you take off the rest of your clothes."

"Even right now?" I whined.

He nodded, something stubborn and anxious seeping

through the Bond. "Clothing is a shield. It is impossible to relax if one is about to jump up."

I cracked my eyes open. So that was his aversion. Not modesty, but the same thing that made these rooms have no windows. He was a lupine. Clothing might have been natural to me, but he had acquired it much later in his life. It was an armor, a guise, a different set of fur to hide the one he had worn in his youth.

"Deal," I agreed. I found the energy to squirm out of my remaining attire.

Gabel watched, and only once I was naked did he take off his own clothes and collapse next to me.

"They outsmarted me," he said, staring at the ceiling, as if he could not believe it. "They ran and hid somewhere. The whole pack."

I moved closer. "Are you more upset that they outsmarted you, or that they did it by running?"

"That an enemy would outsmart me with cowardice." Under his tired, stunned voice there was a thread of cold iron. "What did they hope to accomplish? That I would think they did not exist? Humiliate me? An enemy who is dishonorable I can understand, but not one who is a coward. Cowards submit, or run away to hide. They also don't come back. It doesn't make any sense."

I curled up against his arm and smoothed my palm across his strong chest. "You want it to make more sense than it does. Some things simply are, as illogical as they seem."

"Who would accept an Alpha that is such a coward? How do I deal with a pack who will behave like cowards? I can deal with idiots, fools, weaklings, but how do I deal with such debase cowards?" Gabel's voice rattled around in his throat with frustration.

"You don't," I said gently. "They aren't important. They're

a distraction. Aaron or Magnes are using them to distract you. Don't give the SaltPaw more attention than they're worth."

"You seem very convinced this is Aaron and not Magnes."

I tensed, remembering the tall IceMaw Alpha, and the crush of his prestige against me, and how my Mark had responded to him, slithering and warm under my skin.

Gabel gave me a very, very long look, then turned over onto his belly, and said nothing else.

A VOICE SUMMONED me out of my dreams.

It didn't wake Gabel, who slept on next to me in the dark, grey-tinted room where the air moved like water currents.

I swung my legs over the side of the bed, stood, opened the door.

No one on the other side. Gabel slept on.

Shifting blue-white light washed the hallway, moonlight shining on clear, moving water. The currents pulled, and I drifted towards Gabel's office, up the stairs, through the door. The Moon itself hung in the sky just above the trees, absorbing the whole of the massive window, and bathing the office in moonlight.

How bizarre. Gabel's window faced south.

Light and water played over the empty room, stroking and pulling my hair with a thousand familiar fingers.

No, not empty. Not quite.

Flint stood by Gabel's desk, his eyes distinctive jungle-green in the blue-silver, tattoos gleaming shadowy blue, twisting and moving in the currents. He was completely naked. The tattoos extended to the point of his hips, downward, entangled his groin, genitals, and inner thighs. The moonlight imbued light in the ends of his golden hair, moving over it as one might

fondly stroke a pet. In his hands he held the large blue tourmaline spear Gabel had claimed for himself.

The moonlight flooded the blue stone's surface. Light
brewed within its belly and illuminated Flint's hands. The
edges of his tattoos lifted off his skin to admire the glow.

His meaning was clear. I said, "No."

He offered me the spear of tourmaline.

"No," I repeated.

The Moon hung outside the window, Eye unblinking.

Flint shifted the stone to one hand, and placed the other on
my shoulder. He pushed. The weight of the Tides bent my
knees. He pressed the tourmaline between my breasts. The
rough edges dug into my skin. I could not move forward, nor
back, nor up, or evade the tourmaline's summons.

The currents pulled my resistance away, pulled my fingertips around it.

I cradled it in both hands, looking down into the illuminated depths, my resistance and fear gone, and only obedience
remaining.

~*~ *Through The Stone* ~*~

I needed to scream. I wanted to scream.

I could not scream.

*I clung to the memory that the Tides only went so deep, and that this
rushing blue hell would take me somewhere. I couldn't fall forever, I
wouldn't drown forever, and I clung to it, claws and nails digging into iron
resolve. If I never did anything else, it had to be this thing.*

Do not scream!

*My mind shrieked and screamed, pounding on my chest wall to let the
screams out, to open my mouth.*

BETWEEN

Endless, warm, liquid darkness.

      My eyes adjusted to the dim, red light captured in the liquid that suspended me. I breathed in. Warm liquid rushed over my tongue and into my lungs, but no coughing fit or even a gag came of it.

A shift within the liquid prompted a glance to the side, nudging me in that direction, until I bumped up against a filmy membrane of some kind. I reached out, touched it, saw it was laced with tiny veins flowing with red blood.

Look.

Beyond the filmy membrane was the world I knew, and a yard, and a house I knew extremely well, an overcast winter day. On the porch much of the ranked Shadowless watched a solemn conversation between two smaller groups of wolves.

"Kiery," I breathed the name of the SableFur Oracle, who stood to one side, while Gabel and Flint stood to the other. She had been Anita's replacement as SableFur's serving Oracle, and she had also been one of my teachers. Between them was... me.

On my knees, in the snow, hands behind my back.

Kiery was saying something. I shoved my whole face against the membrane.

The words are not important.

My fingers dug into the membrane, trying to puncture it and rip through it to stop whatever was happening.

It cannot be stopped.

I understood then that this was a thing that would come to pass. Something the Moon Herself would see come to be.

Whatever Future Gabel was saying to Future Me twisted our Bond. I felt the words and regret and anguish and I clung to the membrane, sobbing.

Other Me screamed and wept.

Kiery directed two SableFur warriors pull me off my knees and take me away. Long chains twisted with fangs dragged behind me, endless and impossibly long.

I stabbed and pulled and punched the membrane, but the scene did not change.

Defeated, I pled, "Why?"

Look.

The membrane shifted, rotated, and in the dark murkiness, a single vein extended from the edge of the membrane, to the other side, thick and pulsing.

The Bond. My Bond with Gabel.

A blue thread of light drifted down, draped itself across the Bond like a string, wrapped twice, then yanked tight by unseen hands.

The Bond shuddered. Each end surged with pressure but the constriction point did not budge.

** Look **

I waited for the Bond to wither from lack of blood flow, but it did not. The agony was excruciating, the Bond should have died, but the blue thread did not let it die anymore than it let it thrive.

"I don't understand," I wept to the voice.

The contents of the membrane shifted again, this time splitting into two panes. In one pane I saw Future Gabel once more speaking to Future Me. In the other pane, the blue cord suffocated the Bond.

At that moment of constriction Other Me screamed, and Other Gabel turned away, but put his hand on Flint's shoulder to brace himself against the agony.

All must believe. Even the two of you must only have faith left.

"Why?" I wept to the voice I had known my entire life and never heard in words before now.

Change from within and without. You will understand when it comes to pass. Do not fight it. Your hearts will break, the pain will be great, you will both despise Me for this, but you must each be in the place where I need you most.

"And this isn't together?"

Not in body.

I sobbed.

THE WARMTH OVERPOWERED ME, and the liquid flooded my body again.

I woke up screaming.

I flailed, screaming, sobbing, sunlight stabbing into my eyes, and rough hands grabbed me.

"What were you doing?!"

Gabel's voice.

I grabbed at him. "Gabel!"

He was shouting, almost shaking me, his fingers clamped over my biceps with fury. "I found you in here with that goddamn stone again and—"

"The Moon. She—" I stopped. Where the hell was Flint? Had Flint really been here and handed me the stone? I struggled to sit up all the way.

I was in the office, bright daylight, no moon hanging just outside. I blinked, the rush of blood and air bitterly cold, and I shuddered all over.

"This," Gabel yanked one of my bruised wrists to his lips, kissed it, "this is—"

"Shackles," I whispered. My skin was blue and purple and rubbed raw from the chains in my vision. The skin between my breasts had burn marks in the shape of the tourmaline edges where I had clutched it to me.

The spear had fallen to the side. I reached for it.

Gabel snatched it and flung it away. It smashed into the bookshelf and then to the floor, splintering the wood panels. "I am throwing that into the river!"

"No, no!" I knew he couldn't. He'd need it. I didn't know why or how, I just knew he'd need it. "You can't! I don't know why, Gabel, but you can't! I am going to be taken soon and you need it with you and—"

"Taken! Taken where?!"

"The SableFur."

"What are you talking about? Did you hit your head?" He grabbed my hair and yanked my head towards him, examining me all over for bumps and gashes. "No one is taking you anywhere! Especially not the Moon-damned SableFur! I will die before the SableFur get their hands on you!"

"You'll have to let them take me."

"The fuck I will!" He gathered me up in his arms, ignoring my resistance, got to his feet and stormed down the hallway.

"Where are you—" the rocking motion of being carried made me a little woozy, my brain sort of sloshed and a queasy feeling grabbed my stomach. Gabel's anger rose hot and thick into my nose. He kicked open the door to our room, carried me into the bathroom, and before I realized what was happening, he had stepped into the shower and cold water splattered both of us.

He set me down when my squirming and squealing convinced him I was coherent.

"This is absurd." I tried to get out of the shower. He grabbed me and didn't let go.

"Are you awake yet?" he growled.

"I was awake the moment I woke up! Gabel, I'm freezing." I shivered and my teeth chattered. Unlike the previous time, I had returned to this world with almost total clarity.

"You were gone again." He clutched me against his chest and pinned us both under the ice-cold water. "You hate that tourmaline, and I find you with it?!"

"How long was I gone?" I tried to push away from him because, dammit, the water was cold!

"Two days! You beg me to come to bed so you can sneak off to that damn stone?!"

He thought I was the one out of her mind, well, he wasn't making much sense ranting and shouting under the water and grabbing me like he was going to shake all the sense clear out of me.

"What did you ask it?" He grabbed my face in his hands. "Tell me what you asked it."

I tried to paw at his flailing, grabbing hands but it didn't work. His frantic anger made me dizzy. "I didn't ask it anything! The Moon made me."

"The Moon made you." Scorn dripped from his voice. "Bullshit the Moon made you."

"She called me to Her. So I'd know what is coming. What can't be changed."

"No," Gabel said. "No, Gianna. No. Visions of the future are what *might* happen. Not what will happen."

"Not this future. Not this one, Gabel. The SableFur will

come for me. Kiery will come with them. You'll repudiate me—"

"No!" Gabel shouted and shoved us both under the icy water again. "No! I will not!"

I squirmed out from under the water, gasping, "The Moon needs you to. The SableFur will take me with them!"

"Why?!"

"She told me for change within and without. She wants me inside SableFur, and you outside, and everyone to believe that our Bond has been broken. But it won't be. You'll speak the words, but She won't sever it. It will hurt. Everyone has to believe it. Even we have to know only on faith! It'll happen at Shadowless, very soon."

"No," Gabel snapped. "No, it won't. I won't give you up. She can't make me, Gianna. If She wants you, She'll have to do it Herself. I won't do it. She can't make me say the words!"

"She showed me so that I could tell you, so you know what we have to do."

"No!"

I clawed my way out of the shower, dripping frigid water on the floor, and shivering. The Moon had created this future and promised it would come to pass. Gabel would repudiate me as his mate and Luna when the time came.

He curled in the shower stall like a rabid Hound that no mortal dare defy. "I made those vows before Her, sworn in Her name, in Her light, and I do not break my promises. The future is never set in stone, and I refuse to play along with Her designs."

HER SERVANT

I knocked on Flint's door.

"Luna," he greeted me.

"I need to talk to you. Now." Not that I expected Flint to put me off, but on the off chance he did, no confusion.

He stepped aside and gestured for me to enter. On his coffee table was a battered-looking novel featuring a woman in a skimpy, torn dress and a rather rugged-looking bare-chested man bent over her as she swooned. Flint picked it up, dog-eared a page and set it aside. He sat down on his couch, and it was only then I noticed he wore only a plaid robe that fell just to the tops of his knees, and unlikely anything else under it, and my mind remembered the tattoos that extended to the top of his thigh. Normally they were hidden under the hem of his kilts, so intricate, glossy-blue and unreal, and I frowned, trying to remember and inadvertently staring at his lower body in the process.

"I can disrobe if there's something you want to see." Flint's voice intruded into my thoughts.

That yanked my eyes to his. The tattoos, I wanted to see those, they had lifted off his skin and wrapped through my awareness, but beyond my understanding. But that's not what I had come for. "You were in Gabel's office. That wasn't a vision. You were *there*."

He didn't blink. "Yes."

"Why?"

"I was summoned, as you were."

"Do you know what's coming?" I had never heard of a male Oracle, but given the crazy state of my life, I was willing to believe anything. Gabel was the Comet, I was Balance, I had been to weird places thanks to a tourmaline spike I had only encountered perhaps-not-by-chance.

"No. I am not an Oracle. I am only a servant."

"A servant." That meant nothing to me.

"A servant," Flint repeated. "But you know that. You've seen my tattoos. You know I am pledged to Her service."

"I didn't realize you were in so tight with Her." I finally sat down on the other end of his couch.

"Jealous?" Flint asked wryly.

"No. This is all." I gestured to my head, "This has all become more than just an ambitious male wanting to be a King and having a violent streak."

Flint half-smiled. "Did you want to know if I had been there, or if I had been part of the vision?"

"I need your help. With what I saw. Where I went. Well, I am not the one who will need your help. Gabel will. I will be on my own."

Flint titled his head to the side. "In what way?"

In my vision, I had seen Flint counsel and stand by Gabel, so it seemed reasonable to involve Flint in what I had been shown. "The Moon has created a future that will come to pass. The SableFur, through the Oracles, are going to come for me. It will happen soon. Gabel will be forced to repudiate me. When Gabel abandons me, the Moon will constrict our Bond, but won't sever it. She will keep the Bond just barely alive. Everyone except for you, I, and Gabel will believe it is dead. She told me that even Gabel and I will have to doubt, because everyone has to believe."

Flint's face carved itself into deep frown lines. "To what end?"

"I don't know. She said to cause change within and without. We have to know before it happens so we can play our parts. In the future She showed me, you were at Gabel's side. I've already told Gabel all this, and he's sworn he won't give me up, but the Moon has promised me She will force him to."

"And by extension, I am supposed to encourage him to give you up." Flint's frown deepened.

I nodded.

Flint sighed.

He didn't say anything, and the line of his strong shoulders tightened. Dumbfounded, I asked, "You won't?"

"Why would the SableFur come for you? They are insular. You're too powerful and visible a Luna for Magnes to permit his Oracles to meddle with you," Flint said.

I took a deep breath. "Magnes has a reason to destroy Gabel. A couple of reasons, but one of them is very personal."

"That being?"

"Gabel is Magnes' get."

Flint's green eyes registered shock. His whole body arched with his breath, which he held, then let out very slowly. "Are you sure?"

"I'm certain. Gabel had no idea. I know because the Moon showed me the first time I went beyond the Tides. She is very angry, furious, don't ask me to explain all of it, because I can't. Gabel is the Comet. Anita, and I think Magnes by extension, believes Gabel is the Destroyer."

"If he is truly Magnes' get, and Magnes' knows it," Flint

said slowly, "it gives Gabel a claim to the SableFur throne, and it destroys Magnes' honor. He is a mated wolf and has several other offspring. The stain will affect all of them. It can do great damage to the SableFur. The dishonor and shame of an Alpha bleeds onto the whole pack."

"Do you know anything about Gabel's mother?"

"Only that she herself had the Moon's Gift but never became an Oracle. Gabel has never told me her name. It's possible that she only gave him her wolf-name, not her human one." Flint shook his head.

In wolf-form we obviously couldn't pronounce human speech, or our common names. We had approximate translations of our names, with it understood what the name was. It was complicated, more instinctual than anything else, and I had never considered the possibility that Gabel might only know his mother's wolf-name, and might not know her common name. It might be impossible to deduce who she was by that name alone. What if he had never thought to ask her her name? Like many young children it had not originally occurred to me that my parents had names. I had been about five or six before I had curiously asked my father if he had a name.

Would a lupine even have thought to ask? Did Gabel even know her name? Or had she simply been *Mother*?

Like the pup-ring...

I was getting ahead of myself. Back on task. I asked, "Littermates?"

"Gabel never offered, and I never asked. He doesn't offer anything about his past, if you haven't noticed." Flint rocked back and wrapped his fingers around one knee. "It also isn't by chance I crossed paths with him."

IronMoon wasn't really the sort of pack where you asked

too many questions about the hows and whys. The Doctor was an excellent example of things you'd rather not know.

"Did you know he was the Comet?" I prodded.

Flint shook his head, and for the first time, I sensed him being both pensive and evasive. I had given him new information, things he didn't know, but he still had his own cards close to his chest. "What part do you play in this?"

"Anita told me that I am Balance," I said. "I—again, it's a long story."

But Flint nodded wisely, as if this bit of info made sense of other things he knew. "Balance. The one who keeps Gabel from becoming that lump of iron, and keeps the sword sharp and pointed at the proper targets. But you being taken away from him will make him very angry, and tip Balance. The future is not set in stone, Gianna. You say that yourself. The Moon cannot make him give you up, and if Gabel intends to fight, he will."

"Somehow She will force him."

"The Moon does not normally force us. Compel, yes, but force? No."

"This time She will."

Flint absorbed this, skeptical. "So Anita knows all this. She told you this."

"Not exactly. Anita believes Gabel is the Comet, and will destroy everything. But I suspect Magnes is involved too. When I went to see her before Solstice, she lectured me about Gabel being the Comet, but she was revealing pieces from someone else's vision. She doesn't know that I know Gabel is Magnes' son."

Flint nodded slowly. "And she believes Gabel is a mindless monster?"

"I think she knows deep inside he's not, but it's easier for everyone to keep thinking it. The idea of a clever Gabel is something nobody wants to consider."

Flint shifted his shoulders, causing a crackling sound as the joints cricked into place. The right half of his robe slouched a bit, exposing some of his tattoos to the light. Their gloss had intensified, as if the Moon shone on them constantly.

He was quiet too long. I said, "You don't believe me."

"No, I find it all difficult to believe. Tell me everything."

So I told him: the deal Shadowless struck with SableFur, Anita's summons, the piecemeal vision belonging to some other wolf (probably Magnes) she'd tried to pass off as her own, the rabid she-bitch in MarchMoon that claimed to be an Emerald-Pelt, and how everyone tried to prey on my unwillingness to be with Gabel, except no one wanted to actually save me.

Flint didn't fill in any blanks, and it was hard to say if it was for lack of anything to contribute, or nothing he wanted to share. His expression and scent just grew more troubled, like some old wound slowly peeling open.

When I was done talking, Flint said, "The Moon has laid it all out, and now She tightens the noose."

"Will you help?" His unwillingness seemed greater than ever.

He shifted again. "I am a servant. If you tell me that you saw me bowing to the Moon's will, then I must do this thing. But the pain of losing your mate." He shook his head to and fro, slowly, as if dazed.

"It happens," I offered tentatively. "Bonds wither, they die. Mates part ways."

"Severing a dying limb so life can go on is one thing. It's being forced to give up your mate when every instinct tells you both to stay together. I don't know what it will do to Gabel, I don't know what it will do to you, and I don't know if it's something I can watch."

Bewildered, I said, "It doesn't matter what it does to me. You have to make Gabel do it, and keep a hold of him after it's done."

"You believe it will come to pass. Gabel doesn't, he thinks he can fight it, and I believe that too."

"You were there the other night. You're the one who forced me to go to Her."

He rubbed his unshaven evening scruff, his attention somewhere else. He looked very old, and very tired, as if something had drawn all the life out of him and for a moment, I sensed some flicker of old, draining agony within him. Something familiar, something I had felt recently.

I said, softly, "Your mate is dead. You're living with a broken Bond."

Flint looked sideways at me, his eyes sparkling with a sharp warning to mind myself on delicate ground. His voice raked my skin like claws. "The Moon is asking you to live with a pain beyond imagining. You have no idea, little girl. None. It is an unspeakable pain and it never eases."

I licked my lips. "Never?"

"Never."

"Then why are you still alive?"

"Who said I was?" Flint asked me with a feral wryness that showed a shade of his torment. "I am where the Moon needs me to be. I am Her Servant. One day I have been promised I will be with her again. Just as you've been promised. But it is a cruel promise.

"It's not the daylight, it's not when your mind is occupied with work, it's not when your muscles burn from effort. The cruelty is in the quiet, still moments, when even silence sleeps, and in life it would have been just the two of you, suspended in that silence. In those moments I can still hear her, feel her, just whispers. The Bond doesn't sever. She is still here, reaching for me across the umbra, but all she can do is," he extended his hand and grazed his rough fingertips just along my cheek, "and in those moments you know everything you've lost."

"But death severs the Bond," I whispered.

He barked a laugh. "Yes, that's what they say. It's a lie. The mates are only split between the worlds. The Bond is like a spiderweb. You can walk through it, rip it, tear it, but a few tendrils stretch, stick, and linger. When it's quiet, I feel those tendrils stretched across worlds. I hear her calling me, howling my name, because where she is she is as tormented as I. She endures knowing it is the only way we will ever be together. It's a lie, Gianna, that the dead mate goes to their reward to wait in happiness for their other half to live out their life. That is why the survivors so often die. Their mate is suffering as they are."

He picked up the abused book. "I have not slept well in a very long time, and I have not slept alone for even longer." He flung it down and his jaw hardened. "I will kill, maim, and watch horrors committed in Her Name, but now She asks me to send two souls into an agony that will drive them into madness. And for what? What is so important that She must ask you to do that She dare not do Herself?"

Lacking anything to say, and stunned by what he was saying, I sank back on my haunches, hands on my knees, and tried to understand.

The Moon had promised agony. She had promised I would doubt, question, even we would have to partially believe, it all had to be this way. Sand seemed to parch my throat. I swallowed, but it didn't help.

Flint said, "I am Her Servant, and if I do not obey Her will, I will not be with my love again. But if I do Her will, I know what I'll send both of you to. You two will live as I live, as all who survive do: a Bond just barely alive, a few scant tendrils tethering you together. You think that the Moon is sparing you something because She will tie your Bond with a tourniquet and that is somehow more merciful?"

I licked my lips again. "Well, I—"

"No." Flint spoke over me, "No. She'll simulate death's touch. That is what the Bond across the worlds is like. Only mine is stretched so thin a few stubborn silk threads tether us, yours will be bound so tight that it will be compressed into a few stubborn silk threads."

It didn't matter. "We have to do this."

Flint's lips stretched over his teeth in a ghoulish grin. "It is better you don't know what you're going to. If you did, I don't think you'd be so persistent. I think you'd have Gabel fight Her."

"It has to be this way," I said. "She needs each of us in our place, and that place isn't together."

"And you saw me go with Gabel, not you."

"Yes."

Flint drew in a long, slow breath through his nose, then let it out, equally slow. "SableFur in its time and place, and if the Moon wants you in SableFur to affect changes within, we will need to give you time to do that. I will use that logic to keep Gabel focused, and the promise that one day he will be in a position to come for you, and he has to be ready when that moment comes."

"Thank you."

"*If* that moment comes," Flint amended with great meaning.

There was no guarantee Gabel and I would get things right. If things were that easy She would have shown us what to do. She was going to force this moment to come, but after that, the future unfurled like the future always did. The rest was on the mortals, and there was no guarantee that Gabel and

I would be together again in life, or even in death, if we failed. I picked at my leggings. "Don't let him obsess over the SaltPaw."

Flint nodded. "Have you told Gabel about the Comet? Balance?"

"No. Tell him if you think he needs to know."

"It is not for me to tell him these things. You are Balance, an Oracle, and his mate. If you don't have the courage to tell him the truth of things, then you do not have the courage to face what you're going to."

THE BELL

G abel was already in bed reading. "Where have you been, buttercup?"

"Talking with Flint." I closed the door behind me.

Gabel turned the page. "Did he growl at you for bothering him after-hours?"

"I am the Luna. I can cajole a little indulgence from him."

Gabel chuckled. "How bad of a mood was he in?"

With Hix in the south, Eroth not a suitable First Beta, and Donovan as predictable as a cat, Flint had become the de facto First Beta in many ways. It wasn't official, nor was it permanent, but it didn't please the Master of Arms at all.

"Grouchy."

Gabel watched as I pulled off my top and shook out my hair. Warmth pooled between us, and he set his book on the nightstand table.

"Gabel, we need to talk about something," I said, hoping to chill the moment. Or at least talk to him before he got too distracted.

"Still this? The Moon will not take you from me. She cannot make me give you up."

"She will find a way."

Gabel slid out of bed. He came over to me, gripped my face in his hands. "No."

He made it sound so simple! He pulled me back towards the blankets. "Gabel, please. It's not about that anyway—"

"It can wait. Tell me afterwards."

"After what?"

"After I remind the Moon Herself who you belong to."

I laughed. "The Moon knows!"

"Then I need to remind myself. Right now."

I was not in the mood, but telling Gabel *no* in that moment would have been unwise. He was so rattled, so feral. Even if he didn't know as I did, he knew things were spiraling out of his control.

He kissed a chain down my neck, along my throat. His hands gripped my ass, and his body swelled, trapped between us, and his scent turned feral and savage and rushed.

I pushed against him. "Slow down, Gabel. Just in case you're wrong, I want memories no one will ever exceed."

He shoved me down onto our bed. I squeaked, tumbled into the blankets, and his hands seized my calves and yanked me to the edge of the mattress. He moved over me with hands on either side of my body. I smiled at him anyway, enjoying his strong hips moving against my thighs.

He growled, "Control? You want control when I am about to tear off my own skin?"

It wasn't his skin I was worried about. "Yes."

The tip of his cock pressed against me, and I squirmed against the taunting brush of his flesh. My body moistened for him, and he kissed between my breasts, his own breath faster, harder. He rasped, "I could take you right now. Maybe I should. To remind you who you belong to, so the Moon knows I have no intention of humoring Her whims. Pleasure be damned."

I suppressed a moan. "Maybe you shouldn't punish the wrong woman, Lord-Alpha."

"That title sounds like honey dripping from your lips." He nipped my ear and purred, "Lord-Alpha. Say it again."

"Earn it."

He bit my neck, a sharp quick nip, then ducked backwards, quick as a serpent, and buried his face between my thighs. I yelped in surprise, then moaned as his tongue slid along me, slow and taunting.

He chuckled and used his fingers to spread me a bit to expose my jewel, drew his tongue around it, over it. Shocks and lashes of lightening danced over my nerves. I whimpered. Another skilled finger slid just inside me, pressed upward. I squirmed against his hand, wanting more.

His other hand looped around my thigh and pinned my hips to the bed. "Hold still."

I whined at him and bucked my hips against the restraint. His fingers clenched down like iron, and a warning nip stung the softest part of my thigh. I gasped. Fresh dampness rewarded him.

He inhaled my scent, kissed the stinging skin where he'd just bitten me, and kissed a light, breathy trail of kisses along my inner thighs while his teasing finger carved a shallow, slow path just inside me.

His tongue bathed me again and I moaned in tormented relief. Warmth spooled within me as my core ached for him. He shifted up onto one arm, the other hand still moving between my thighs. I reached up to meet his lips, and he offered me his tongue.

"Taste yourself, buttercup," he murmured.

I twisted my tongue against his, catching my scent and taste against his. A second finger slid into me, and he gripped me, the heel of his palm rubbing against my jewel while his fingers stroked my core. He looked down at me, reeking of triumph and desire, as I turned molten in his grip.

I melted around him as he replaced his fingers with his cock. He sighed against my neck, ragged and trembling. I pulled my thighs higher on his hips, drawing him deep into me.

"You are mine, buttercup," he panted raggedy as he drew back just to fill me again. "Mine, and I swore it, and I will tear the cosmos apart to be with you."

I mewled in response, trembling with starlight as he drew back once more, his cock angled *just so* it sent sweet fiery agony through my whole body.

I scratched deep gouges in his shoulders as I clung to him, dizzy on the howling between us and his body within mine. I arched up to meet his thrust. The reflection of the stinging pain on his skin throbbed along my awareness of his pleasure. He groaned.

"Again," he rasped.

"Beast," I whispered back.

"But yours. Always…yours…"

Starlight tore through my body and I cried out around my release. A moment later he met me, his body spasming within mine while he growled something I didn't understand by my ear.

We collapsed onto the blankets, sweaty, damp, and exhausted. Neither of us spoke for quite a while. I got up to rinse off. Returned to find the blankets straightened. Curled up next to him.

"Gabel," I murmured. "You need to know something."

He twisted onto his elbow and looked down at me. "What, buttercup?"

"There is more going on here than appears to be."

"You won't convince me."

"Humor me a moment."

He grumbled, "A moment."

"Do you know the old rune, the Comet?"

"No, but comets are historic symbols of destruction and divine wrath. Is this any different?"

"Not really. It's fallen out of use, I didn't know it the first time I saw it, but Flint recognized it, and Anita has seen it as well. It means the Moon's anger and wrath, something She has flung to Earth to destroy what has corrupted and angered Her. I started seeing the Comet in my visions almost as soon as I got here. One of them was the rune appearing on a hastily constructed pup-ring. It was in a battered lock box, left in the ruins of an ancient farm house."

He kept watching.

"Anita had the same vision. She doesn't know that I've also seen the ring."

"Your point?" Gabel twitched with impatience.

"You're the Comet, Gabel. The Destroyer."

Gabel frowned.

"This isn't just about Magnes," I went on very slowly. "This is about something else. You and I have—"

"a role to play? Be good little puppets?"

I tucked my lips together.

Gabel growled, "No. If She takes you from me, I will tear this world apart, build a tower from the rubble so I can crawl up to the sky and smash my claws into Her Eye. You are mine, and I will never let you go."

So much for thinking Gabel might budge a degree if he thought the Moon had a purpose. If anything, it incensed him even more. He glared at me, face darkening, rage building. "I will not be used. I will not let you be used. She can't make me, Gianna, and I've already resolved to not do Her bidding."

Then he changed the subject entirely. "GleamingFang deserves our attention right now. I don't trust Anders as far as I can throw him, but I still don't know why. In the vision, you saw him wearing multiple collars. I wonder if when you can scry again how many of those collars he'd be wearing now."

"You think many collars, many masters?"

"That's the obvious deduction, isn't it?"

"It's your vision."

Gabel's fingers pulled at the sheets as he stared at the ceiling. "Your mind is already elsewhere. You've already left."

"That isn't true! It is an old vision, from months ago, a great deal might have changed, and it's your vision. You know that! Only you can say what you think it means. I'm not putting you off, I just can't help you like you want, and I can't scry to check up on the current state of things."

"You've met Anders. You have an opinion," Gabel pressed.

Exactly three times. The first time I didn't care to remember, the second time I had been introduced and only seen him from a distance, and the third time I had other things to worry about at Solstice. I hadn't sat down and shared food with him, or any kind of conversation. "My opinion of him is I don't have an opinion."

"None." Gabel's eyes slid sideways.

"No. None. He's just... there. Another face in the crowd. But he's a powerful Alpha. GleamingFang is pretty large. Almost as big as Shadowless."

"Big in terms of territory, their population is spread out. Not so many of them. But he has never impressed you when you met him."

"No, I can't say he did," I admitted.

"Maybe that's the key," Gabel mused.

"You mean he's gutless."

"You weren't impressed, were you? You didn't sense his prestige?"

"No..."

"But what?"

"I'm not the best judge anymore."

"Oh, am I that impressive?" Gabel smirked.

I rolled my eyes.

"So you no longer sense what you used to."

"No. I guess I can only really sense those that rival you. All the others are..." I shrugged.

"That's inconvenient," Gabel said.

"I don't know, perhaps I will only perceive the ones who are the biggest threats, even if they don't appear to be?"

"You mean Aaron."

"You don't need me to tell you that."

"They're all threats."

"So kill them all," I grumbled into my pillow.

"Maybe I will," he said to the ceiling.

As IF THEY had heard our conversation, a card from Gleaming-Fang arrived the next day, affirming their loyalty to Gabel.

Gabel tore it up and flung it into the trash.

"Cowards," he diagnosed. "Anders is on whatever side won't get him disemboweled. Not willing to bleed! Dammit, buttercup. Why is it so difficult for these Alphas to understand? You fight, you bleed. You surrender when you're beaten. You honor your agreements! What do they think is going to happen? That I'm not going to come back and beat them into the ground again?! Look at all of them," he gestured to his map, "plotting and scheming, making agreements with each other."

I shifted on the couch, annoyed.

"What?" Gabel asked me.

I pursed my lips. I had sworn to myself I'd never speak of Anders, Gardenia, or that entire horrible episode again, but like a sore that just wouldn't heal, it was there again, raw and bloody.

"You're angry," Gabel stated.

"Just that of all the Alphas I don't want to ever deal with, it's Anders. It'd have been better if you had presented Gardenia to an Alpha with some courage, but you put your stupidity on display for that gutless slug. To hear you incensed at his actions just angers me given the history there."

Gabel's expression darkened.

Well, I meant it. Being humiliated in front of Anders. Even Marcus would have been better, because Marcus had had the courage to call Gabel out. The SpringHide Alpha who had been willing to die (stupidly, but, well, it was something). But Anders. Humiliated like that in front of Anders.

A knock on the door.

"What?" Gabel barked.

The warrior was young, nervous at being in the Alpha's private space, and surely bearing unwelcome information. "There is a messenger here for Luna Gianna."

Gabel's features stretched, and his biceps pulled at the seams of his shirt. "Who?"

"An- An Oracle. She is in the foyer."

An Oracle. Gabel gnashed his teeth, and stormed past the wolf.

Technically our visitor wasn't a SableFur, and she definitely wasn't an Oracle. It was a young acolyte, still a girl, maybe fifteen at best.

Gabel stared at her with appalled disgust, and she shriveled before him, cowering, head drawn between her shoulders and a submissive whine drawing out her words.

"A girl! So Anita sends a little girl to speak to the IronMoon Luna?!"

The girl managed to whimper, "O-oracle Gianna."

Every syllable she uttered incensed Gabel further. "Is that old bat delusional or has no one informed her *Oracle* Gianna is now *Luna* Gianna? Her attempt to stop our vows failed. Completely."

"Anita knows." Her voice quaked.

I put a hand on Gabel's bicep. He clenched from jaw to ankle.

The girl stumbled on. "Gianna has been charged with violation of her vows—"

I gasped in horror.

"Go home to your corrupt mistress," Gabel growled.

"K-Kiery sent me—"

Gabel's growl deepened. "And we all know who holds Kiery's leash, you stupid puppy. Get out of my territory."

I squeezed Gabel's arm harder, a sickness brewing under my heart, and I managed to just barely keep my voice from shaking. It was here. This was how it would happen. It was starting. "Gabel, she's still a kid."

"Which is why I won't send her home in pieces. How dare that withered old bitch insult you this way! Stupid pup, in a few years you won't have your youth to defend you. If you keep doing the bidding of corrupt bitches, you'll die."

The acolyte shook. Oracles were a tough breed, but Gabel's presence was overwhelming, and his dark fury had eroded all her training and toughness. She opened her mouth to say one more thing.

"Leave!" Gabel shouted.

She shrieked in terror, spun, slammed into the front door. She scrambled back, yanked it open, then bolted out into the snow.

Gabel slammed the door behind her.

"Don't say it, Gianna," he warned me. "Don't you dare say it!"

I didn't say it. I asked, "Where are you going?"

"Outside. To train. To bleed." He ripped at the button of his shirt and succeeded only in tearing a hole in the fabric. He cursed and ripped the whole thing off, threw it into the koi pond, then stormed upstairs.

This was how SableFur would come for me. Through my Oracle sisters.

Upstairs something shattered. Inside the Bond he shouted and howled at the Moon. *No! I won't! You cannot make me!*

Maybe She couldn't.

He came back from working out steaming with sweat, strips of skin peeled off his back and thighs, his lip split and a gash on his scalp stained his hair red. He growled, "So lovely to know where your true loyalties lie."

Anguish pressed fingers against my throat. "It's the Moon's will. You've fought the Moon before, so you know—"

"I know what?" he hissed.

I bit my lower lip. "You need stitches."

"Fuck stitches."

"If you have to fight the SableFur you should be in good repair."

He hissed something, and I sent for Ana.

As he sat there on our bed, bleeding, I asked, "How do your partners look?"

Gabel snorted, annoyed. "Flint is fine."

The Master of Arms was also indestructible, it seemed. What had he traded for those tattoos?

"Usually Flint doesn't spar," I commented.

"I was not allowed to play with the children today." He barred his teeth at me.

"Flint giving you a tune-up doesn't sound so bad." I didn't know what else to say, words failed me, and there wasn't anything to mollify him. His smoldering anger was dark, but frantic at the same time.

Gabel scratching and clawing and grasping frightened me.

He knew.

Would it drive him mad?

Ana flung open the door and marched in. "Well fuck, this is why Violet is always doing so much damn laundry! You fucking bleed on it. I hope you got a rubber sheet under that. Flint's got a few scratches and you look like you got into a fight with a hibachi chef. A losing fight."

Gabel glared at her. "I am not in the mood for your colorful candor."

"Just doesn't bite me. You haven't had your rabies shot." Ana was not impressed.

"Do you not remember me ripping a man's head off? Are you too stupid for that to have left an impression?"

"Gabel." I swatted his shoulder.

Ana rolled her eyes. "Sure, I remember. But self preservation and intelligence are two different things."

"You seem to lack one of them."

"Hahaha. No. I'm a female. That guy was a man. You won't touch lil' old female human me. Nope." She swaggered over to him, a twitch in her hips. "All these hips, you ain't gonna touch 'em, one way or the other!"

Gabel and I collectively had no response to that.

She grabbed his neck, pulled his head down and pawed through his hair. "Yep. There it is. Still pumping blood. I'll put a stitch or two in it and you can wash out this sexy hair dye. Strawberry blond is not your color."

Gabel turned his head enough so that one blue eye glared at me, even more annoyed with Ana man-handling him and his honor making it impossible for him to disagree with her. As Gabel had said, we couldn't be picky about certain things. A mouthy, crude human vet was a better addition than the doctor who liked to carve his name into female flesh.

"This has nothing to do with my loyalty," I told Gabel quietly. "I made my promises, Gabel."

"Yes, you did. To *me*. Dammit, Gianna. There is always a choice. Or are you still looking for an escape?"

"No!" My voice cracked. How could he accuse me of that? "Me being here, us having made those vows, doesn't that prove the Moon's power and my loyalty? I wouldn't have taken those vows if I hadn't intended to honor them."

"I know how hard you'll fight when you want to."

"That's not fair! What am I supposed to do when She breaks Her own rules?!"

"Not submit! Wouldn't be the first time. Maybe I should play along and give you what you want."

"I don't want this! I just know it's going to happen. How horrible do you have to make it?!"

"You are my mate, and you will fight at my side, not Hers!"

Ana kept her focus strictly on her work.

I chewed on my lip, tears swimming across my eyes, threatening to fall. "The Oracles have accused me of violating my vows. Do you think I'm just going to confess to a crime I didn't commit?"

"Are you?"

"No, you stupid prick!"

Gabel flinched, but it was from something else.

"Sorry," Ana said sweetly as she tugged on the thread.

In the vision I had been fighting, it was Gabel who hadn't, and had walked away. So I could say, without guilt, "I won't go quietly! Remember what Flint says about the courage of females!"

Gabel smiled a bit at me, but there was no warmth to it. "Your courage is what frightens me, buttercup."

CLINCH

The next day another messenger arrived. Yet again from SableFur, but this time one of the full-fledged Oracles: Thessa. She was the Oracle from the far south of SableFur, and from the shadows under her eyes, she'd been summoned on short notice.

Thessa was about ten years older than I was, give or take, and I had only met her a few times. She hadn't changed much, petite and curly-haired, sharp features and a keen eye taking in all of Gabel's office. She didn't have the schooled expression Kiery would have had, and it was easy to see she was surprised to see that Gabel was far more civilized than anyone cared to realize. She paid no attention to the blue tourmaline on his desk; she was more interested in the map and books.

Gabel did not stand to greet her. "What nonsense brings you here, Oracle?"

"I am here for Oracle Gianna."

"You mean *Luna* Gianna," Gabel corrected, voice having a dangerous edge that shaved a few layers off her skin and mine. "As much as Anita may have tried to prevent that from happening."

Thessa cocked her head.

I didn't buy her feigned innocence. "You didn't know? That I was in SableFur a month ago? Anita wanted me to leave Gabel."

Gabel's expression clouded. "If that old bitch is so worried about me being the Dark Comet, bringer of Destruction, she's doing a damn good job provoking my anger."

Thessa's attempt at not knowing evaporated. To me, in a clipped tone, she said, "You were not supposed to tell him. The vision was not for sharing."

I tossed my hair, in no mood to humor her. "Ah, and that is what I didn't tell Anita. I'd already had the vision of the pup-ring and the house. It was very entertaining listening to her feed me snippets of a dream I'd already had. That's how I know it wasn't her vision, it belonged to someone else."

Thessa's lips thinned. "You are to come to Shadowless in two days time to be judged for violating your vows of silence and secrecy. If you are found guilty, you will be stripped and dishonored. If your Alpha still wants you after that that is his concern."

"I have not violated any vows," I snapped.

"Very doubtful, given Alpha Gabel knew Marcus was consorting with Aaron of IceMaw," Thessa said dryly. She gave Gabel a meaningful look.

Gabel's fingers dug into the wood of his desk. "Get out."

Thessa didn't budge. "She will be expected in Shadowless in two days time to defend herself. If she doesn't show up, she will be marked guilty. It is not a crime, Alpha Gabel, in the sense she needs to be punished. It's just dishonor. The Luna of IronMoon will be a disgraced Oracle who violated her vows. If you both do not care about that, fine."

"She never violated her vows. Do you think I am such an idiot I cannot figure out for myself what it means when another male says he will stop at nothing to have my mate for himself?" Gabel growled.

"Two days. Shadowless. If you fail to appear no one will be surprised, nor will anyone really care."

Gabel's fingernails splintered the wood. "Crawl back to Anita, you corrupt bitch. Tell her that I know what this is. Tell Magnes, while you're at it. Tell him I know he's using the Oracles to pull my teeth because he doesn't have the courage to come for me himself. I'm not playing along."

"This has nothing to do with Alpha Magnes," Thessa said so dryly I actually believed her. Could Anita have crafted circumstantial evidence and moved the Oracles against me while her true motivations remained hidden?

Perhaps the Moon was even guiding her into the trap.

Gabel surged to his feet. He tore a hunk of the desk with him, and flung it off his elongated fingers. It missed Thessa's head by inches and smashed into the wall. "If it is a monster you want, SableFur, it is a monster I will give you! Shall I send you back to SableFur bone by bone?"

"Gabel," I interrupted him. "If you kill her it will just make things worse."

"I doubt the Moon will begrudge me one corrupt Oracle," Gabel snarled.

"I still have my gifts, Alpha," Thessa said, holding up her unnaturally pale forearms in demonstration. "Be careful who you call corrupt."

"And my Luna still has hers."

"If that is the case, she will be given a chance to vindicate herself."

"Oh, vindicate herself. You mean after you say she's guilty. This isn't a trial. It's an execution. Will I get your body as collateral against hers? That pale skin of yours will make a lovely canvas on which to paint."

Thessa recoiled.

Time for Thessa to go. "Leave. Or else you will go home in that little box. Gabel's temper is well... his temper."

Thessa left with haste.

"Dammit, Gianna!" Gabel shouted. "You know what Magnes is doing!"

I rubbed my head. "An idiot could see what they're doing. They're also going to win, Gabel. Unless you plan on having a disgraced Luna. If I can see it, you can!"

Gabel snarled, "Of course I do, but—"

"Gabel, the only advantage I'm going to have inside SableFur is if Magnes doesn't know I know his secrets. You can't run your damn mouth!"

"I am not letting you go. I issued that challenge to Magnes."

"He won't answer it." I rolled my eyes, frustrated. "Do you really think you'd stand any chance against the full might of SableFur?"

He tore off another piece of his desk. "You've already given up!"

"I told you I haven't, but I know I've been found guilty! They won't let me be innocent! You can't have a disgraced Luna, and you're not ready to challenge SableFur for my honor! We already know Magnes is dishonorable. How do we fight that?"

Gabel's expression was terrible. Inside, he crumbled, piece by piece, the horrible choices leaders have to make, and the even worse sacrifices, and his refusal to accept there was not a way out of this. "I don't know, buttercup. But I'm going to figure it out."

It was a very long two days. Gabel seethed, insisting that he would not be forced to give me up. He raged when I packed a bag the night before because I wanted to at least have some panties and a change of clothes.

"No!" He flung my bag against the wall. The contents spilled out. "You are not leaving! I am not giving you up!"

I picked up the clothes. Gabel hadn't come up with any solutions he had shared with me, and had only become more frazzled. He knew when he was getting backed into a corner, and I worried it would drive him insane. It had also required a few more sets of stitches since Flint let him work out the burning stress, and Flint could apparently take on anything this side of the living world, up to and including the Dark Comet.

Actually, Flint had a few scratches and gashes. Ana had stitched up the first set, but Crazy Doctor did the other.

"I made him uncomfortable," Ana had told me.

"Ana, he's made it clear he's not into you."

"I know, I know! And I was very professional, but he said he could smell it. Oh the fuck well, what can I do about that? The guy is fucking hot, and ink gets me boiling." Ana had pouted.

"Welcome to life with werewolves."

"No privacy," she had muttered.

Now I picked up a pair of panties. Gabel yanked them out of my hands and flung them away. He grabbed me, blue eyes churning and roiling, the Bond howling. "No, Gianna. I won't. She can't make me."

"You can't have a dishonored Luna," I told him. "The Gabel Romero wanted could, but not you. You know that. You've killed in the name of honor. I have to be held to at least the same standard as Marcus."

"The truth is its own defense!" he raged. "Do you want to go? Why aren't you going to fight?!"

"I'm an Oracle, and I know the Moon's will. Twice now She's taken me beyond the Tides. You and I are Her servants. We each have our part to play."

He grabbed my right wrist and raised it to his lips. The bruises were still there, dark violet and red. "I will fight this, Gianna. You are my Luna, and you are coming back with me. I will not give you up. The Moon did not hear my vows to make me give you up. That is not the way of things!"

If anyone could resist the Moon's design, it would be Her Comet. I smiled at him. Fair enough, if he succeeded in defying Her, I was not under any mandate to sabotage him. "As you say, my Alpha."

"We have a pack to run, a kingdom to build, and pups to raise." Gabel nipped the inside of my wrist, "I have no time for the Moon's divine designs."

"Even if this is the way to my crown?" I baited him gently.

Gabel didn't hesitate. "Not if it means divine handouts and giving you up. I will win our kingdom myself, and not as a prize for being the lapdog of a goddess!"

I slid my hand out of his grasp and around his neck. "Let me finish packing, Gabel."

"Packing? No—"

"It is an Oracle matter. You have to let me take my tools. It will be humiliation if I show up without them, and confirm my guilt."

He scowled. "They will know about the bowls. That will not help things, I suppose."

"I don't have to present my tools, but I have to have them just in case I'm asked. And yes, not having my bowls is a very bad thing. I will be faulted for not having protected them more carefully. Most Oracles don't have workrooms where they can safekeep their things. We are supposed to be very careful."

"You were careful."

"It will still be seen as my fault. I have to bring what I have."

Gabel growled.

"It'll only take a minute. Wait for me in the bath."

"The bath?"

I waited for him to realize what I meant.

"Oh," he said. The promise of splashing about thoroughly distracted him and dissolved his sour mood, and he went to fill the tub.

I fetched my bag of runes, the bag of RedWater fangs, and after a moment of consideration, the smaller tourmaline spear. I also took the larger chunk of obsidian.

My thumb rubbed the tip of the spear. I hadn't paid much attention to the smaller one, but yes. I'd need it where I was going. And the large chunk of obsidian, which slumbered quietly in its velvet, almost ready to be made into a bowl, full of secrets and truths to be revealed.

The rough tip of the tourmaline reminded me the Oracles couldn't punish me more than I'd tolerate. I always had the option to return to IronMoon, disgraced or not. The smear forgotten in time, and if I had been any other she-wolf, or a less prominent Luna, being a fallen Oracle would be only a little ugly blemish. My bowls would be shattered, people would assume the Moon had stripped me of Her gift, and for a while it would be disgraceful, but in time it'd fade.

But for the Luna of IronMoon, disgrace wasn't an option. Gabel styled himself as an Alpha of kept promises and honor, and a disgraced Luna could not rule at his side. He could not be seen to have benefited from a corrupt Oracle whispering forbidden knowledge to him.

I had two options: admit my guilt and atone for my sins, or to maintain my innocence and pursue vindication. For either I had to return to the oversight of a senior Oracle. If I chose vindication, it challenged those who had accused me, and I would have a limited amount of time to pass four specific tests to prove the Moon's favor. If I admitted guilt, I'd have the rest of my natural life to atone and try to regain my gifts.

Most did not choose to pursue vindication, and true vindication was rare. The Oracles were the ones who determined if the four tests had been passed—and it was in their interest to say the tests had not been passed. I'd need to expose no less than Anita's corruption, and possibly Magnes' shameful past. If I chose vindication, Anita would know I could prove myself. I had revealed to Thessa I had seen the pup-ring.

My "retraining" would be horrible. If I succeeded in vindication, I'd dismantle the SableFur from the inside... and I'd be able to throw the gates open for Gabel.

But if I chose atonement, Anita could hold me the rest of my life, saying I had not atoned enough for my sins.

If I failed in either, I'd die. Horribly. Gabel would probably die as well, and the Moon's anger would not be answered.

I tucked the tourmaline into the velvet, carried everything back downstairs and went to join Gabel in the tub.

FLINT WAS RIGHT

Shadowless had been chosen because of its proximity to the SableFur border while still being in IronMoon territory. It wasn't neutral ground, but it was the best possible compromise. There was also that small detail of Shadowless being in SableFur's pocket, but SableFur didn't know IronMoon knew that detail. Probably not many of Shadowless knew about the attempt to make off with me from my own vow-making.

When we arrived the SableFur Oracles were already there: Kiery and Thessa, plus three acolytes. A cluster of Shadowless stood around on the front porch of the house, including my father and Alpha Jermain. This had nothing to do with them, but they were just there to watch.

Well, wasn't this just cozy.

Flint had come with us to handle Gabel. The Oracles had not been expecting to see him, with his tattooed torso on display in the bitter winter cold.

Gabel clutched my hand so tightly my fingers went numb, and his fingers trembled. His teeth ground together. His ocean blue eyes were the brightest thing in the wintry world just then, too bright, almost wild.

"I have nothing to confess," I told him under my breath. "I have committed no crimes. Let me go, Gabel. You know your Luna cannot duck an accusation like this."

He pried his fingers off my hand. I gathered myself, then stepped apart from the IronMoon. I crossed the snow between us until I was right in the center. I was supposed to go all the way over to Kiery, but I refused to do that much. I knelt in the snow, but did not bow my head. "I am here."

Gabel's snarl reached me through our Bond.

Thessa scowled openly at my defiance and disrespect. Elder Oracle Kiery didn't care, and simply said, "You have violated the vow of silence, and revealed a vision to someone other than the wolf it belonged to."

I raised my voice very slightly. "I have never done such a thing."

"Alpha Gabel only knew about the MarchMoon's duplicity because you revealed their involvement with Aaron of IceMaw to him." Kiery's tone was bland, as if I were a stupid criminal to even try to talk around my guilt.

The rabid she-bitch from MarchMoon had to have played a part in this. With great care, I chose the words of my defense. "I did not ask the petitioner wolf his name, nor his pack. His question, his answer. No one else's."

"But Gabel knew he was MarchMoon."

The implied stupidity angered me. "Are you dense? Lord-Alpha Gabel demanded he reveal who he was before the petitioner met me. One does not enter the IronMoon den without giving a name and pack rank. The MarchMoon put him onto their scent by showing up at all. I never had to tell Lord-Alpha Gabel anything! It was there to be pieced together, the March-Moon offered it freely!"

Kiery was not impressed. "We do not believe that Gabel

could have put together the MarchMoon's duplicity without your help. He was too aware of their every move, too suspicious, too quick to put together evidence that we could not piece together without knowing key facts he should not have known."

"What does SableFur have to do with this?" I asked. "How do you know what the MarchMoon knew? How do you know about the vision? I have never told anyone what I saw, save the wolf who asked!"

Kiery refused to answer my challenge.

Even so, a tiny little grain of guilt twinged in my heart. I had never told Gabel anything, but my reactions to certain provocations had put him onto one scent after the other. Aaron, at Anders' party, had been one such thing. But wasn't that unavoidable? I had been Bound to him. Of course he would have sensed such things.

Kiery said, "Regardless, we are certain that you betrayed information to him in some fashion."

"No. That is not true." Guilt nettled me even a little more. There was no prohibition against Oracles taking mates, but most never did, or they traded their Oracle mantle for a family. The inherent conflict, the realization they couldn't truly, and completely, keep secrets from their mates. I pushed the prick of guilt away. I had done everything in my power to honor my vows, it wasn't even like I had chosen Gabel, dammit!

There was no evidence I could offer of my innocence without betraying my vows. I couldn't tell them Magnes was Gabel's father. That Anita had to know who Gabel's mother was, that Anita knew who Gabel was, and if they were looking for corruption, they were looking in the wrong place.

I had nothing to exonerate me.

Gabel's helpless fury clashed into my despair.

Oh, there was such a cruel irony to this! And this was how

the Moon would make it come to pass: bid Her Oracles to do this. Had She even sent them visions of what they must do and say to make things come out the way She designed?

My faith crumbled for a second. What if I had seen a lie? What if I was not the one in the right?

Tears sprang in my eyes. For a moment it was more than I could bear.

Gabel's expression was terrible. Helpless and furious, his hands limp at his sides. Flint stood at his arm, but his gaze was on me, calm and jungle-green, and in my head I heard the song, his song, calling a Queen to battle.

But my body shivered, and the Bond howled, and everything began to hurt as the moment crashed down on us, as we both knew what was about to happen, what had to happen.

"She is guilty, Alpha Gabel," Kiery said. "Whatever she revealed to you violated her vows, and the manner in which you were told is of no consequence. We take from her her Oracle rank and her honor, and leave her marked in disgrace. She broke her promises."

And that was how the SableFur applied leverage to Gabel: they used his honor against him.

Gabel exploded, "I know what this is, Oracle!"

"It is exactly what it looks like." Kiery didn't relent. "She is still your Luna and your mate. She also is an oath-breaker."

"It's not true!" I shouted without thought. "It's not true!"

Gabel lunged. Flint snared him and hauled him backwards several steps. Gabel resisted. Flint grabbed him by the back of his neck and yanked Gabel's head down to his own, lips moving and speaking something I couldn't hear.

There was no way, no hope. Gabel could fight the Sable-Fur, but he couldn't fight the Oracles. The MarchMoon. Damn them! Had it always been a trap? The SableFur knew more than they should. Was Aaron working with them after all? Or had the SableFur somehow pulled a string within MarchMoon, spinning both IceMaw and IronMoon to its use?

Gabel fought. Inside he tugged and yanked and the Bond howled, even though physically he stood, head bowed and Flint spoke to him in whispers. I shivered.

Whatever Flint said to him, I never knew, but the moment Gabel caved and bowed to the chains that would bind both of us, the pain cut through the Bond like glass, and I sobbed once.

Gabel turned back around, and it was all I could do to raise my head to meet his gaze, my eyes watering with tears, and his eyes were so bright, bright and horrible and he had been beaten.

We had been bested. We had surrendered.

And it was just glass, glass, glass, a thousand pieces of glass coursing like blood cells up and down the Bond.

Gabel's voice was not steady, the edges of it seemed to crumble around each word. "The IronMoon only ask that those among us keep their promises and honor their obligations. I cannot have a Luna who does not carry this in her heart. Gianna never told me anything, but—"

A final yank between us as Gabel flung himself against the Moon's will, the pressure, and flirted with refusing to obey, and a violent urge to rip Kiery into two pieces.

Flint grabbed his bicep and spoke low, forceful by his ear.

Gabel found his voice again, and it was more unsteady than before. "But if she somehow conveyed more meaning to me than she should have, it was her responsibility to know where such lines exist."

I crumbled inside and almost believed him. His words toppled everything inside me, and I sobbed, "No, Gabel, I—"

His words stretched tight, uneven. "You may come back to IronMoon. But... I..."

I tried to prepare myself for what was coming.

"May the Moon hear me: I repudiate you as my Luna and my Bound. I do not know you."

The pain of those words is excruciating.

Flint was right. If I had known what he knew, I would never have had the courage.

I curled over and screamed. Gabel staggered and Flint caught him. The Bond twisted, constricted, and my mind swam red, then bright, bright blue. The blue filament snapped tight around our Bond, binding it across the middle and knotted tight, and I screamed again.

Gabel was gone.

He was just gone from my awareness, part of me gone, beyond my reach, a void, and my soul fled down the Bond, chasing after phantoms.

He turned his back and walked away, limping with Flint holding him up and his knees barely worked, but I couldn't feel his pain, or his suffering, his anger, his feral rage, the burning coal that he had been in my awareness, and he was gone, and the Bond dangled in the breeze, and it was still there, but oh the Moon—

You have no idea what She's asking of you.

Instinct grabbed my throat, yanked me upright. "Gabel, no!"

It was too late, and just like in the vision, I screamed and pled, and Flint half-pulled, half-guided Gabel away.

The pain intensified, and my soul tried to squeeze through the remains of the Bond.

It ran up against the tourniquet created by the blue filament.

If the knot had not been there, I would have died, bleeding into the chasm between souls.

Flint was right: death didn't free any of us.

**You must both do this. Your hearts will break,

the pain will be great, you may both despise Me, but you must each be in the place where I need you most.**

The agony, the wrongness of it, it was too much.

Flint's bare feet appeared by my face. Two items dropped onto the snow: my chunk of obsidian, and the small canvas bag holding my bag of runes, my blue tourmaline spear and the RedWater fangs. I grabbed his ankle. "Flint—"

"You are not coming back to IronMoon," he told me, his voice a cord that pulled through my awareness.

I rolled my eyes up to him, saw the blue-gloss tattoos swimming in my vision. They curled towards me. I reached for them, shaking violently.

Vindication. I had to vindicate myself.

Vindication. Justice. Balance.

I would force the Oracles, and the SableFur, to give Gabel and I justice.

Flint grabbed my hand and pulled me back to my knees.

He leaned down to my ear and whispered, "I warned you, Gianna. It is a pain almost beyond bearing, but we must, and it will not last forever. Say your final words to Gabel and choose them well."

Tears blurred my vision. His hand squeezed my bicep so tight my fingers tingled and went numb, and his old grief sank against my skin. He knew this pain, he survived it, he fought through it for the promise of being with her again.

I grabbed his forearm, the pain in my belly so intense, my soul revolted and flailed. I wasn't guilty. I was where the Moon needed me to be, and all needed to believe: that my Bond was dead, that Gabel hated me, and that I had been wrongly accused.

My awareness swam in hot agony, lashed by wires and toxins, as the agony of the knotted Bond grew. I dug my hand into Flint's bicep, unaware that my fingers elongated and extended, nails drawing blood as fury buoyed my awareness for one last effort. "I will prove my innocence and vindicate myself. Tell Gabel he will regret this! Tell him he will regret taking the word of Oracles over his Luna! He knows my gifts are intact and that the Moon does not punish me! I choose vindication, and the Moon will grant me justice!"

Grant all of us justice.

Flint didn't respond except to release me. He turned and walked away, and I managed to not double over and groan. Feigning anger over Gabel's trust in me had taken the last of my strength, and while I managed to stay upright, I wept uncontrollably.

Flint had been right.

They were all gone.

And I was alone.

SABLEFUR: INTERLUDE

"She opted for vindication," Kiery told Magnes.

The SableFur Alpha rarely concerned himself with these matters, but the former IronMoon Luna was of special interest. "Gabel repudiated her?"

"Yes. The Bond is broken."

"Did she survive?"

"She is very sick, but alive." Kiery sounded annoyed. "She is in delirium, raving about knots and vindication."

Magnes eyed the Oracle. "Can she prove herself innocent?"

Kiery sat down despite the lack of invitation. Magnes' expression pinched a few degrees. They'd always had a difficult relationship. The SableFur Alpha and Luna would have preferred the more demure, SableFur-bred Thessa to replace Anita as the premier Oracle in the pack, not the foreign-bred, outspoken Kiery.

But Kiery was an Elder Oracle, having achieved the distinction after training an Oracle herself. The irony wasn't lost on Kiery that the Oracle she'd helped train was the very one now residing in disgrace a few hours north.

Being a young Oracle (and an even younger Elder) was a challenge Kiery didn't enjoy, especially when she had to deal with an Alpha almost old enough to be her father, over a matter that she didn't think he should be involved in at all. "Probably. Having met Gabel," Kiery pondered the SableFur Alpha for a moment, then said, "he's not the idiot everyone thinks he is. Thessa reported his office is full of books, maps, plans, antiques. Gabel also had another older wolf with them, covered in old-order runes with blue-gloss ink. Gabel heeded this wolf's counsel. My bet is that wolf advised Gabel to let Gianna go so she could clear her name."

"So you don't believe she's guilty."

Kiery bristled with aggravation but kept her tone civil. "I've *never* believed she was guilty. You asked me to defer to Anita, but I maintain this was a serious mistake. The time for the Oracles to be concerned about her was months ago."

"She's your student, wasn't she?" Magnes inquired.

There were days when she fantasized about throttling Magnes, and this was one of those days. "Anita and I both trained her, but yes, she was my first student. Gianna was devoted to becoming an Oracle. She wouldn't have betrayed her vows."

"Nobody is suggesting Gianna did it carelessly. I believe it's more likely that Gabel wore her down, tormented her, and warped her perception of things. Maybe he threatened her, maybe he did worse. She might have crossed the line just to survive. I know you say that Oracles are supposed to die before they betray their vow of silence, but let's be realistic, Kiery," Magnes said.

Kiery pondered him another moment, then her face smoothed over as she schooled her emotions away from the surface. "I suppose we'll see. Gianna wants vindication."

"You could just not let that happen."

"It's her right to demand it."

"With so much at stake?" Magnes tapped his fingertips on his desk.

"This is exactly why I'm opposed to this. I understand why Anita asked you for help, and I deferred to you when you asked me to back her." Kiery growled silently to herself, then continued in a steady voice, "But you saw an opportunity, too. You wouldn't have gotten SableFur involved if there wasn't an upside for you."

"Don't accuse me of using my Oracles to deal with the likes of Gabel." Magnes dismissed her statement.

Kiery raised a brow. "Anita appealed to you for help, and you took the opportunity like you hunt rabbit. Gabel having a rebellious Oracle wouldn't have lasted. The Moon would have dealt with Gianna in time. As I said, the time to be concerned for her was months ago."

Magnes' expression hardened. "You are assuming Gabel survives."

Kiery couldn't keep the bitterness out of her voice. "I'm going to defer my anger. If Gabel's the Dark Comet and she's the Balance-Keeper, they'll both survive, and she'll vindicate herself."

"If," Magnes said like Kiery had just suggested they fart rainbows and eat glitter. "Gabel is a violent thug, Kiery. He just happens to be a bit smarter than the average thug."

Kiery snorted and shook her head. "Males. You're the Alpha, and you're just as obnoxious to talk to as Lucas. Gabel is rumored to be a lupine. If that's true, then he's brilliant and mentally disciplined to overcome his early life. That wolf with the tattoos." She mulled it over. "I do not know him. Do you?"

"Flint. The IronMoon Master of Arms. I don't know anything else about him, except that he is older and has a repu-tation for being a skilled warrior."

"His tattoos have the old-order blue-gloss." Kiery gestured to her own arm. "To get that gloss it has to be done in a certain holy way. The technique was lost hundreds of years ago. His seem to move if I stared at them long enough, and legend has it if an Oracle does try to scry in them, the ink will tell her what it's bound the wearer to. The biggest one was service to the Moon, and I doubt he'd be in a pack like IronMoon unless he had a reason. Flint is the one who told him to let Gianna go."

"So he has sense," Magnes said. "A disgraced Oracle isn't an appropriate Luna."

"Or Flint knows Gianna will be vindicated and will eventually return to IronMoon with the honor of the SableFur Oracles around her neck," Kiery said with a mild shrug. "I told you before indulging Anita was unwise, and I tell you again."

"But the Moon did not warn you off this," Magnes reminded her.

Kiery hid a scowl. And that was where Magnes nailed her paw into the ground every single time. Three times Kiery had tried to get the Moon to offer guidance on this subject, and three times Her Eye had been closed. "And that is the *only* reason I am going along with this."

"Then you and I should both trust Anita to know her business. You're young to be an Elder Oracle. I've learned to trust my Oracles. I have my oldest Oracle telling me of a rogue Oracle, and the Alpha bound to her is the Destroyer, while the Moon is otherwise silent. Do you disagree *some* action had to be taken?"

Kiery stood. She was done irritating herself on this, because Magnes was right: Anita was the one who had had the visions. Kiery was the one the Moon didn't want to talk to. "I won't hinder or help Gianna vindicate herself. I also think you're talking out of both sides of your mouth. This time you've crossed a line. I don't appreciate it."

Magnes smiled. "Then I suggest, Oracle, to take your annoyance to the Moon, and perhaps ask yourself why you aren't the one She wants to talk to. Perhaps you are too fond of your old student."

Kiery stalked towards the door, seething. "You should find out more about this Flint. We should know who did his tattoos."

"Why does that matter?"

"The warriors who wore the blue-gloss were Her Chosen," Kiery growled. "When lost knowledge suddenly re-appears I think it's worth investigating. If you don't, Magnes, I'm going to start wondering why you're so determined to not care."

The SableFur Alpha didn't flinch, or betray any emotion at all. "I'm not determined to not care, Oracle. I simply don't."

NOT SO FAST

The pain kept me alive: it wouldn't let me die.

Was this what Flint had experienced? My soul kept trying to flee down the shattered Bond, slip into the chasm between souls and into the next world, but it couldn't. The Moon had tied that one escape off, bringing it into death throes that could never end.

My body remained stuffed full of flailing, burning, agonized soul.

The SableFur, believing me to be legitimately repudiated, expected me to die. Maybe even hoped Gabel would die.

I did not die. I could not die.

My next memory was daylight streaming through thin, ugly curtains.

Curtains. There are no curtains in our room.

It hit me all over again. I doubled over onto the thin mattress. My throat choked as I tried to scream.

Anita's bungalow. The tiny little attic room, barely large enough for the mattress and not even tall enough to stand in because of the dramatic slope to the roof. The world swam through water and moonlight.

Get up.

There wasn't much: a mattress on the floor, a single bar bolted to the wall to hang clothing, a few extra blankets folded in a corner. Piled onto the blankets were my bag of runestones, and the velvet-wrapped chunk of obsidian. I wept with relief and crawled over to them. I picked up the obsidian chunk and clutched it to my breasts.

It slumbered in my arms, a void of secrets waiting for their time.

Flint had been right. If I had had any idea my courage would have failed me. I'd have told Gabel to fight.

I wept over the obsidian chunk.

Without a bowl it would be impossible to vindicate myself. The chunk would not be ready for carving for another six weeks, and then however long it took the stonecutter to do the work, then yet more time to imbue the bowl. I was weeks, *months*, away from my prize.

Anita had succeeded in getting me away from Gabel. She lived out here with the other advanced acolytes in isolation. She was queen here, and so old that if the Moon stripped her of her Gift for her sins, she could simply retire or fake it.

I was her prisoner.

First order of business: escape.

I could only go as far as the care of another Oracle. Neither of the other options were a good choice. Kiery had been one of my teachers, and Thessa was Anita's little toad. But both lived within earshot of other SableFur, and if they tried to keep me from vindicating myself someone would hear me howl.

"You'd be proud of me, Gabel," I whispered to the obsidian orb. "Cunning is your job."

Time to drag myself downstairs. I rolled the obsidian back

to the corner, then tried to stand. I got halfway upright before a wave knocked me back to my knees.

Trembling seized me.

Too weak to stand. Too sick to stand.

I crawled across the floor, opened the door, eased myself down the narrow staircase that opened up onto the second floor. The attic room wasn't a prison, and it wasn't the first time I had been up there. It was saved for Oracles or students who needed peace and stillness, usually after a bad time on the Tides.

"Gianna!" a young voice said.

I twisted and saw one of the young acolytes who had been at my disgrace. I snarled at her as she tried to come close, and she leapt back, hands outstretched but fingers drawn back, unsure what to do.

Oh, and I was naked.

...Gabel...

I laid my head down and moaned in pain.

"Gianna is awake!" the acolyte shouted down the hall.

I dragged myself up onto all fours, and crawled down the hallway to the stairs. The acolyte followed me. Another young acolyte appeared, and she was equally useless.

I sort of slid down the stairs, landed in a crumpled heap at the bottom, barely paid attention given my soul hurt so much worse than my body, and through bleary, watery eyes, crawled to the tiny living room where Anita lectured two more acolytes.

Fury replaced some of my pain, washed my brain in stupidity, crippled me, and dropped me to the ground. I rolled over, stared at the ceiling, grasping for something that wasn't there.

Anita, sitting in her favorite chair, spoke to me. She didn't get up. Her voice carried. "You're finally awake."

Oh yes, you old bitch. I am awake.

I tried to say something but my awareness couldn't swim through the fever-wash. I pulled myself onto my belly so I could at least face her.

Her old eyes were narrow slits. "Gabel is not going to put that crown of shattered obsidian on your head, Gianna. I've made sure that won't happen."

That's what you think.

My body couldn't obey my brain, so I just drooled and stared at her instead of howling. Was she confessing her motive to me? Or just trying to make it sound like she got me out of a bad situation for my own good? I closed my eyes and shook my head, hoping to clear it.

Anita had green socks on her feet. Green socks with little textured rubber grip things so she wouldn't slip and fall.

The acolytes hovered like nervous birds.

"When that bowl is prepared, you can start your retaining and atonement," Anita said.

Atonement.

The word yanked on my spine. Who told her atonement! I snarled and lifted myself onto one elbow. "Vindication!"

Anita's lips curled. "What did you say?"

"I am innocent." My voice was hoarse from screaming. "I want vindication!"

She scowled.

The acolytes twittered nervously. I looked at the second one. She had been there. She knew what I had said. I had said *vindication* and never admitted to guilt. The acolyte squeaked in terror. Would I have been so useless? So terrified of the old bat?

Anita, you horrid sow, are you trying to put words in my mouth? I publicly declared I wanted vindication. You think that's somehow going to change because you tell me it will?

Anita's face scrunched up into a mass of compressed wrinkles. "Child, he took you by force. It's understandable if you twisted things around in your head so you could endure—"

Child? I was no child! I was an adult, I was an Oracle, I was... or had been... a Luna! I panted, "I am not guilty."

She knew I wasn't guilty, she knew I'd pass all the tests and vindicate myself, and they'd never be able to come at me again. The only chance she had would be to make me think I was confused, that I had somehow made a mistake, and I was too traumatized to see it. I laid my head down on the floor and laughed a miserable laugh.

"You're out of your mind." Anita clucked her tongue. She grunted to the two terrified acolytes. "Take her back upstairs to her room."

"Will she die?" one asked.

"She's survived the first few days of a broken Bond, but it doesn't mean the pain won't drive her mad. She has already suffered a great deal of torment at Alpha Gabel's claws." Anita's voice sounded heavy with grave prophecy.

And that was her fail-safe. If I refused atonement, she'd declare my mind broken. I'd be stripped of all blame, all responsibility, all dishonor, my title, and any hope of redeeming myself.

I laughed at how amateur her plan was. Did she really think I was such a fool I couldn't see through her?

Pain and weakness did make me a little mad, and I drooled and stumbled and hummed to myself, out of my mind with fever as my soul scrambled around inside my body trying to find a way out.

The acolytes were kind, and managed to wrestle me up the stairs to my room. They made sure I had some water and some food, and one even smoothed my blankets. One tried to help me into some clothes.

I refused.

I'd sleep naked.

TWO MORE DAYS passed while I flopped around in a fever state.
Now my mind was mostly clear, although pain permeated
every part of me. My thoughts kept turning backwards towards
the abyss. Flint had warned me of the dangers of silence.

The punishment my body had endured from the shattered
Bond left me weak and sick. Right now I had the advantage of
being considered out of my mind with pain, but that wouldn't
last. I had to escape Anita.

My fevered brain shakily sorted through escape options.
There was one conclusion: violence.

Better get moving on that before I couldn't play the "out of
her head with pain" card.

I still slid down the stairs because I felt so weak. For
measure I went naked, hair unbrushed.

Anita was in the front room again, in those stupid green
socks, giving another lecture.

"Gianna," Anita said. "Sit. You can begin your
atonement."

I growled at her. I didn't even have to fake it. "No.
Vindication."

Anita sighed.

My fingernails dug into the wall, fingers elongating and
sharpening without my even trying. The anger bubbled up
from the Bond, the pain, everything that couldn't escape
trapped within me. And this bitch was the cause of all of it. I
howled and staggered forward towards her. "Vindication!"

The acolytes scrambled to get out of the way. Anita held
her ground in her chair. "Gian—"

"Vindication!"

My left hand elongated and silvery fur shimmered over the back of my palm, my nails extended, and my teeth sharpened. Anita seized the arms of her chair, eyes riveted on my claw.

I raked her across the chest, ripping her blouse to ribbons and drawing lines of blood across her sagging skin. She shrieked and yanked her hands up to shield her face The acolytes screamed. My vision wavered and unfocused, the fevered exhaustion mingling with my anger.

I raised my hand to rake Anita's face into shreds but my strength failed, my joints melted, and I crumbled to the floor, weak and fevered again.

They left me where I fell. I drifted on the fever-pain for hours. But it had worked. Through the hot haze I overheard Anita declare me violent, and her shaky, panicked voice speaking into the phone as she summoned SableFur to retrieve me.

A day later two SableFur came, bound my wrists with silver-inlaid ropes and put a silver-bar leather restraint collar around my neck. The pain was laughable compared to what my soul felt.

Then they took me exactly where I wanted to go: to Kiery. To the heart of SableFur.

MARCHMOON: CURRENCY

The rabid she-bitch's name was Lulu. According to her.

Hix only half-believed her. The gleam in her already-too-bright eyes all but dared him to take issue with her name. He didn't take the bait. Reasonably speaking (and he was inclined to be reasonable from time to time) he couldn't just lock her up or tie her to a chair for the rest of her natural life. He had bigger things to do making sense of the MarchMoon.

Or what had once been the MarchMoon, and now was the IronMoon. Alpha Gabel had been clear on that.

Try telling that to the MarchMoon. Hix didn't much care what they called themselves, or were called, and he cared even less what they thought of it. As far as he was concerned, they were traitors, cowards, or children. They got no say in the matter. It was a matter of names, and Hix didn't give much weight to names. Names were words. Words were useless more often than they were useful. Words meant nothing without physical will behind them.

He had been ordered to make sense of what the March-

Moon had left. All they had left were words. So now he was compelled to sit in a chair, with notepad and pen, and collect those words.

Right now a young male sat across from him, trying not to fidget and making such an effort that his muscles twitched. Hix's own face was so tired of scowling he couldn't even manage a glare. He flipped to a new page. Asked the usual questions. Name. Age. Rank. Schooling. Occupation. Relatives within two degrees of separation, alive or dead. Their age. Name. Manner of death. Then he threw in a few random questions, hoping to find holes in what the other wolves had told him.

"When did Lulu come to MarchMoon?"

The male frowned. "Um... a year ago? No. Wait. A little longer."

"Where did she come from?"

"I dunno. She just showed up one day, I guess?" The youngster said this with the casual boredom of a youth who thought details like that were stupid, and the adults asking them obnoxious pests.

Everyone agreed Lulu had been born an EmeraldPelt, but nobody seemed to know why she'd come to MarchMoon, or if she'd even come directly from EmeraldPelt. The senior members would have known those details, but they were all inconveniently dead.

Hix didn't buy her half-crazy act either. She had been a little too quick to still her viper tongue when Luna Gianna had punched the old dustbag. Those sorts of females were the most dangerous troublemakers. They weren't stupid enough to get caught in their own trap.

He dismissed the male with a grunt when his phone rang. Gabel's number. "Alpha."

"It is not," the voice said.

Hix stood. His pad fell to the floor. "Flint. Where is Gabel?"

"Not in a talking mood. Return to IronMoon."

"Why?"

"Gabel repudiated her, and she has been taken to SableFur with the Oracles. There is not time to explain more. Return home."

"Are those Gabel's orders?"

"They are mine. Your Alpha is unfit to lead, and you are First Beta. You are needed here."

His fingers pressed into the phone's smooth metallic case. He went over to the window, and looked at the world outside. Instinct nagged at the back of his mind, whispering half-formed words. His Luna had been wrongfully disgraced and repudiated. Now his Alpha was in no condition to avenge the wrong that had been done.

The duty fell to him.

"I outrank you, Master of Arms. I am not done here. You will have to lead IronMoon for now. I am on the scent of something."

Time to find Lulu.

Donovan took a drag on his cigar. From the scent it was a cheap affair he had picked up at a truckstop for a few bucks. "So you have nothing to go on."

Hix folded his arms across his chest and adjusted his hips a bit, hoping to hide the discomfort of the torn stitches in his abdomen. "Female, very capable, presumably born an EmeraldPelt. She is likely heading towards SableFur, via RedWater or IceMaw, and does not want to be spotted. How is that nothing?"

Lulu had disappeared from MarchMoon. It could not be a coincidence.

Donovan shifted the cigar in his teeth. "To mourn a mischief that is past and gone/Is the next way to draw new mischief on."

Hix was short on patience at that moment. "Your point?"

"That's a fancy way of asking why you want to cause headaches. The crazy wolf is gone. Let her go, who cares why. Good riddance."

"She was here to make false charges against Luna Gianna. Now that her work is done she's returned to her master. Find that master."

"So you think the MarchMoon were SableFur toadies?"

"We know the Shadowless are."

"That means nothing, and tracking anything to SableFur is dangerous."

"Quit complaining and get on her trail."

Donovan dropped his cigar butt onto the ground and twisted it into soot with the toe of his boot. "If she's smart like you say, and a plant like you think, she's not going straight to SableFur. Too obvious."

Hix grumbled in frustration. "It's all I have. It's a lead. Track it."

"Maybe it was your charming personality that made her move on."

"Our Luna is being held prisoner in SableFur for a crime she didn't commit, and I have to convince you to do your part?"

"She is not being held prisoner," Donovan said. "She's an Oracle. She didn't commit a *crime*. She's either there to atone, or she's going to try to pass the Four Tests and vindicate herself. That means prove she's innocent and reclaim her honor."

"I know what *vindicate* means."

"Just checking. It's a big word for an IronMoon."

Hix barred his teeth at the Hunter.

Donovan shrugged. "This is my way of warning you not to give me shit if your hunch about Lulu is wrong. If Lulu's work here was done, and she has no payload for SableFur, she won't risk returning there."

"And I would not have risked leaving MarchMoon and drawing suspicion at all."

"Nor would I, so there's a reason she's going back, if you're right about her at all."

"Speak to no one, Hunter, except myself or Flint or Alpha Gabel."

"I almost never do, Beta." Donovan pulled out a fresh cigar. He unwrapped it, ran it under his nose and chomped off the end.

"How can you hunt with that in your nose?"

"You have no scent for me to go on, it disguises my scent and wolves never smoke." Donovan grinned. "Unless you have a pair of her panties for me to sniff?"

"If I had them, I would give them to you. She took everything."

"Pity. Panties really are the best way to track a female."

"Do not be disgusting."

"I should drag you to a titty bar and have the girls get that stick out of your ass."

"I'm sure they wouldn't have anything to do with you if you weren't paying them."

Donovan clamped down on the unlit cigar. "So how pissed off were you, Champion of Female Kind, when Alpha Gabel Marked up a female without her consent? Or paraded that little blue-eyed tart in front of Anders just to torture his actual mate?"

"That trail is not getting any warmer," Hix answered instead.

"Thought so." Donovan sauntered out, as if he were a tomcat with tail held high. "Everyone has their price, Hix. The currency varies, but everyone has their price."

THE REST of IronMoon reeled under all the news. Most didn't know what to think, much less believe. Many hadn't even realized that an Oracle's vow of silence extended to the Alpha and matters of pack safety. Most of the conversations revolved more about the horror Oracles could keep such secrets, and how could any Luna possibly serve as an Oracle.

Many believed Gabel needed to go reclaim Gianna and to hell if she was "tarnished" or not. They were all tarnished in IronMoon, and Gianna's "crime" was hardly a crime in the eyes of most.

Hix had returned a week later (it had taken that long to locate the Hunter), and Flint's lecturing tone annoyed him. If Alpha Gabel could not avenge his Luna, then it fell to the First Beta, Moon-nonsense or not. Hix had only one question for the Master of Arms: "How long until she comes back?"

"She might not come back," Flint said. "The Moon didn't promise them they would be together again."

Hix drew back. "I don't understand your meaning."

"The Moon only told them what She was going to do so they would each be in the place She needed them. Being together again wasn't promised. It also wasn't ruled out. She bound up their Bond so that it simulates death. I think that means that the possibility exists, but the outcome is not assured. I presume they will be together again in death." Flint shrugged, and added in a sober tone, "If it comes to that."

"But how long will this vindication take? How long until she *can* return?"

"I don't know. Perhaps a long time. She needs her new bowls, which I think will take several turns of the Moon, and then she has to pass the tests."

"What are these Four Tests she has to pass?"

"She has to discover a secret, find something hidden, predict an event that comes to pass, and prove she still has the Moon's favor. She only gets one chance at each test, and her sisters judge if she's passed or not."

"Then it is corrupt," Hix said coldly. "They found her guilty with no evidence, and they'll never say she has passed any of them."

"We will have to hope the Moon provides irrefutable evidence," Flint said heavily.

Hix ground his teeth together. "Where is Alpha Gabel?"

Flint raised a hand to settle the First Beta. "He doesn't need your anger. IronMoon has executed wolves for betrayal. Gianna couldn't stay his Luna with this cloud over her head."

"Flimsy at best, and the pack agrees!" Hix spat.

"And most of the wolves here can barely read," Flint retorted. "They don't understand what's at stake. Gabel's entire kingdom is founded on the idea that promises are to be kept. There can be no exceptions, especially for the Alpha."

Hix gripped the fabric of his jeans, anger knotting and unknotting within him. "If the SableFur want Gabel, Magnes should just come for him. Alpha to Alpha. Using his mate is disgusting."

"I agree, but that's not all that's happening here. The Moon showed Gianna the truth of what is driving all of this. I can't tell you more than that."

"Then she will never come back because SableFur will keep moving the shells!"

Flint nodded. "We have to figure out what the Moon wants us to do. Solve the puzzle. If we——"

Hix got out of his chair and marched up to Gabel's office. Flint followed him in silence.

Hix had half-expected chaos and squalor, the crazed insanity of a male with a broken Bond. He had seen that insanity more than once. The only symptom of grief was the scent of suffering in the air. The First Beta snarled under his breath. Gabel didn't care? He was up and about and in one piece not eight days after he had given up his mate?

Gabel looked over his shoulder. He was shaven, but raw patches of skin from where the razor had sliced up layers of skin striped his jaw, and there was a ghastly shadow around each eye. His face reminded Hix of someone who had been deathly fevered for a month, including the crazed gleam and bright gloss to his eyes.

Soul-sick or not, Hix didn't care. "Get out of this office and go get your Luna back!"

Gabel shook his head as if dazed.

"You were careless with her many times, and the one time she needs you to defend her, you roll over! I do not care what the Moon wanted. Tell the Moon to solve Her own problems!"

Flint did not correct Hix.

"I would never ask Gianna to give up being an Oracle." Gabel's voice was hoarse and raw. "That is her choice. She did not choose it."

"So you're just going to stand at that window and wait while the pack falls apart around you? I am not holding it together for you! Not like this! I will go to SableFur today and bring her home. Put your Mark back on her arm—*properly this time*—and force Magnes to use his claws and not his Oracles!"

Gabel limped a few paces away from the window. There was blood on his pants where Aaron had stabbed him, and his other shoulder, and he walked as if every internal organ was tender and every half-healed wound had torn open. He rested his hands on the back of the other couch, his fingertips pressing into the fabric. The crazed gleam in his eyes brightened a degree.

"You think I am going to do nothing, First Beta?" he asked in a quiet, deadly tone.

"I see you doing nothing," Hix snarled.

Gabel's lips stretched into a ghoulish, horrific smile straight from the Void itself. "I told Gianna that if the Moon took her from me, I would lay waste to Her creation and build a tower so I could climb to the heavens to smash Her Eye. And that is exactly what I am going to do."

IN/SANE

The SableFur dungeon (because let's face it: that's what it was) was nothing compared to the IronMoon basement.

It was as impeccably clean as old stones can be, and frighteningly ancient. The sort of dark, dank hole sixty feet under that spoke about innumerable lives that had simply disappeared into it. Half a dozen cages lined one long side, and the other side dotted by pairs of shackles. The end of the rectangular room was curiously devoid of anything. It wasn't too difficult to imagine any number of punishments that could be enacted in the bare, smooth space.

To complete the dungeon decor were torches, which gave the air a faint oily haze that eventually stung the eyes and nose. Twice a day a male wolf wearing a black executioner's hood came to change them.

They had stripped me of my clothing and left me on the uneven, ancient stone floor of the centermost cell. Iron bars were driven into the stone, each bar wrapped with silver bands, but instead of bars overhead, the cage had an open top. The bars ended in sharp spikes coated in silver. There was about a foot of clearance between the top spike and the ceiling. A determined wolf could have crawled out, but would have sliced themselves getting between the stone ceiling and the spikes.

The flickering torchlight made the shadows jump and leap, and in the haze of silver sickness caused by my collar, I'd sometimes startle and have to remind myself they were just shadows, although I swore I saw ghostly wolves moving in the unsteady light. Spectral and translucent, blue-white like the Moon's light, they seemed strangely familiar in my fevered dreams.

Or maybe I was seeing some of the old ghosts that haunted this pit ready to welcome another to their pack, and they knew I'd be one of them soon.

My hands were free, at least, but bruised from wearing silver-inlaid shackles for hours. The collar's six bars of silver pressed into the skin of my neck, and my skin had formed huge blisters that had popped, then ulcerated. Blood and weeping fluid crept down my chest and back while the silver seeped through the ulcers to poison my blood stream.

Unlike the collar I had put on Gardenia, these were designed for restraint and torment. The silver exposure would eventually kill me, but not before I died from gangrene.

Every breath or swallow pushed my skin against the silver of my collar. My lungs ached from hours of shallow breathing, and when they rebelled so I'd inhale a deep breath, my throat burned and the thick scent of the torches mixed with the scent of sizzling skin, blood, fluid and ulcerated flesh edged with festering. True sleep was impossible. A feverish doze was all that I could manage.

Assuming the torch-bearer came twice a day, I had been here perhaps two, three days. It might have been five, or one. I had no idea, time meant nothing in the burning pain of the torn Bond and my ruined neck. No Kiery, no Oracles, nothing except the torch-bearers, who also brought me food and water.

There was no where to escape the pain. If I tried to retreat into myself, I only met the remains of the Bond. If I turned away to the outside, I met the burning pain of the collar. So I stayed between the two, in a wretched umbra where time meant nothing, and I needed it to mean nothing.

The SableFur couldn't honestly propose to keep me down here forever, could they? Lock me up, throw away the key?

Doubt needled my brain.

I needed to get out of here. I needed to be above ground, figuring out how to do whatever it was the Moon wanted me to do.

This dungeon was not the IronMoon basement. It was not that concrete, godless, bereft sarcophagus. This was just a dungeon on the shadowy side of the Moon.

The heavy metal door at the top of the long stairwell creaked open above me, then closed again. Footsteps picked their way down the steps, and Elder Oracle Kiery came into the torchlight.

I tried to push myself up off the floor, trembling with the effort. The collar rubbed into my neck and I couldn't not whimper. The angry red lines of the toxin had moved down to my breasts and probably up to my face. I gave up trying to sit and stared at Kiery from my place on the floor. Hours of laying on the stones had caused sores to open up on my skin, and large bruises to form. The effects of the silver worsened it, and my whole body was wracked with dull, throbbing pain.

Kiery was no stranger to me: she'd helped Anita finish my training. She'd made me an Oracle, and my success had made her an Elder Oracle. Medium height, auburn hair kept back in a tight braid, and like me, unnaturally pale. Her skin seemed luminescent in the flickering torchlight. It was hard to focus my eyes on her.

"Hello, Gianna," she said, cautiously.

"Kiery," I rasped. You might not realize how much the skin of your neck moves when you talk, but the collar made sure to educate me on the more subtle points of torment.

She crouched down so her eyes were level with mine. "You recognize me. Do you remember what happened?"

Of course I recognized her. Of course I remembered what happened. If they thought I had been in my right mind when I had attacked Anita, they'd hang me for it. But if I had been out of my mind, I wasn't wholly responsible. Would Kiery believe me if I accused Anita of not giving me what I wanted, and that had driven me into a feverish rage? Or should I just play dumb?

Lying seemed like such a bad idea. I wasn't a very good liar. And in this condition I didn't think I could keep my lies straight. I played for a little more time. "What part?"

"Attacking Anita."

Pain burned up and down my throat, seeping into my face and down my chest. The collar forced me to pause again, recovering from the wash of pain, which blanked out my mind as well as blanking out whatever I was going to blabber. I decided on a half-truth, because I remembered everything quite clearly until I had collapsed in exhaustion. "Some."

"Do you remember how you got here?"

"No." That was true. Most of my memories from the past week were incomplete. Things out of focus, or only one sense remembered, like a scent or sound with nothing else, outright holes and blackness, very little was coherent and clear. I barely remembered anything after attacking Anita, and once they had put the collar and bindings on me, everything had become a blank.

Kiery shifted her weight. "How long have you been here?"

Oracles get used to strange questions, but not usually from

other Oracles. Was her question a quiz, or did she not know? I couldn't tell from her expression. "... a day? Two?"

Kiery got out of her crouch. She retrieved the iron ring of keys (after all, it was a dungeon, and no dungeon is complete without a ring of keys) and unlocked my cell. Then she knelt down next to me, and felt along the collar for the buckle. I whimpered in pain. She didn't mean to hurt me, but the buckle had slid around to the back of my neck and her fingers fumbled with the stiff, unfamiliar leather. But then she pulled it off and cool air brushed my skin and I breathed in, and while my wrecked skin protested, the silver burn didn't follow.

I collapsed, limp, onto the stones and closed my eyes.

"I don't think we need that anymore." Kiery had distaste on her tone. Holding it between two fingers she took it over to the long, low wooden table under where the keys had hung. She dropped it there.

I was far too weak to shift forms even without the collar. She came back into my cell, and using her phone's light, examined my neck. I shied away from the scalding brightness.

"I can't bring you upstairs just yet." Kiery tucked her phone into her pocket. "But there's no reason you have to wear that collar."

"Why?" I cracked open one aching eyeball. Why did I have to stay down in the dungeon? Why had they left the collar on me at all? It wasn't the special hell of the basement, but it *was* a dungeon, and they hadn't even spared me a blanket or burlap sack. There were worse places to be, and worse things that could happen down here, but it didn't mean I wanted to stay.

"Questionable mental stability and you partially shift in your violence," Kiery said.

I had never been able to do that before. Pure anger has its perks. Not knowing what to say in my defense, I just said, "Oh."

Kiery seemed satisfied that I didn't have full recollection of what I had done to Anita.

I couldn't overplay the insanity card, though. If I was questionably sane, and mentally not fit, they wouldn't let me pursue vindication. Oracles legitimately did go insane, or at least mentally fracture under the stress of our gifts, and letting an Oracle go into the Tides when their mind wasn't healthy ended badly. I needed to somehow convince everyone that I had just been sick, and my actions had been the result of my broken Bond, and not a broken mind.

"How badly hurt is Anita?" I whispered, figuring that showing a little remorse would buy me some good will with Kiery.

"Not too bad. You swiped at her and peeled up some skin." Kiery didn't seem very concerned.

So I hadn't hurt Anita more than I had scared the crap out of her. Good. Now I had to make sure Kiery didn't send me back there.

Kiery got up and left, her footsteps disappearing up the staircase to the heavy door above. It creaked open, creaked closed, and I was alone in the red-light darkness again.

I had endured Gabel, fighting with him and his crazed plans, I could endure this quiet a little longer. The difficult part would be when I had to move among the SableFur, and insist on my innocence while knowing that certain individuals wanted no part of it.

In the silence, the fog stole over my brain, lulling me to sleep, pulling me down into the stillness of slumber.

...*Gianna*...

His voice. A whisper from the back of my brain, from a coming dream.

Or was it?

The Bond's fragment thumped to life, and the prickling rush of adrenaline came with it.

"Gabel?" I whispered.

Of course he didn't answer. I waited in the darkness but couldn't hear anything else over the thumping of my heart, echoing the thumping of the Bond as it twisted and squirmed against its binding.

The spasm of pain Flint had warned about hit, and I doubled over.

...Gianna...

That was my imagination. It had to be my imagination! I had silver going through my system.

I wrestled myself to all fours and crawled to the corner of my cell. I snatched the velvet bag that contained the obsidian chunk and curled my body around it. The chunk was real. Like a young Seer I clung to something fixed from the waking world, something I understood that would anchor me in reality. The rough, unhewn block of obsidian with all its sharp edges and unforgiving surfaces was that thing. When it was ready the work could begin.

I had to survive until then.

BOSS ENCOUNTER

A doctor-type woke me out of my fitful sleep an unknown number of hours later. She pried the obsidian chunk away from me and unfolded me so she could look at my neck.

I opened my eyes, stared up, saw the ceiling, the doctor, and two ghostly wolves peering down at me.

Wait.

I recognize you two.

Even though they were now ghostly and translucent, I recognized the RedWater wolves. The two I had defied Gabel to defend. They'd guided me through the dark grotto on the Edge of the Tides to the house with the pup-ring.

They perked their ears that I had roused, and wagged their tails.

I tried to move one arm to touch one. I wasn't alone. Not completely. Not entirely. Had the Moon sent them, or were their fates bound to mine because I owned their fangs?

I'm sorry if that's true.

I felt drained of everything, and like sand had been poured in where blood had been, and my hands hurt from holding the rough obsidian chunk, and my neck burned and scalded with each breath. And my soul—my *soul* hurt.

But I needed to demonstrate some coherence and not just be a withdrawn lump. The doctor-type might report back that I was a husk. I couldn't be a husk.

"How bad is it?" I whispered.

"Oh, it's not too bad," she replied with the insincerity of all doctors who don't want to be dealing with a particular patient.

"It hurts worse than bad." I wheezed out the last word around the pain.

Her eyes flickered, but still didn't meet mine. Her gloved fingers felt along the skin very gently. Her silence confirmed to me it was very ugly. My whole neck hurt, and my lower jaw and the base of my skull.

"Is it infected?" I prodded again.

"A little. You have a slight fever, but that's normal."

Normal. Because everything about this was so normal.

I am going to dismantle your pack and throw the gates open for IronMoon.

Do you know what your Alpha did?

How many SableFur knew? How many SableFur had known Gabel's mother? Who had questioned her disappearance? Had there been rumors? Questions?

I needed to find out. Maybe if there had been rumors, or more than rumors, or some kind of records, or witnesses, or evidence, or something... some kind of trail to follow, maybe that was what I was supposed to find. From what the Moon had shown me, Gabel's mother had been an acolyte and disappeared with a trace. Surely someone had to remember her, there had to have been questions... there had to have been other Oracles, or other acolytes that had known her. I had to find them. Figure out what they knew.

Unless she had been kept with Anita, or Magnes had

chased her to Anita, and Anita had disposed of his little problem... or problems, as it were.

The cream the doctor slathered on the wounds was
exquisite. I sighed and relaxed onto the stones.

"Don't move too much. You'll make the scaring worse."

No worry of that. I wasn't pacing the cell, and what did I
care about the scars anyway? No, I hoped there would be scars!
So when all this was over, there'd be a permanent, visible
reminder of what had been done. So nobody could pretend it
hadn't happened.

The doctor gathered up her things and left without another
word. The torch-bearer came and brought dinner, then
changed the torches. I slept, freed briefly from the pain by the
thick goop all over my neck, until the creaking of the door
woke me once more.

The RedWater wolves disappeared into the shadows.

Heavier footsteps this time. A male. It wasn't time for the
torch-bearer to come back.

The male's large frame melted out of the shadows into the
red-tinged light. I stared, my eyes focusing on him, but it was
his presence that my senses understood. I had never seen him
before.

But I had. Parts of him. I had seen that sandy blond hair,
the jaw, the frame, the bearing, the raw force of his presence,
the iron will that I would be unwise to challenge, and the
authority he wielded in both hands.

Inside I quaked from sheer common sense.

He waited, staring at me, face made of stone.

I pulled myself onto my hip, then onto my knees. I wanted
to stand, but I didn't think I could manage it. Maybe it would
appease him if he thought I was more inclined to be the
obedient little Oracle, and not the former Luna.

He had blue eyes. Not ocean-blue eyes like his son, more

like the summer sky. A chasm cut across his left cheek, like a channel of liquid silver had eroded away most of the skin, and the wound had filled in with glossy, mottled scar tissue. It didn't diminish his good looks, it only made him seem that much more... prestigious.

Oh, Alpha Magnes left an impression.

One I had never thought I'd feel again after being Bound to his son.

Was he as intense as his son? I wavered, not quite sure. They were different in a way.

No matter. I felt it, the force of him, what he was willing to do to me if I made even the slightest misstep.

He'd crack my spine and leave me to rot down here, and like Gabel, wouldn't even think about it twice. He'd probably not even think about it once.

Except the difference between Magnes and Gabel was Gabel had honor. Magnes didn't. Gabel had his limits, and he never crossed them. It made him predictable. There were things he'd never do. Magnes... Magnes could do anything.

My unease satisfied him. I hadn't expected to see him at all.

He would kill me. The longer he stared at me, the more absolutely certain I was he would kill me. I had never confronted anyone who I knew would kill me. Assault me, abuse me, abduct me, *then* kill me, but never just twist my head off like a chicken's.

Oddly, I didn't sense he *wanted* to kill me, only that he *would*. It was a peculiar difference.

"Oracle Kiery has said you should be let out of here."

I shuddered at the sound of his voice. Not in a good way. This was the wolf I needed to destroy, and I was about to wet myself with how frightened I was.

He very slowly titled his head to the left, eyeing me more sharply as if the vision from his left eye were slightly better.

Did he suspect what I knew?

"Why did you attack Anita?" he asked.

Did I risk lying? Gabel would have sensed the lie. But I had been... no, *was*, Gabel's Luna. I wasn't some little itty bitty she-wolf. I was a Luna, an Oracle. Did I risk a little lie? If Magnes figured out I knew all about his dirty little secret, he'd just kill me and tell Kiery that my mental state had required him doing what Alphas must do.

I bought a second by pushing a strand of hair back behind my ear. "I think I was angry."

"About what?" His tone made me think of a needle coming straight for my eye.

"I don't really remember. Anita's accusations, I think. I want vindication."

Magnes' presence shifted oh so slightly, and if I hadn't been so used to another powerful Alpha, I might not have noticed it at all. *Vindication* prodded him. It shouldn't matter to him if Anita had made a mistake. A minor embarrassment that should have very little to do with him—in theory. But the word found purchase in his guilt, and he had to shift under the weight.

He looked at the small pile of velvet in the corner. "Your bowls are broken. There is no vindication."

"Those aren't shards. That is a stone being prepared." He couldn't deny me access to a stone cutter to make the bowl. Technically.

Gabel never would have acted so dishonorably, but Magnes might.

Magnes asked, "And what happens if you succeed?"

I hadn't thought of that. I was *supposed* to be angry at my mate siding with obvious lies. Everyone in SableFur had to believe the only way I'd have Gabel back in my life was as a rug for a floor.

"I don't know," I said. IronMoon and SableFur would look very different when Gabel and I were done. I wanted to believe we'd be together again. It seemed impossible (and improbable) it could be that simple.

Magnes was about to say something. I jumped ahead. "I don't know, and I don't care. I've been accused of a crime I didn't commit. Proving my innocence is all I care about right now."

He did not smile but his scent did. In a way that sent a shudder across my skin. "You are more sensible than I expected. I was expecting some girlish answer of running back to IronMoon with flowers in your hair."

"Gabel is the one who put Kiery's word ahead of mine." My voice cracked. The Bond throbbed and convulsed, and I closed my eyes, gasping for breath. "I owe him nothing!"

Magnes went to retrieve the keys.

I instinctively shrank back from him. I was completely naked, and more than a little exposed. Magnes grabbed my arm. I shrieked and lashed out, catching him with a fist in the thigh. He didn't seem to notice. His fingers clamped down until my bone creaked.

His eyes were so blue.

He cranked my arm to look at the Mark.

I focused on not sobbing and whimpering. I was an Oracle, dammit, but only an idiot wouldn't have been afraid of him, locked in a dungeon that he ruled over, and my life his to end or not.

Satisfied by what he saw, he released me.

He tossed the keys onto their peg and went back up the stairs.

My arm throbbed. With a shaking hand I reached up and felt the Mark. Or what was left of it.

In nine days it had already started to fade, the scars receding into my flesh. Soon it would be gone.

Tears welled up and spilled over, and I couldn't stop the sobs. In the private emptiness of the dungeon, no one heard me weep.

All must believe.

GABEL: RUN, FIGHT, DIE

G abel would have preferred to crush one of his territories, and rip from them their names, as he had flayed the MarchMoon from the world. But he could not shed his honor. The other packs under his rule had not given him reason to rip them into pieces. It would not be right to suddenly change the terms of their previous submission. He would have to build that tower to the Moon from pieces found elsewhere, and wait for the other packs to betray him.

He stood on a hill overlooking the small cluster of houses and buildings below. Smoke came from a few, a few street fires, and screams. Bodies tumbling over each other as some fled, others cowered, others ripped and tore into those who fled.

Was this what the human hell was like? Bodies screaming and twisting and writhing while creatures tore at them?

He tapped his teeth together. He wanted to be down there, but the anger was too raw. He just wanted death and violence, feeling bodies pulling apart and breaking, blood soaking him, and it was hollow rage. It was not these wolves he was angry with. The anger ate a hole in him, gnawing around and around like one of those bottom-feeding fish scouring scum from the bottom of a tank. The dark fury sat at odds with the weakness of his body, the aching pain that invaded every joint and muscle and organ.

Gianna's loss had ripped life from him. Consumed and burned part of him away.

So he supervised from the hill. And if Eroth lost control of the IronMoon hordes, and perhaps some who weren't supposed to die did... he would not care.

The GrassClaw. That was the name of this pack. A small pack that had been on his to-do list. He had intended to offer them a bloodless deal made of words and promises, but no. No more promises. Not when the Moon broke Her word. No.

Brutalize the GrassClaw until their pack was nothing but tatters, and when he descended from the hill and gave them their new name, and their new Alpha, they would grovel at his feet and kiss them for his graciousness and mercy.

And those who did not would die.

Rip this place apart. Find them all.

If it fights, it dies.

If it runs, it dies.

Everything else lives.

"I should have included an order for children," Gabel mused.

Flint glanced sideways at him. "You would have a child cut down for being a child?"

Gabel glared at the chaos below him. A few cries of surrender reached his ears. He ignored them. No surrender. Not until they were all dead or prostrate. He was not going to accept less than cruel, brutal, bloody triumph. He would beat it out of them until they begged him to accept it.

They must be broken, and he must be willing to break them.

Flint said, "The fastest way to make a female despise you is to kill her offspring. You will never break a female that way."

"I must be willing to go as far as needed."

"That is a fool's talk. You cannot go somewhere from where you cannot return. Pups are a bigger threat dead than alive. Didn't Gianna teach you anything about a female's heart?"

"Do not say her name," Gabel snapped as his entire body twisted in a spasm, and his soul howled for her. The howling rung in his ears and mind. He shook his head violently to try to clear it. He was the one who had repudiated her, he should have been protected from the agony.

Maybe if it had been a real repudiation, not with him cornered and his own principles used against him, and his soul tugged and yanked at its shackles, and howled at its bonds.

His enemies couldn't see. If this was the Moon's will, didn't She know Her Comet couldn't be weak? What did the silvery sky-bitch want?

He was going to ask Her personally. With the tip of his goddess-forged claws.

Flint went on in a matter-of-fact tone, "You want to build a tower, not create a void that will consume you. You build the tower and fall off—which you will—you still built the tower. This is a void. You can do nothing with a void. Except throw bodies in it, and what then? You are no closer to the Moon than before, and invariably you will fall into the void and be forgotten."

There was a void inside him. He knew the futility of a void. "I made my promises before the Moon, and I meant them. This is how She answers faith?"

Flint did not reply.

Gabel snorted in disgust. "Your faith is obnoxious, old

man. What has She done for you except bind you to the same hell I'm in?"

"Faith is believing there is a larger purpose to our suffering, and that there is purpose beyond our own lifespan," Flint said. "One day, when you have pups, you'll understand."

"Oh, like you?" Gabel barred his teeth.

"Yes. Like me," Flint growled back.

Ana worked up the will to approach the edge and look down at the masses. "Fuck."

"We are not human," Gabel reminded her with warning.

"You think wolves got the monopoly on cruelty? Yeah, right. There's a reason I'm a vet, not a doctor. I hate people. Can't say I much like you wolves either. Different species, same fucked up shit. And here I am fucking standing here watching it. What does that say about me?"

"It says you are more honest than most."

A war-form splattered with blood loped up the slope on all fours. A few scratches had peeled up strips of hide from his shoulders, but he was otherwise unharmed. He shifted back into human form. "Alpha, they are howling to surrender."

"No. No surrender. If it fights, it dies. If it runs, it dies. It must *cower*. Break them until they are shards and ripped skin that beg to submit."

The wolf shifted back into war-form and bounded down the hill, the howl to continue combat shaking the tips of the trees.

Two hours later Gabel stood in the center of the decimated buildings, the surviving GrassClaw huddled in front of him. Mostly females, some shielding children with their bodies. There were some males too, a few badly injured.

Ana pulled one over. He gurgled from the hole in his side.

"Leave him," Gabel said. "Leave all them."

"This is a shit way to die. At least have someone come rip his head off so he doesn't suffer."

"Let him suffer. Tend to the IronMoon warriors."

Ana stood up.

"Do not test me, human. I wasn't the one who wanted you around," Gabel growled.

Ana threw up her hands. "Fine. Fine. *Alpha.*"

She stepped over the dying GrassClaw male and further into the organized, destructive chaos of IronMoon swarming over the buildings like a hive of termites.

The void inside him twisted around itself like a spiral-armed galaxy, a black hole in its center. A hole was right through him, and there would never be enough blood or death or agony to ever balance or fill it. He looked at the darkening winter sky. The Moon would rise soon. Good. Let Her see this.

I will destroy everything You profess to love. I will rip apart all You value, and we will see what You truly think.

"This is IronMoon territory now," he told the wolves. "And all this will be razed back to the earth. You may go east, towards IronMoon, and call yourself that. Or you can leave. I do not care where you go. Do not think you can find safety anywhere else. I will come for those packs too, in time, and do to them what I have done here."

A few war-form IronMoon warriors began to destroy an outbuilding with claws and snarls.

"Destroy everything!" Gabel shouted to them. "I want this place reduced to rubble! Burn it, splinter it, shatter it! Any who try to stop you, kill them!"

Some of the females with younger children squeaked and clutched their babies closer.

"You will leave us out in the winter?" one with two slightly older children tucked against her side asked.

"If you would call me your Alpha, then go to IronMoon."
He pointed to the east. "Or you and your spawn can rot into
the earth."

"What do you want?" one of the uninjured males asked,
barely old enough to shave and skinny and undeveloped.

"I have what I want from you," Gabel replied

"What about a treaty?" another voice asked from the back.

"No more treaties. They are not honored. Alphas get on
their knees and say nice words to me, but they mean none of it
and make arrangements and plot. No more treaties. I have
learned my lesson. Not even the Moon protects promises made
in good faith! I will make no more bargains with anyone!"
Gabel raged.

He returned to his hilltop perch to watch the destruction of
GrassClaw, holding one arm across the ache in his ribs, feeling
considerably older and haggard. He growled under his breath.

The survivors huddled like idiots for another hour until
they realized that it was over for them. Gabel ground his teeth
together, disgust bubbling in his gut. "I should kill them for
being so stupid."

"They are dazed," Flint said.

"They are idiots!" Gabel snapped. In the moonlight Flint's
tattoos swam and shifted, like underwater plants. This aching,
dull pain ate at his sanity. There was no triumph over this pain.
There was nothing to best. There was nothing to fight against.
It was just a void.

The darkness turned to orange and yellow as GrassClaw
burned.

Gabel turned his back.

The RockTail waited.

READY OR NOT, HERE I COME

The next time I saw Kiery she came to let me out of the cage.

She wasn't alone: she had two SableFur warriors with her. They were older men, going grey, and glared at me in a way that made it clear they weren't happy about being anywhere near me. They also did not give me their names, and Kiery didn't introduce them.

Goon A.

Goon B.

Kiery unlocked my cage and swung the door open. "Alpha Magnes has decided you may be released. However, given your past behavior, and where you're from, you're not a welcome guest. You'll be kept in SableFur's heart so we can keep an eye on you."

My heart surged. I was not only in SableFur's heart—I was *living* with the ranked members of the pack.

So that's why the Goons were grumpy. They had drawn some short straws. Nobody wanted to follow around a questionably sane Oracle that should have been miles away in a little cottage with Anita, and not underfoot in SableFur proper.

Too bad for them.

SableFur's heart had originally been an expansive estate, with a huge central ski-lodge type house. Over the years a few more houses and buildings had popped up, and the whole property sat a mile off a remote road and was fenced with an old palisade fence. The rest of SableFur was scattered throughout their huge territory.

Northern SableFur was rough open tundra, difficult to get across if the handful of existing roads didn't get you close to where you wanted to be. Mountains wrapped the south, west, and most of the east.

SableFur, simply because of its geography, kept mostly to itself. A long time ago they had gobbled up packs and built that huge territory within the safe valley, but since then, they had been quiet. As long as trouble hadn't come to their borders, they ignored everyone and everything around them. With a pack and territory so vast, they were practically their own country.

The silence of the main house struck me. Like IronMoon, very few wolves actually lived within its walls. This still bewildered me. Was it something large, powerful packs did? Shadowless hadn't been so... selective.

The SableFur gave me a room on the third floor. A small room, nothing special, and it smelled dusty. The only prominent feature was a large, east-facing window that gave a view of the forests beyond the fence.

The trees poked into the sky, swaying slightly in the breeze.

Just like...

"Don't wander around the house." Kiery pulled me out of my thoughts. "Your meals will be brought to you."

"Am I being held prisoner?" I asked, taking in the room, and looking for the RedWater ghosts. They'd flickered in and out only once since I'd seen Magnes. Perhaps they hadn't mastered the art of making themselves known.

Or my broken mind was just trying to fill in some cracks.

"No, but you're not a guest," she told me, voice dry.

The trees swayed in the breeze, pulling me back in my memories. "Can I go outside?"

"Yes, as long as your wandering is beyond the fenceline. Your guards will follow you everywhere you go and prevent you from going where you shouldn't. There are candles and salt on the top shelf of the closet for your work."

This room, despite its awesome view, was tiny, and I was going to risk my meditative space getting inadvertently trampled. Well, nobody said the SableFur had to make vindication easy.

I couldn't fail.

"Don't wander around within the fence," Kiery warned me again.

"Why? Fear I might spy?" I asked, unable to sound less than bitter.

"No, this isn't your home. Don't be rude." She slammed the door behind her.

I flinched at the noise, then the realization I had no home, and the SableFur could ship me back to Anita if I wasn't careful.

I needed to move fast, before Anita tried to get me back, or Magnes decided I was getting close to something dangerous.

But without a bowl what was I going to do?

I unwrapped the smaller spear of tourmaline. It had a good weight in my palm.

The blue color drew me in, blue like the ocean, blue like—

...*Gianna*...

I shoved it back into the velvet. Not yet. It wasn't a replacement for the bowl. It served some other purpose. The damn blue stone! I wished I hadn't brought it, but I hadn't been able to leave it behind. Gabel had the other one. Hopefully he wouldn't do something with it, and it was just a paperweight on his desk.

Will the tourmaline take me to him? He has the other one, perhaps—

The ache started under my ribs and spread outward. My body twisted around it in a single large cramp. I heard the faint howl in my head and caught the scent of blood and burning. Burning. Something was on fire—

Focus. How can we de-fang Magnes?

Stiff-legged, I turned around and took stock of everything in my room. There was a small bathroom with a tiny medicine cabinet, and a long, narrow mirror hanging behind the door.

I could use a mirror. A handful of Oracles did resonate with mirrors. Mirrors were far more dangerous and unreliable. Their flat surface couldn't protect the Oracle on the Tides. The Oracle would be completely exposed. Mirrors were lighter, easier to toss about, faster... or so it was said.

I had immediately resonated with a bowl, so I'd never risked a mirror. Mirrors were the last option for Seers who couldn't make a bowl work. Most took it as a sign they weren't powerful enough, or didn't have the Moon's favor, and simply withdrew from further training. Very few Oracles used a mirror by choice, and even fewer survived.

Mirrors didn't need to be carved, just consecrated, and that was simple. Broken mirrors were easy to replace. Actually, *any* reflective surface would do in a pinch. Even a crappy old mirror with nasty rust spots.

...What are you doing, Gabel?...

"You look like shit," I croaked to my reflection. I was gaunt, my skin covered in dusky, oily soot from the haze of the torches and general squalor; huge, ghoulish bags under my eyes. My neck was a necklace of ulcerated wounds. I looked like I belonged in a hospital. I probably did.

My fingers pulled at the sleeve of my far-too-large shirt, trying to get up the courage to see my Mark.

The hideous, crude, bars slashed into my arm had faded. The ridges sank back into the skin. I pushed my fingers into them, but they felt more faded and receded than when Magnes had done it.

I yanked the curtains closed and pulled the obsidian chunk from velvet. The rough edges raked my skin, threatening to slice me like a blade, but the cool well of secrets rose to my palm, a piece of the night sky without stars.

The Oracle was the one who decided when a stone was ready. Choosing that moment was our first major test since the later training all required a bowl. Acolytes who chose the wrong stone, did not purify it correctly, sent it to be cut too soon, all failed. It was always better to wait than to guess. A flawed bowl was useless, or dangerous.

Was I powerful and experienced enough to risk using a flawed bowl? Should I use the mirror instead? Should I wait?

The Moon had sent me here. The Moon would have to preserve me.

I returned the obsidian to the velvet and went to shower. I had not had a proper bath in... um... a while, and the water ran murky around my toes, and turned my neck into burning, acrid, agony.

...*Gianna*...

In the quiet of the shower, the steady pulse of water and steam lured my brain back into the recesses of the Bond, deluding me.

He had plunged me into water swearing this wouldn't happen, and I, so glib, had insisted it would. If I had even stopped a moment to think...

...Gianna....

He was here. He had to be, somewhere, he was close. The tile wall, was he behind the wall? I pushed, pressing, leaning. He was here, I could feel him, I could smell him even through the steam, he was here. I scratched at the grout. One of my fingernails ripped off the nail bed. I stared at the blood.

Flint had warned me. Flint had warned me.

...Gianna...

"Stop it! Stop it!" I shouted. "Stop it! Is this enough pain for you, Gabel?! Is this enough of a risk?!"

Why was I even shouting? I was the one who had told him to let me go and play along with the Moon's plan! I had no one to blame but myself. I could have fought. I could have refused.

It's better you don't know what you're going to...

Flint had been right. I wept into my hands. Flint had been right.

And even though I knew it was crazy, I somehow knew Gabel was coming. I could feel him pressing against the Bond, sort of like the heat from a fire behind a closed door.

I had to do whatever it was I was supposed to do here, so that when Gabel showed up, SableFur was ready.

Think.

The path to vindication involved four tests. One of those was find something hidden.

Which wasn't to be confused with a different test: discover a secret.

I had never spent a lot of time thinking about vindication, or learning anything about it besides it was an option, and what the tests were, or what the difference between hidden and secret was. It hadn't mattered. I had never thought I'd need to know.

The trees outside my window were just like the trees in the place beyond the Tides. Had I gone back in time itself and that place was real? If I could go there, I'd discover something hidden. How finding that hidden place was supposed to help me I had no idea, because what would I tell Kiery? *Oh, by the way, I found the place where your Alpha knocked up an acolyte?*

Outside the window, the trees swayed, luring me back into my memories of that Other Place. My mind stilled, my blood calmed. I needed to find it. That was what was hidden. That was what the Moon wanted me to find.

But first: the bowl. Chances would have to be taken.

I poked my head out my door. Goon A was absent, Goon B glared. I glared right back. "So. Who'd you annoy to get this job?"

His scowl increased several times over.

"Send word to Oracle Kiery that my obsidian chunk is ready to go to the stonecutter," I stated.

He harumph'd. I closed the door.

There. Done. The chunk was going to the cutter. First test of how far Magnes was willing to go to obstruct me. Time to find out if Kiery was one of Anita's little toadies like Thessa, or if Kiery was just an innocent Oracle caught up in this. Or a gutless one.

The trees danced around in the corner of my vision, but it wasn't time yet. I was still physically unwell, and I didn't have the faintest clue where to go. I could start prowling in a few days, but I'd need the bowl to help me divine the location of the grove, unless the Moon spoke to me in my dreams.

Try not to destroy the world, Gabel. I need a few days yet...

THE FIRST TEST

Bog, river, thicket.

I thumbed through the survival guide I had picked off Gabel's shelf. Bog, river, thicket. I read a few paragraphs of a chapter on creating a search pattern, and orienting oneself to new, unknown surroundings. Not what I was looking for. I needed information on the best ways to get across thickets, rivers, and bogs of sucking mud. Or, more to the point, try to figure out which one was the least dangerous option.

"Donovan makes you nervous. Or are you just reading survival books for dinner conversation?"

I closed the book and walked to the railing. Gabel stood in the center of the lower floor. Outside it was a misty, grey night. Gabel gave me an expectant look, arms akimbo, wanting his answer.

"I had a dream. I'm looking something up."

I retreated out of his sight and flipped back through the book.

Bog, river, thicket. Three roads, three challenges, only one outcome.

"Buttercup." His voice came closer as he came up the spiral staircase.

His presence felt huge, and hot, and everything dimmed, like gas lanterns flickering. I squinted at the text. Gah, I had gone too far, and was *back at that orientate-yourself-to-your-surroundings chapter again. "Gabel, I'm busy."*

His hand touched my arm, reaching out through the darkness. I twisted away, trying to find my place in the book again. He was such a pest—

"Buttercup. Is that the name he calls you?"

I dropped the book and whirled around.

Magnes looked back at me.

"Buttercup." He pushed me against the books. The weight of his body pinned me. "How adorable. A little pet name for his little pet Oracle."

"Don't call me that! Get away from me," I rasped, unable to breathe around his body pressing me flat against the shelves. The lights dimmed even further, with just the flickering wall sconce at my right to illuminate the dark space.

"I will never let you go, buttercup." Magnes curled the words at me around the fangs that extended from his jaws. His eyes tinged green like summer storm clouds.

He bent forward, and I screamed, kicked him, it didn't matter. His fangs glowed dull in the sconce light.

I screamed and pushed back—

I SURGED out of my covers mid-scream. I flung the covers off before I realized they were not Magnes.

I clamped my hands over my mouth to hold in the screams.

A dream. It had been a dream. A horrible, horrible, horrible dream. But a dream.

I rubbed my arms. Only Gabel's fading mark. Not—

It had been a dream. Just a dream.

Just a dream.

I retrieved my blankets and huddled into my bed. The

room seemed too big now, just a vast empty box. Almost every other time I had woken from a nightmare someone had been there. Shaking me out of it, waiting, or I had gone to them. Even Gabel had always been there.

The Moon had shown me that dream for a reason. I closed my eyes. I'd lived it, after having the dream about the bog, river, and thicket. I'd argued with Gabel about his public antics with me, and how Donovan would spot we'd consummated our bond, and he'd confessed to doing it all deliberately.

The book. The book was what I was supposed to have remembered! I had read a chapter about scouting unfamiliar territory and orienting myself.

The door opened.

"It's Kiery," the figure said. In her hand the light of her phone popped up, casting her in a faint blue glow.

I watched her from my huddle of blankets.

"I heard screaming." Kiery approached the bed.

"Nightmare," I answered.

"Are you better now?"

Did she actually care, or did it just worry her that I might have my gifts left? Hard to say. I looked at the drawn curtains across from my bed. "I am going to find something hidden."

There. I had declared that I was undertaking the first test. I would have a turn of the moon to find the hidden thing.

Unlike the others, the test of finding something hidden had to be declared. It wasn't like you could just show up with something and claim it had been hidden. You had to put the Oracles on notice that you had been shown the hidden thing, and you were going to find it.

Kiery didn't object, and she also didn't seem to care, but it was the dark of night and I had woken up that wing of the house with screaming. Satisfied I was not dying (nor killing anyone), she just shrugged it off and went back to bed.

THE NEXT MORNING I set out in wolf-form with my grumpy goons in tow.

With a little while to think about it, trying to find the meadow where Gabel had been conceived seemed reasonable. Magnes had always lived in SableFur's heart, so the meadow couldn't be too far away. Maybe he could have snuck away overnight, but acolytes were closely supervised, so it would have had to have been within half a day of the heart.

My goons had shown me a basic map of the surrounding area. There were no rivers, and no bogs within the logical distance. Thickets weren't noted on the map. There were several ponds. With the exception of the trees, and the meadow, there hadn't been any clues as to direction or location of the place I needed to find. After some thought, I decided to set up a modified grid search: trot out a mile, turn right (or left), then trot back and forth like I was weaving. Then the next day, trot out two miles, track the squares I hadn't before, over and over, for about five miles out, then rotate around to the next cardinal direction.

It might not have been the way Donovan would do it, but it was the best plan I had.

After four days of searching (and my muscles aching, my paws tender, and my ulcerated neck blistered, raw, infected glory) I caught the scent of something. I sniffed around the rock, unable to describe what I was smelling, but I did smell it, and the trail on the trees led me deep into the forest, wriggling under brush and scrambling over rocks.

"Where are we going?" Goon B growled, annoyed. They were sick of following me around for days on end.

"Wherever this scent takes me," I retorted.

"I don't smell anything." Goon A sniffed.

"You're not an Oracle," I flung back. If a male couldn't smell it, it wasn't a scent for their noses. I slid down a snowy slope, then wriggled under some more brush. It tore at my fur and neck. Didn't care. The scent was what mattered. The Goons swore and cursed as their larger bodies left tufts of fur behind on the stickers.

Males could be so vain about their pelts.

The forest was dense here, and very dark, and we picked our way along mostly by feel. Then, after an hour of scrambling, the trees grew thinner, and opened up onto a flat-ish plain of snow. I barked and bolted forward. The meadow from the vision!

Minus the pond, but the pond hadn't really been a pond, it'd been Her Eye, or a bridge back to my world.

I bounded down the hill with a shout of triumph.

The Goons were not impressed, and sat off to the side while I trotted around the clearing, my snout in the snow.

Surely the Moon had not just brought me here to find the damn place? I needed evidence! I *needed* the hidden thing, and this meadow was not hidden.

"It's getting late," Goon B told me.

I ignored him.

A new scent caught my nose, and out of the corner of one eye, I saw a glimmer. Just a brief gleam. I trotted over, but there was nothing there. I dug at the snow, rooting around in the frozen earth underneath.

The Goons looked on with interest while I dug with my forepaws.

"Come here and help!" I demanded.

They didn't move.

"The sooner you come help the sooner we can go back," I growled.

Reluctantly, they came over and helped. They were bigger, heavier, stronger and their large claws ripped at the packed, frozen dirt.

One claw caught a pebble, it flipped over—

"Stop!" I barked. I shifted into human form (damn, it was cold) and picked up the pebble. It was a sliver of quartz. A runestone.

Balance.

"A runestone?" Goon B asked.

"*Balance.*" I showed it to him, unable to hide how excited I was. "Keep digging. Carefully. There will be more."

Goon A hesitated. I shifted back to wolf and snapped at him, and, reluctantly, they continued to rake at the dirt.

We unearthed four more runes: *love, betrayal, pup* and *faith.*

In this case, the *love* rune was the one that symbolized passionate love between mates.

The Goons didn't recognize the runes, or they might have killed me right then. The runes were old, and had been there a long time, the edges softened by years, but their power intact. I could not use them, they were not mine, but someone once had.

Gabel's mother.

We dug some more, and found a small leather bag, filthy and half-rotted, and then, the claws of Goon B struck something hard. A jagged, broken piece of mirror.

"What is it?" Good B asked.

"A piece of a scrying mirror." The power of the mirror was firmly intact. Gabel's mother had used a mirror! I could barely breathe.

She had been far along in her training if she had had a mirror and a set of runes. Could she have been a full fledged Oracle, and had "left abruptly" under the guise of a calling?

Was that what she had said? Or was that what Magnes had told everyone?

Or what Anita had told everyone?

Someone had to have known where a late-stage acolyte or an Oracle had gone. They just had to! And an Oracle that used a mirror. Anita had to have known her, and couldn't possibly have forgotten her.

Anita, I am coming for you.

The remains of the mirror were the size of my palm, and I was able to put it in the leather rune bag. I told the other two wolves, "We've found the tools of an Oracle. Or an acolyte in the final stages of training. Some of them, at least. This is not a complete mirror or set of runes."

I picked the straps of the leather bag up in my teeth very carefully.

I had it. I had found something hidden, and I had (for whatever they were worth!) witnesses. The goons were very uncomfortable, ears slicking and unslicking, pawing at the dirt. They would be much more uncomfortable if they knew what those runes said! But that would be going too far. I had to be careful not to let on that I knew where all this was leading.

"It's late," Goon B said uneasily.

"Lead the way back," I said. "I'm done here."

We bounded through the snow. Getting back went quickly, but not before night had fallen and we entered the house coated in snow and ice, dirty and grimy, and the Goons had missed their evening meal with the pack.

I shifted into human form, dripping wet in the mudroom, the bag dangling from my fingers. I did need to report my find to Kiery no matter what, and I even had the Goons with me.

Did I dare do it with Magnes present? Would that stir up the hornets?

No good choices. If I delayed, it could be doubted. If I

stirred up hornets, I'd get stung. Better to march right into the dining room ass-naked and filthy with my prize.

After all. It was just flesh.

I followed the sounds of dinner. Goon B tried to tell me I should put on some clothes. I snapped at him to get out of my way. "It's just skin. You have it too."

"But—" He faltered.

I went right into the dining room, head held high. I had been the IronMoon Luna, and if I had anything to say about it, I would be again. Dinner stopped and silence glossed over the assembled senior members of SableFur. Oh, I was going to have an audience. Even better!

"Apologies, Alpha," Goon B said uneasily, trying to cover himself as best he could. He looked absurd, and it wasn't like his body was a squishy lump to be ashamed of. "She insisted on seeing Oracle Kiery."

I didn't wait for Kiery or Magnes or anyone else to acknowledge me. I walked right over to her. She sat several seats down from Magnes, who presided at the head of the table, Luna Adrianna on his right and his First Beta on his left. Luna Adrianna watched me.

Do you know?

I focused on not looking at anyone but Kiery. I had to play innocent and ignorant. "I have found something hidden."

"Excuse us, Alpha—" Kiery started to say.

I dropped the bag right in front of her plate before she could get up and get me out of the room.

My hair dripped water down my back as it thawed.

Kiery pushed her plate to the side, gave Magnes an apologetic look, and gingerly picked up the rotting leather bag. "Apologies, Alpha. The test does demand she come to me without delay. Gianna, where did you find... this?"

"A clearing about four hours northeast of here, through the

forest, across a meadow, and down a slope. My guards can tell you exactly where. Careful, there is glass in there."

Magnes and Adrianna just watched, but the First Beta showed far more interest. Kiery loosened the ties. With care, she withdrew the mirror shard, and her eyes instantly widened. Its speckled, ruined appearance did not disguise the power still imbued into it. She turned it over once, then carefully set it aside. She fished out the runes next and lined them up side by side on the table.

balance, love, betrayal, pup, faith

Even for an Oracle she went several shades paler.

I stared at her. I could not look at Magnes. Instead, I inquired of Kiery, "Do you know who they might have belonged to?"

"No," she said in a breathless, horrified tone. "I don't."

Oh I wanted to stare straight at Magnes as I spoke, but I restrained myself. "They had to have belonged to an Oracle or a late-stage acolyte. Their power is still intact. Has there ever been a SableFur Oracle who used a mirror?"

Kiery leaned her chin on her hand.

I stared down at her, cold-fire anger and triumph inside me. I had succeeded! The first test. And there was the Moon's accusation, the crime that had been committed, right there in front of Kiery, Magnes, his family, all of them! They wouldn't be able to make this go away or hush it up.

Triumph made me giddy and a little shaky. The First Beta gave me a curious look, but what did he care if he smelled my cruel, furious triumph? That's what I was here for, wasn't it?

Kiery stared at the mirror shard, but I couldn't tell if she knew who it belonged to or not. Kiery couldn't have known Gabel's mother—she would have been just a baby when all this had happened. But maybe she had heard something or learned something.

I bit my lower lip and focused on keeping my face calm. Kiery picked over the runes.

"Are the runes significant?" the First Beta inquired.

"I don't know," Kiery said.

How could she say that! I blurted out, "They tell a damning story."

"Four runes out of a set of how many?" Kiery glanced up at me. "Maybe they do, and maybe they don't, Gianna."

"What are the runes for?" the First Beta pressed, tone curious.

Kiery tapped each off in turn. "Justice. Mates. Betrayal. Pup. Faith."

Justice? That rune wasn't *justice*. It was *balance*. It could be (and often was) translated as *justice*, but not in the literal sense. There was a rune for that.

Kiery hadn't made a mistake. Anita had told her about my association with *balance*. Or the Moon had shown Kiery something.

Kiery didn't look at me, she was looking at the First Beta.

The shreds of the Bond within me twisted. My voice cracked as my lungs struggled to breathe around the pain twisting inside of me. "Surely there would be memory of an Oracle who used a mirror and just went missing, or left suddenly."

Kiery glanced up at me again, this time a sharpness to her expression. "I don't know offhand. You have found something hidden, Gianna, but it could have been there for a long time. Glass mirrors have been around for hundreds of years. I will look into it. After dinner."

Dazed, I gathered up the items. They were part of my test, and I was entitled to keep them in case I needed them to understand later tests. I bid the room goodbye, apologized for interrupting the meal, and went back to my room, with my subdued goons in tow.

I was grimy and filthy and cold, and the hot shower was amazing.

Victory.

THE GROVE: MEETING

Air like water currents woke me.

The Moon hung low in the sky, absorbing the whole window, throwing blue/silver light over the walls, washing, shifting, moving.

I slipped out of bed, moved towards my velvet-wrapped tools. The chunk of obsidian was gone, but my fingers, drifting through air, found the blue tourmaline spear.

The air pressed on me, pushing me down onto my knees, the currents closing my fingers around the stone.

Look.

~*~ Through The Stone ~*~

A tiny island of grass, suspended in a dark, endless void. The edges of the island simply ended, grass that stopped, the roots dangling into the void and flicks of dirt falling down. No sky, no ground, no walls. Just a little chunk of meadow, maybe ten feet in diameter.

"You're distracted, buttercup."

Gabel sat in the center of the island, watching me.

"You took your time," he added.

"Gabel?" This didn't feel like a dream, or a vision, or anything, it felt... real. Just like everything else the tourmaline had brought me to in the past. I looked around again, but there was nothing to see.

He held out a hand to me.

Could it be him? For the first time in two weeks the pain was gone, I could breathe, I felt him, aware of him again. The faint ache that permeated his body, the ache that hurt mine. I slid my hand into his, and he pulled me down next to him. Before I could react, he kissed me warmly.

This was real.

This was absolutely, completely, totally somehow real.

The dark void shifted and stars punctured the darkness. The sky began to rotate. Time ticking. We didn't have much of it in this place.

"If She thinks this brief visit will mollify me," Gabel told me, "she is wrong."

"She knows what you are."

"I like it even less that you think I'm doing what She wants."

"Gabel, do we have to argue?" I had full awareness of him, my brain was clear, everything was so clear, so real, so plain. He was thinner. A hollow in his cheeks that hadn't been there before.

"She dangles you in front of me like a bone," Gabel said. He studied me, his fingertips moved over where the Mark had faded, then the sores around my neck. "Silver. The SableFur used silver on you. Is this how Oracles are punished?"

"All must believe," I whispered.

"I believe, buttercup. I also do not like what I see."

"There is nothing for that."

He changed the subject, grasping for information in the stolen moments. "Where are you, buttercup?"

"SableFur's heart. They had me with Anita, but I attacked her and she decided I was too dangerous to be around. I've passed the test of finding something hidden."

"What did you find?"

"A few of your mother's runes and a piece of her mirror. Gabel, was she an acolyte, or an Oracle?"

Gabel frowned. "I don't know. She never spoke about anything from before. I didn't ask. I didn't know those are questions that get asked of parents. Maybe they do of humans, but not lupines. It is not... I suppose the easiest way to say it is the mind is not the same before the first shift. The curiosity is different. The things you ask about are different."

The silence was like a warm summer night. He buried his head in my shoulder. I closed my eyes.

Gabel pulled back and looked down at me. "Does he suspect what you know?"

"No, not yet. I'm sniffing around something I shouldn't be, but he doesn't realize I know what I'm looking for. If the next test digs deeper, he'll strike. He can't let me get close to the truth. He has children with Adrianna."

Gabel nodded. "That is reasonable. Do any other SableFur suspect?"

"No, and that is very strange. Anita knows, and I'm fairly certain Luna Adrianna knows, but nobody else has a clue." I told him how I had handed over the findings at dinner, in front of the elder members of the pack, and nobody had reacted beyond gee-whiz curiosity. A mystery worth looking into, but hardly something that might involve any of them. "How can an Oracle just disappear without a trace?"

Gabel, though, was satisfied. "That gives you room while he sizes you up. When is the next test?"

"When the Moon offers it. I sent my obsidian chunk out for cutting, but I won't have it for another month. I might have to use a mirror. I just don't feel like I have much time."

"I will pressure Magnes from the outside. If he is distracted by me, he'll have less time to worry about you."

That would only go on so long before SableFur swatted IronMoon. It couldn't happen too quickly. Somehow, my work and Gabel's had to collide at the same moment.

A red tinge colored the dome. "Dawn must be coming."

Going back to the pain made me shake, and Gabel's face drew in, suddenly gaunt.

The red dome washed down over us, a curtain of sky falling between us and the pain. The knots returned, made me scream as the darkness wretched me backwards towards the tourmaline anchor.

GABEL: THE ENEMY OF MY ENEMY IS

Aaron declined the invitation to sit. He stood in the center of the office. Gabel glared at him from his place by the window. The Master of Arms waited off to the side.

"You look like death." Aaron believed the rumors Gabel had gone insane. The IronMoon Alpha had a twitchy edge to him, and while he seemed healthy at first, when he moved it was as if his whole body ached badly enough he could not disguise it, and his attention twitched as if something constantly distracted him.

Gabel asked, "What do you want? You came here under parlay, but I have little patience."

"I want to discuss this tower you are building."

"I see you have spies everywhere," Gabel hissed.

"I don't need spies when you've talked about it in the open."

"You said you would stop me from building an empire. I beat you once, Aaron, what makes you think having a nice conversation will stop me now?"

Aaron gestured with one hand. "Because that was a cock fight."

"A cock fight that meant nothing? You claimed you could smell my mate's lure-scent and that you would take her from me. That meant something," Gabel growled.

"I *can* smell her scent. She smells of the night-blooming cereus," Aaron retorted.

Gabel snarled. Flint flicked his left hand—a classic gesture to focus on the matter at hand. Gianna had begged him not to be distracted by the SaltPaw. He struggled under the agony and jealousy, then told Aaron, "You made the trip here. I'm listening."

"SableFur."

Gabel snarled, his face rippling with the flutter of a shift before he gained hold of his humanity again. "What about the SableFur?"

"Haven't you wondered why they're just letting you gobble up packs right to their northern border? Even the SableFur can't ignore that."

"They are SableFur and arrogant enough to think they can get away with it. They pried my Luna from me like a soup can lid," Gabel spat.

"And have you not asked yourself *why*?"

"They are cowards."

Aaron sighed with forced patience. "No. It's because you're doing Magnes' work for him."

Gabel froze. He stalked across the space. The name ripped fury off his skin, some dark and smoldering scent lifting to Aaron's nose. "What did you say, IceMaw? I am not Magnes' lapdog!"

Aaron didn't budge. "You heard me. He used his Oracles to take your Luna from you. He lets you crush all the packs on this side of the mountain, and when you have done all the filthy work for him, he will pop you like a boil, come for my pack and my allies and crown himself King-Alpha with all our bones. He will not be a conqueror. He will be a hero."

Gabel shifted backwards a degree. "How do you know that?"

"You're the forest, I see the trees. Your little tower to the Moon has driven refugees flooding into SableFur. The SableFur don't want them there. They aren't SableFur. Yet Magnes refuses to raise a single finger against you despite the trouble you are causing his pack. Why?"

Gabel snarled. His vocal cords trembled on a growl and words he didn't want to speak.

Aaron raised both brows. "The SableFur never get involved outside their borders. You don't bother them, they don't bother you. You are bothering them with your burned-earth policy. Think about it. If IronMoon does all the dirty work of crushing, conquering, and killing, that means Magnes won't have to get his hands dirty. You're destroying packs and stripping them of their names, and that plays into things perfectly. When SableFur does come for IronMoon, Magnes will crush you, and he will get everything by right of conquest. He'll do exactly what you're doing, only he'll look like a damn hero doing it."

Gabel's eyes slid towards him. "But there are still packs under my control who are sworn to IronMoon under an older arrangement. If he takes IronMoon, those packs still exist."

"So what? How many are there? Four? Five? Maybe he'll liberate them. Maybe he'll play them to betray you and you'll destroy them for him. You are not being ignored. You are being played. Nobody is ever going to look between you and Magnes and call Magnes the criminal. You're either the monster, or you're the Alpha driven half-mad from his Luna's betrayal—"

"She never betrayed me or her vows!" Gabel shouted. He stormed across the office, face twisting and fingers stretching, and with a roar he swiped at Aaron.

The IceMaw Alpha leapt back, ducked right. Gabel snarled, gathering himself just barely. Harming someone who had come under parlay was disgraceful. "She never betrayed me or those vows. It was all SableFur! When they couldn't lure her away, they stole her! I was forced to do what I did for Iron-Moon because I still care about honor, and she will vindicate herself!"

Aaron strafed to the right, putting distance between himself and Gabel's claws. "Oracles don't let Alphas use them that way. She told you to go to hell."

"This is your fault, IceMaw!" Gabel snarled. "You want Gianna for yourself, this is just you making a play to get her! You are the Alpha who sent that MarchMoon wolf here to lay the trap for Gianna! You are the reason all of this has happened!"

Aaron snorted in disgust. "I would never win my Luna with such deceit. Yes, I told the RedWater to hunt on your land. Yes, I told the MarchMoon to send the petitioner wolf here. I did it to undermine *you*."

"And your strategy worked so well, didn't it. Go crawl back to the south, Aaron. I'll come for you in time. Enjoy your freedom. Or go crawl into bed with Magnes!"

Aaron didn't move. "I will call no wolf my Alpha, my Lord, or my King. I am here because the SableFur are playing you, and when they're done, they will come for me and my southern allies. Calling you King would be bad enough, but having Magnes steal the crown while being called a hero? That is worse. If I have to make deals with devils to prevent it, I will."

Gabel withdrew slowly, backed up a step, paced one way,

then the next, eyes never leaving Aaron. In an ugly tone he asked, "So what are you suggesting?"

"A temporary alliance. We work together to squeeze Sable-Fur's ambitions down to size."

"Not a direct assault."

"No. We secure the two access points in the south to destabilize the area. Their problem right now is in the north. Refugees taking up space in their northern lands. At the moment Magnes is ignoring it all. Pressure in the south will force Magnes to act when we want him to, not when he deigns to."

"You mean GleamingFang and RedWater," Gabel said. "I have GleamingFang in name."

"Exactly."

Gabel paused again, then limped over to his map, unable to completely hide the ache in his body. He gestured for Aaron to follow.

The IceMaw Alpha observed Gabel's slightly hunched stance, then said, "I thought you repudiated Gianna."

The name made Gabel flinch. He composed himself in the next moment and put his finger over RedWater's territory. "What dealings do you have with Holden?"

Aaron hesitated. "If we are going to trust each other."

"I am going to go for Magnes' throat," Gabel told Aaron. "He will not get mine. I do not care about anything other than destroying the SableFur."

"I will never call you King," Aaron said. "And I will never let you have SableFur."

Gabel snorted a laugh. "Then there's nothing to talk about. I want SableFur. Either under my foot or burned to the ground. You can have the ashes for all I care."

Aaron looked at the map. His own IceMaw were on it.

"You want things to stay the same, IceMaw," Gabel said,

"but they won't. Too much has been set into motion that cannot be stopped. I will crown myself with Magnes' bones, or I will die trying."

"And the rest of your pack?"

"The rest of IronMoon? The wolves no other pack wanted. They aren't tame and civilized like you. They will obey. To the death."

Aaron's face bent into lines of anger.

"Enough." Flint stepped between the two Alphas, voice calm. "Alpha Aaron, you have come a long way, and Alpha Gabel has a short temper. Stay the night, and once everyone has had a chance to think this over, revisit it in the morning."

AARON CIRCLED over to the map. Gabel seemed less frazzled that morning, but moved like he ached, which must have meant his whole body hurt far more than just an ache.

Gabel gave Aaron a long, long look, then repeated what he had said the day before, in a calm tone, "I will crown myself with Magnes' bones, or I will die trying."

"I do not believe we can dismantle the SableFur." Aaron decided to humor Gabel for a few minutes. "Just contain them and disarm Magnes' ambitions."

Gabel said, "No. It's personal between Magnes and I."

"Because you believe he took Gianna from you deliberately?"

"No." Gabel paused, then said, "Because Magnes is my father."

Aaron rocked back on his heels. He studied Gabel a moment, sharply, and said, "I've heard it said you bear a resemblance to Magnes. Having met the wolf multiple times, I agree. It's hard to argue you aren't his get."

"You might be right about Magnes' ultimate ambition, but you're wrong about what is driving him now. I must destroy him, or he will destroy me. I will take his crown, or he will take mine. There is nothing else."

Aaron frowned. "This does complicate matters."

"My mother always told me my father had died in the winter, as many wolves do. I never thought anything more of it. Such is the mind of lupines. Gianna had a vision where she saw Magnes coerce my mother to stand for him, and when it resulted in a belly full of pups, he drove her away. My mother was an Oracle or an acolyte, so Anita must have known her, and Anita and Gianna have had some of the same visions from the Moon regarding this matter, and that I am the Destroyer, the instrument of the Moon's vengeance. The Moon gave Gianna a vision where She warned Gianna that the Oracles would come for her, and I'd be forced to repudiate her. Put all this together, Aaron."

"To what end?" Aaron pressed with care, wary of what Gabel was saying, or not saying.

Gabel barked a laugh. "That She needs us both where we need to be, and that's not together. The silvery sky-bitch is going to regret the day I die, because I will have words for Her!"

"This still doesn't make sense." Aaron looked at Flint, who stood quiet and serene, blue-gloss tattoos on display.

"Gabel is the Moon's Comet, the instrument of divine anger." Flint answered the unspoken question. "That is the vision both Gianna and Anita had. Anita, apparently, has always known Gianna has a greater destiny than just being an Oracle. She is Balance, the point at which light and dark pivot. Oracle Kiery had a vision that Gabel would mate a Shadowless female, but the vision didn't show Gianna as the mate. The SableFur promised to help the Shadowless get their girl back should it come to pass. Gabel apparently chose differently than the vision foretold. Anita then demanded Gianna leave Gabel for the safety of all. She refused, and that was when the Moon revealed the SableFur's true motivation, and all of this was set into motion."

Aaron grimaced at Gabel. If it was true, then Magnes' was guilty of a number of serious crimes and Gabel was the rightful heir to SableFur, and that made Magnes' current Luna and offspring disgraced or even illegitimate. "Does Luna Adrianna know?"

Gabel weighed his answer. Then, he said, "We believe she knows, but only her, and Elder Oracle Anita."

"This is a hell of a secret to keep contained for almost thirty years. Not even a rumor," Aaron said, skeptical.

"If you don't believe, then there's nothing to talk about," Gabel said. "But go ahead, open your mouth and get those rumors going, Aaron."

Aaron ground his teeth together. "Let's say I believe you. That you're Magnes' bastard, and he needs to keep that a secret, and he's being a smart Alpha and listening when his Elder Oracle warns him that you'll destroy him, and Gianna is the one who can reveal the secret. Why let Gianna live at all?"

Flint said, "Our guess is that he can't risk the questions. He had a spy in MarchMoon, and your game with the petitioner wolf gave Magnes what he needed."

"Unless you knew about the MarchMoon spy," Gabel growled.

"I knew about her. There are spies everywhere. We all spy on each other. I didn't know Magnes had such an extreme motivation for wanting to take so much risk with removing you."

Gabel put a finger on RedWater. "Why stop at removing his bastard when he can have the bastard's crown?"

Aaron grunted.

"You have a nice, clean reputation. I do not. Demand that RedWater formally declare themselves IceMaw allies. When they refuse, attack them as IronMoon thralls. Nobody will question your motives."

Aaron nodded, and his lips curled. "RedWater will do whatever they think benefits them the most. No loyalty. It will be easy for me to sell my allies on dealing with RedWater."

"Exactly. Now, for GleamingFang—"

"Another gutless Alpha."

"I know you are his master, but I've never been able to prove it. Give me proof, and I'll destroy him like I destroyed MarchMoon. That will remove another slippery Alpha, put the two of us at direct odds with each other, and put pressure on SableFur."

Aaron looked at the map. "Your plan isn't complete. If I am seen as gnawing on your territory successfully, Magnes will have no reason to come for you. That buys Gianna time. Give me these two packs." He pointed to the two Gabel had planned to annex after SaltPaw. "Attack something in the north, or I will take it while you are in GleamingFang. Send a token IronMoon force to put up a bit of a fight, I will beat them, and then take the old SpringHide territory. Make it look convincing."

"Just enough of a fight to make it look like you got something of mine." The idea of losing to Aaron was noxious, but he could deal with the IceMaw later. Keeping the SableFur confused and unsure of just what the real threat was was the most important thing. It would keep Gianna safe, and buy her time. "Make a great deal of noise about how you will never bow to any King-Alpha."

"It would not be noise. I will not."

Gabel grinned at him. "I know. We can discuss that after we deal with Magnes."

"You dealing with Magnes might not give you SableFur, or even let you keep your life," Aaron said.

"Dividing up the spoils is an argument for another time," Flint interrupted. "If you two agree that SableFur and Magnes must be dealt with, then you can work together until then. Then you two can resume fighting with each other."

Gabel gave Aaron a hard look. "Are we agreed?"

"We are agreed, IronMoon," Aaron replied.

HIX : EXCUSE ME SIR, WHAT'S IN THE TRUNK?

Hix pushed his way through the bar crowds. The light was the unnatural pink-red all bars like this seemed to share, complete with dark corners and choking haze. The crowd thinned towards the pool tables, no doubt because of the hostile-looking individuals each bent over their own tables, or watching from the shadows.

Donovan sat on a stool, slouched against the far wall, beer on one knee and a dark-haired woman on the other. He watched a couple of guys play pool while the woman rested her head against his shoulder and teased the collar of his shirt. She opened her eyes as Hix approached, but didn't lift her head.

Hix sat down.

Donovan took a long drink. "I've got winner."

"You know what I'm here for." Hix was in no mood for Donovan's bullshit. The woman-de-jour sighed and murmured something to him.

"And it can wait for a bit. Fuck, don't you even know how to have a good time? I have a beer, a pool table, and a little company." He patted suspiciously low on her torso, almost between her thighs. "And you want to ride me about things you know I'm good for?"

Hix snarled, "Give me what I came for, or else I'm putting you through that pool table."

Donovan handed his beer to his date. "Hold this for me, hmm?"

She brought the tip of the bottle to her lips, leaned forward and eyed Hix as she licked and worked the neck of the bottle.

Hix was not amused. Donovan chortled. The Hunter fished around in his back pocket, pulled out his wallet and removed a few bills. He held up the cash between two fingers. "Want to go double or nothing? Double says the big guy there scratches the next shot."

Hix snatched the sweaty, moist bills. "No. We're done. Enjoy the rest of your evening."

"Aye aye, Mr Professional Thug," Donovan said. His date saluted him with the beer bottle.

Hix pushed his way out of the bar. The cold air was a welcome relief from the hot haze within. He crunched across the empty parking lot, got into the cab of his—*ahem*— borrowed truck and unfolded the bills. On the center most one, scrawled in purple marker, was an address:

127 Holly Briar
3rd (?) floor

The address lead to a squat three-level apartment building six blocks from the bar. "Apartment building" would have been a compliment, and only a minor technicality based on the fact that the condemned, broken-down building had rooms for rent. Humans lounged outside despite the frigid winter night. They did not bother to stir out of their drug hazes. A few gave him a cursory look, but upon realizing he probably wasn't the sort to share any drugs he had, nor the sort that could be *made* to share, opted to not ruin their highs.

The squalor of the building hit his nose from the outside, and the entire block was permeated by a chemical scent like paint thinner. Not a block any werewolf would want to hang out. Which was exactly why it seemed logical his hunt had brought him here.

The doors to many of the apartments were open. Many of the TVs were loud, people shouted, various kids ran up and down the hall unattended. A few kids made a game of jumping over the legs of a passed out drunk. Hix stepped over that body himself and continued slow progress around the halls until the scent he was after drifted from a stairwell. He tracked it to one apartment where the scent clung around the door frame.

He knocked and stepped to the side to avoid the peep hole.

He knocked again.

The door opened a crack.

He kicked in the door. A female shout and curse, footsteps scrambling back. Hix smashed forward and ripped the remains of the door off its hinges. The cheap wood splintered. She cursed and swore and bolted into the filthy one-room apartment, headed for the single window.

He lunged through the room and grabbed a handful of her hair. She screamed, swung around and punched him in the jaw, and her knee snapped up, but caught him in the thigh. He slammed her back against the wall by the throat. He pushed his fingers into her throat, cutting off the blood to her brain.

"Remember me?" he hissed at her.

She grinned and wheezed. "I'm not your type, remember?."

"Running back home to SableFur like a stupid coward."

She tried to kick him.

He didn't release her throat, but did release her hair, and punched her in the left breast.

She choked and gagged.

He eased up on her neck a degree so she could breathe. He didn't want her dead. Yet.

She wheezed and swung at him with a floppy hand, cursing in breathless tones about the size of his manhood, how good he was with it, how many knotholes in fences he had violated, and if he had ever been married to a sheep or goat. Her determination was admirable. He said, "We are leaving."

"Where are we going, big man?"

"SableFur."

She yanked against his hand. He followed her motion and smashed her back into the wall. Her skull left an indent in the sheetrock. She groaned. "SableFur? Why?"

"You are a SableFur spy." Hix pulled her close again. "You were born EmeraldPelt, but you're a SableFur Hunter, aren't you? You didn't cover your trail well enough. Donovan was disappointed."

"You think I care about getting caught? Alpha Magnes won't care. I was Magnes' eyes and ears, and Marcus knew it." She rounded her lips at him and blew him a kiss. "Alpha Gabel killed him for being a traitor. Big deal. None of this is news to anyone, big boy."

"So who sent the petitioner wolf to IronMoon?" Hix asked. "Was that Magnes, or was it Aaron of IceMaw?"

"Don't know, don't care, just know the answer he brought back." She smoothed her tongue over her teeth.

Hix grinned at her in return. He reached into his pocket and pulled out a length of silver-laced cord. He dangled it in front of her face. "Are you going to be a good girl, or am I going to have to tie you up and carry you out of here?"

"You know what I like." She blew him another kiss. "The police will be on you, wolf."

"Humans do not concern me."

He turned her around and neatly tethered her wrists together. She hissed as the silver bit into her skin. "Do it a little rougher, big boy."

His spun her back around. "Now, one last thing since I can't trust you."

"Oh?"

He punched her in the face.

She slumped against the wall, blood pouring out of her lips, and brain reeling. Hix hefted her over his shoulder and proceeded out of the building.

She barred her teeth at him and lunged against her silver-laced tethers.

"We have been through this thirty times," Hix said tolerantly. His shirt was torn, and he had some bloody bite marks from where she had managed to squirm and rip into his skin with her teeth, but he now had her tied up nicely in a little bow. She could just squirm and snap at him from her place in the passenger seat.

"Twenty-seven," she growled. She flipped hair out of her face. Her head pounded, and her brain was a little foggy. "You gave me a concussion, you piece of shit."

Hix ignored her.

"Why are you taking me to SableFur's heart?" she asked around her split lips. "There's no reward coming your way."

Hix ignored her.

Lulu scrunched herself against the car door. "Come on, big

guy, what's this about? Nobody's going to care you found me. Marcus is already dead as a traitor."

"Your testimony was what the Oracles used to dishonor Luna Gianna," Hix said calmly. "If everyone in SableFur knows you're a Hunter implanted into MarchMoon that's exactly what I need."

"So what? Everyone knows I was there." She shoved her feet up onto the dash and rolled her eyes.

"Exactly. I know Marcus served two masters. Alpha Aaron of IceMaw had him send the petitioner to IronMoon, and once the petitioner returned with his fake question— because he was just there to test how easily Alpha Gabel would grant access to Luna Gianna—and *you* sent all that information back to Magnes. Alpha Magnes used *you* to ensnare and discredit an enemy Luna, knowing it would weaken his rival. I cannot free my Luna, but I can shame your Alpha."

"They'll never let you leave alive."

"No, they won't. But you'll be dead before then," Hix said.

"Don't threaten me, big boy."

"The only reason you are not dead is that having a dead body in the truck bed would be conspicuous. I do not actually need nor want you alive."

Lulu pushed back more against the car door. "You're serious."

Hix did not reply.

"How about I start telling you what I know?"

"It does not matter. I will be killed and never be able to give the information back to IronMoon."

"You crazy fuck, you think Magnes will let you die? You'll get tortured for every piece of information you've got in that thick skull of yours!"

"I have seen Alpha Gabel wield pain like a weapon," Hix

said. "Your Magnes cannot possibly be worse than the Moon's Dark Comet."

"Is that what he's calling himself now?"

"That is what he is, and that's why Magnes is so afraid to face him openly."

"That's a lie! Magnes doesn't give two shits about that snaggle-toothed pup."

"Ask the Moon Herself. I will send you to Her quite soon."

"You don't have the balls," Lulu sneered.

"I promise to make it quick and painless. Your suffering doesn't interest me."

"Whatever you say."

Hix kept driving.

Lulu had been quite forthcoming about how to find the heart of SableFur as discretely as possible. Hix was sure they had been noticed, but nobody tried to stop them. Arrival at the heart had been a bit too easy, but then again, he had only been one wolf with one prisoner. They could afford to let him in. They would probably not let him out, but he did not intend to leave.

Hix hefted Lulu's body over his shoulder. Dead weight was a very different thing than live weight, as anyone who had lifted a corpse would attest. Lulu was still warm.

Whatever her real name had been didn't matter. The Moon was the only one who cared, and She already knew.

He carried it up the walk to the main house. A few faces peaked out of windows. It was quiet. Good.

"Magnes!"

His voice bounced through the silence and back at him.

More faces at more windows, peering around doors.

"SableFur! I have something of yours!"

He had to shout a few more summons before the front door opened, and a single wolf emerged. A male, tall, broad, warrior, thirties. By now other wolves had gathered around their doors and porches to watch.

Hix slung the corpse into the snow. He kicked her over. Lulu's neck bent at a sick angle, but her face was intact. "This she-wolf's words were the main evidence against Luna Gianna of IronMoon. A SableFur posing as a MarchMoon. Alpha Magnes used his Oracles to attack his rival's mate instead of using his own claws!"

The wolf at the door came a bit further out into the snow, then stopped.

Hix pointed at him. "You can kill me now, but all these other wolves," he pointed at the eyes peering at him, "are listening to me! Get your Alpha down here! Have him explain how he hides behind lies and spies! Come here, all of you, look for yourself! This is how the SableFur deal with threats! Not with combat, but with spies and liars and moles! Your Alpha doesn't attack another Alpha with courage, he attacks his Luna with his corrupt Oracles!"

The single wolf outside the front door quickly ducked his head back inside.

Within minutes another wolf appeared, wearing far more prestige on his shoulders, calm and stern. "Your accusations are not welcome, IronMoon."

Hix snarled, "Nor are they unfounded."

More warriors stepped out of the house.

Hix snarled at all of them. "Your Alpha is a coward protecting his own skin! He fights without honor! He lies and hides and skitters side to side like a crab!"

They charged at him, stretching into war-form. Hix leapt forward to meet them.

His life didn't matter. He had done what he set out to do. Claws raked into flesh and violence screamed in his blood.

The wolves fell upon him and ripped into his flesh.

Hix swiped at one. His claws ripped up strips of hide as one bit down on his shoulder. He barely felt it. Pest! If he could maim even one before they killed him he'd go to the Moon with his head held high. He howled and grabbed one by the jaw, claws wrapped around the lower mandible and tried to pry the wolf's mouth open. He'd crack this wolf's jaw and rip out his fangs!

A claw stabbed into his left eye. His field of vision narrowed, but there wasn't any pain. He barely felt anything except the hunt and the coming kill. He twisted his hands, and the wolf's jaw cracked.

"Enough," a single female voice commanded over the din.

Instantly the wolves broke and shifted to pin him. Except for the one Hix had maimed, who collapsed into a bloody, slack-jawed heap.

Luna Adrianna of SableFur came one step out of the house, flanked by more warriors. She surveyed the scene, then looked at Hix. "Don't kill him. Collar him and lock him up. The First Beta of IronMoon is too useful to be killed quickly."

He had not died soon enough! He had failed.

Another wolf brought a collar and clamped it around his neck. The silver singed his skin, forcing him back into his human form. "My Alpha doesn't know I am here. I know nothing!"

Adrianna didn't flinch. "Then you will tell us all about this nothing. Take him inside."

THE SECOND TEST

I didn't have to beg to go down to the dungeon. It took two days for them to get around to saying yes, but it had been a simple *yes*. I didn't even have to take my two goons. They waited upstairs by the door, and I descended the stone staircase alone.

There was no reason to trust why they'd let me down here. For all I knew there would be some little spy curled up in a dark corner, listening to everything I had to say, watching everything that happened.

But I couldn't stay away. That fool First Beta—had Gabel sent him? It had been a suicide mission if he had!

Hix, in naked human form, curled in the center of the cell I had been in. His skin was savaged and covered in shadowy bruises, his injuries only half-tended. The shadow of the silver-backed collar obscured his neck, and the flickering torchlight cloaked his body in shifting shadows.

He raised his head, and immediately shuffled over to the silver-wrapped bars. Chains scraped stone. He had a cuff around each ankle, bolted to a plate in the far corner. He came within a hair-distance of the bars and croaked, "Luna."

One of his eyes was sewn shut with six crude stitches, and a trickle of blood had crusted at the corner, and the socket itself... realization jolted me that he had lost the eye. His jaw hung loose on one side, completely broken, and it slurred his words as he tried to speak. The gash across his belly had been restitched for the how many-th time? I couldn't bear to inventory it all, and could barely speak. "Not here. I am no one's Luna here."

"Always. Anywhere," he rasped.

The iron keys were still on the hook. I retrieved them and yanked the door open. I didn't care who heard. I stepped into the cell and knelt down next to him. "What have you done, Hix?"

I had heard what he had done, of course. It was all over SableFur. The house had become like a drum, everything stretched tight and sounding much louder than it was. Even from my little dusty corner I had caught my goons whispering to each other, and seen small groups talking outside. Not in the casual laughing nice-to-see-you way, but in the close-leaning, serious, hushed way.

Lulu.

It seemed so long ago, it was hard to remember what she had even said. It was another lifetime ago.

I leaned as close as I dared. The proximity to silver burned my skin like the fizz off a soda. "Why? You had to know it won't change anything, and they'd kill you."

"I did to them what Lulu did to us. Doubt. Questions." Hix shaped each word with careful pain.

"But your life for so little?" I pleaded with him. It wasn't fair to make him speak, but I couldn't stop myself. Oh, his jaw! I reached towards him through the bars. I cradled his face, trying to do something for him, but he flinched and I withdrew, helpless.

"It is more than zero."

My eyes pooled tears. Stupid, literal wolf! He looked at the raw wounds on my neck with his good eye, and started to rasp, "Luna—"

"Did Gabel send you?"

"No. He knows I hunted Lulu. I told him I would not return."

"Don't speak that way," I pleaded.

"Do not let them hold me prisoner, *güzelim*," he whispered his one request.

I had no idea what the last word was, but I knew exactly what he wanted me to do. I whispered a plea, "The first responsibility of any prisoner is to escape."

He shuffled a little closer. "You plan to attempt escape?"

Getting him out of the cage was easy. But he wasn't going to get far with his injuries. One eye gouged out, shattered jaw, silver sickness, who knew what else. I couldn't even look at the wound on his belly. My fingertips brushed the stiff beard sprouting on his jaw. No, escape for him would be hopeless. I could just walk out of SableFur anytime I wanted, but I couldn't take Hix with me.

I gulped and answered instead, "No, I can't leave. I have to clear my name. You could try."

Was that why they had let me down here? If I let him out, Magnes would have an excuse to kill me. Maybe they thought I wouldn't dare.

"No," Hix said. "I will die for you, but I will not leave you."

I shook my head, trying not to blubber, and whispered, "It might not matter. I have to work quickly, or we'll both be down here."

My vision shimmered like rain off a glass window, and the RedWater ghosts materialized. Hix did not see them as they slid through the bars and circled around him, sniffing out each injury and wound. Azure blue tendrils of light flicked off their coats, caressing Hix's skin, illuminating each part they touched. What were they doing, and why show themselves now?

It wasn't fair that he'd die for so little. He deserved a glorious warrior's death and funeral. Not to die like... like this, poking a bee hive with a stick just to piss off the bees so someone else could run in and get the honey while he was stung to death.

Stupidly, I clung to the hope I could save all of us.

"Does he suspect?" Hix's whisper pulled me back to him.

"Not yet, but he will." The frantic urgency gripped my throat even thinking about it.

The RedWater wolves sat on opposite sides of Hix and stared at him. The blue glimmer on the tips of their ghostly pelts remained.

"Then I will not leave you to die alone," he whispered.

My lips trembled and my fingers did too. "I'm so sorry. I can't. I—"

I wasn't brave enough to be alone. Even though I knew Magnes would torture him, and make him suffer, I didn't have the courage or the bravery I needed. The will to do what I had done for the RedWater wasn't there. I couldn't do it. I couldn't even think it. Hix had been my guardian, even willing to fight with Gabel. Even if he often chose the wrong moments and hills to die on.

Hix sank down onto the stones. "All I want is a good death, because I have not led a good life. I know what they will do to me. I am not afraid. It is for my Luna. I should have done more, sooner. But I was not brave enough when it counted. I will not fail again. If my life still serves you, then I will remain."

"Stop talking." I feared for his mangled jaw. Every word must have hurt him. The tears were hot and thick now. Soon

I'd be blubbering like an idiot. I bit on my lips and fought the shaking in my throat. The RedWater ghosts watched, blue-tinted, and Hix's one good eye was glassy-bright. My hands trembled with realization. "You found the secret for me, Hix. This was the second test."

The secret. Lulu hadn't been the secret, she had been the evidence of the secret: Magnes' secret. I'd follow the trail of blood the rest of the way.

His lips couldn't smile, but somehow his face did even through the swelling and blood.

"I could let you out. I could, I could do what you wanted, but—" It was too much. So many had died, I had ordered some to their death, I had killed, my soul ached, every part of me hurt, and I couldn't do it. I couldn't put Hix out of his misery. And maybe, if I did, Magnes would believe I was still the IronMoon Luna in some way, and maybe this was all just a trap.

Maybe that was an excuse I made to myself.

"Save your courage," Hix said. "I have my own."

My hands fell to my sides. Hix, exhausted, shuffled back to the center of the cell. They had at least given him a blanket. That was an improvement, or was it? The RedWater ghosts sniffed at him, he didn't seem to notice, then they slid back through the bars to sit on either side of me.

Upstairs, my goons gave me looks I didn't appreciate. I snarled at one, "You will be so lucky if your Luna even knows who you are when you die in her service! Would you do what Hix did for her, if she were me?"

He hesitated before he said, "I would."

"Liar, coward!" I spat.

The RedWater wolves wove around their legs, their fur-tips now haloed in reddish-orange-yellow.

"You can say whatever you want about him," I snarled,

"but he isn't a coward, and I'm not guilty. He'll die a warrior, and I'll vindicate myself. You, however, are going to be following me around and when I'm gone, because I *will* be gone, you will still be here doing whatever menial shit goons like you do. If you want to figure out how to be a wolf worth something, go look at the one you just spit on!"

My insides twisted and hurt, almost spinning as they twisted around themselves in a huge knot.

...Gianna...

"Get away from me!" I snapped my foot into Goon A's knee. "Mongrel lapdogs! So worthless they didn't even bother to tell me your names! I doubt the Moon cares either!"

I stormed away before I could do anything else stupid, the RedWater wolves trotting behind me.

DEMENTED EASTER BUNNY

I huddled over the little piece of mirror.

Gabel's mother's mirror.

An Oracle who had used a mirror, and no one remembered. I pulled my finger along the sharp edges.

And Hix in the dungeon. Hix who had found the secret for me, in my name. The SableFur wouldn't see it that way, so I'd have to make them see it that way. I couldn't let Hix's sacrifice go forgotten. I couldn't let the SableFur go back to sleep and pretend it hadn't happened.

The RedWater wolves sat across from me, sunlight playing golden games on the tips of their ghostly pelts.

I had never questioned the Moon before; I had just accepted that deities were beyond my understanding, but the longer this went on, the less it made sense. The ghosts of two wolves I had put down months earlier seemed the most normal thing in all of this. If the Moon had wanted to destroy Magnes, She could have done so.

Perhaps She had already tried.

I only knew that Kiery had seen Gabel choose a Shadowless

female for a mate. She had known me from before, and hadn't seen me, so it must have been Amber she'd seen. Gabel must have changed paths at the last minute and chosen me. That was why visions were unreliable. They only showed a likely future, not a certain one. A single choice could change everything.

Just like I could choose to leave SableFur and return to IronMoon.

Lulu made the SableFur very uncomfortable. Lulu hadn't been her real name, but that's the name everyone had called her, and she had been a well-known and trusted Hunter for Magnes. Her being in MarchMoon for so long, posing as one of them, knowing something as personal as a vision, and having been the voice that had incriminated me... it shocked people.

Gabel was a monster. Nobody in SableFur disputed that. Magnes dealing with him was important. Nobody disagreed on that either.

But incriminating Gabel's Luna using the Oracles and a spy?

Hix had made it more difficult for Magnes to simply throw me into a pit. There might be some questions as to why, but those questions wouldn't be too loud. He'd find a way to smooth them over or push them aside.

It was going to be a race to the finish. No time to wait for my bowls. I needed to know my next move, and my choice in tools was a mirror or the tourmaline.

I set the old piece of mirror aside. There was a vague feeling about it, like it wasn't quite real, or that it was dangerous. It had belonged to another Oracle, and we couldn't swap tools between each other. In theory the tools could be purified again after a very long time, and having been buried for about thirty years might have been good enough, but the mirror was angry. It was still an Oracle's tool, and I wasn't the Oracle it had chosen.

That left the mirror off the back of my door. This mirror was rust-spotted, old and generally derelict, but didn't send an ominous prickle up my senses like the other one.

I smoothed the surface with salt and wrestled it out of its wooden frame. Mirrors didn't need to be purified like stones, their reflective surface meant they were difficult to contaminate. This one felt inert and well... dead. Dead could work. I brushed the salt away and selected my runes. *Protection*, of course. *Mercy* seemed reasonable. Not a rune often used. It could mean various things, literal mercy, or intervention, or supplication. I had no idea what I was even looking for, aside from my next clue.

I was afraid. I was so afraid. Hix in the dungeon, Gabel setting fire to the countryside, Magnes closing in on me. Using an old rusty mirror. The ghosts of two wolves I had put down staring at me from the corner of my tiny room. My fingers trembled as I fished through my runes, unsure which one to use. I settled on *courage* because the Moon knew I needed it right then.

Runes aligned along the top of the mirror, I knelt, and leaned over the reflective surface.

I clung to the edge of something. The mirror's sharp edges. The Tides churned and bounced, threatening to topple me off balance into the waves. I clung to the mirror and tried to stay within the center of the motion, not let myself panic or cry out. I had to keep focused, and not capsize into the Tides, or get lost.

I could do this.

I had to.

I was at Sablefur. Specifically, outside the main house, standing on the porch of one of the other houses, looking inside a window.

Inside, a little girl was tearing apart her room. I pressed my face to the glass and heard her sobbing.

The Tides hadn't taken me far.

I turned and looked around, trying to figure out what I was supposed to see, because I didn't sense it was the little girl, beyond she was a little girl looking for something. At the corner of the porch was a large tree. I went towards it and looked up into the evergreen branches, and spied what the girl was looking for: a sock doll.

A toy. She was looking for a toy that had been thrown up into the branches.

A toy?

A shout from across the way. Angry. Male. Then answered by a female.

Bewildered, I walked towards the argument. It was behind another house, a man and woman having a snarling, not-quite-shouting fight in their kitchen. I peered through the window.

"I told you he won't pay us back!" she was shouting at him.

"He'll pay us back," he snapped. "He's my brother, he's good for it."

"When are you going to stop? He's not good for it and never has been!"

"He'll be here with the money tomorrow," the man insisted, red-faced and furious.

The scene made the hole in my soul ache, but at the same time I laughed. Gabel and I would have been lucky to argue over unpaid debts. The argument seemed to end, with the players pausing like a stilled movie. I pushed off the window and walked around to the back of the house. Tucked into the door jamb was an envelope with the rune for the brother in red ink. I opened it.

Half today, the rest when I can.

The mirror shifted under my feet, and everything wobbled. I gasped and dropped to my knees. My fingers slid through the wood, finding the sharp edges of the mirror instead, as the vision dissolved into mist and darkness

---

I HAD SLICED my fingers open grabbing the actual physical mirror.

The blood coursed down my hand and wrist.

Still woozy and disoriented from being sucked out of the vision so abruptly, and exhausted from wrestling the Tides, I stared at my hands, dumbfounded by the sheer amount of blood, and the lack of any pain to go with the deep gashes.

After a few moments of bleeding, my senses returned, and I went to my bathroom. The water hitting the open wounds made me yelp in pain, and once my body realized how deep the gashes were, the amount of pain caught up.

And the bleeding wasn't stopping.

I wrapped each of my hands in a washcloth, which quickly soaked red.

Goon B was on duty that time of night. I held up my towel-wrapped hands. "I think I need stitches."

"What the hell?" he asked, taking in the damage and the blood dripping onto the floor.

"I grabbed the sharp edge of a mirror," I explained.

"Go sit down and try not to bleed on anything else," he said gruffly.

Lacking a bathtub I went and sat in the shower stall, fingers clenched around the towels, and damn, had it all started to hurt. I tried to distract myself by figuring out how to pad the edges of the mirror so I wouldn't slice myself open the next time I used it.

Now a headache had set in, and the exhaustion from the vision. I just wanted to sleep and wait for my brain to stop sloshing around.

Goon B returned with Kiery. Kiery couldn't do stitches, so why had the Goon brought her? She unwrapped one hand, then quickly rewrapped it. "What did you do?"

"I was scrying with the mirror and must have grabbed it on the Tides."

"With a mirror? Are you insane? Your bowls will be done in a month," Kiery groused. She looked up at Goon B. "Call the doctor. We have to take her."

Goon B was mildly annoyed at the late night jaunt a few miles down the road to a small brick building. The doctor wasn't much happier having been dragged out of bed to sew up my fingers. My fingers, once they were washed down, were cut deep: a gash across the middle three fingers on each hand. The bleeding had slowed down to a persistent ooze.

"What were you doing using a mirror?" Kiery demanded while the doctor numbed my fingers.

"Scrying." I felt more than a little fuzzy.

"With a mirror?" Her voice cracked on her agitation.

"I had to. What do you care if I use a mirror and die in the attempt? I'm an Oracle. I know the risk I'm taking."

She growled, "Did you see anything?"

"Yes."

"What did you see?"

"A toy in a tree and a note in a door." The numbing injection had also had some painkillers in it, and that turned my brain into soup. The doctor also checked the slow-healing necklace of ulcers.

The RedWater wolves materialized in the bright light and sniffed Kiery, the tips of their fur green/blue. One of the wolves put his paws up on the bench and sniffed the hand the doctor wasn't currently stitching.

I half-expected Kiery to at least be partially aware of the wolves, but she clearly wasn't.

Kiery didn't ask any more questions, and I drifted into la-la land while my hands were stitched and bandaged. Somehow I ended up back in my bed, and the next thing I really remember was waking up in the yellow-dark of my little room in daylight, my hands hurting like they had been hit with a hammer, my head splitting, and a rotten taste in my mouth.

And the RedWater ghosts curled up at the foot of my bed.

I propped myself up on my elbows. I needed to go outside and see if that toy was in the tree.

The RedWater wolves looked at me, shimmering and translucent, and expectant.

I still had their fangs. The seat of courage, the warrior's fight. But now them sleeping on my bed seemed so... personal.

I also got dragged back in time to Places Beyond The Tides, and groves suspended in a void to see Gabel, and my Bond blocked off and twisted, and trying to unravel the secrets of a Goddess. A couple of wolf-spectres... but perhaps I should stop just taking them at face value.

"If I asked you to do something," I ventured to the spectres. "Would you?"

Both tails wagged slowly to affirm they would, in fact, entertain requests.

"Will one of you go down to the dungeon and check on Hix?" I asked.

The one on the left hopped down off the bed and disappeared through the door.

As much as I wanted to stay in bed, and moving sent a pulse through my fingers, and my head was a sloppy mess, I needed to go find that toy and that note. The note had said *tomorrow*, and that implied "pretty damn soon," so I needed to arrive before the note.

Getting dressed with my hands bandaged into mittens was difficult. Shoes were impossible. A bra was impossible.

Goon A greeted me outside the door.

"Rough night," I told him, holding up my bandaged hands. "Don't judge."

I knew I wasn't allowed to prowl around within the fence, but I was going to break the rules. I wasn't prowling, really. I was looking for something. Goon A followed close behind. It was easy enough to find the first house with the toy, it wasn't far from the main house, and my vision had been flawless.

"You aren't supposed to be out here," he reminded me.

"I had a vision," I snapped. "This won't take long."

I peered up at the trees around the house, and right where the vision had said, I spied a little sock doll in the branches of an evergreen.

"What's going on?" a female voice asked as a screen door creaked open.

"The toy." I pointed at the tree. "The toy the little girl was looking for. It's up there."

She gave me a totally bewildered look.

"The sock doll toy. It's up there on the branch. She's been looking for it, hasn't she?" I kept pointing at the tree.

Well, if Magnes thought I was merrily, harmlessly insane, he might be less quick to kill me... maybe that was the Moon's ploy. To make me look a wee bit crazy. But then Magnes could just put me down, so that sounded bad too...

But the woman walked over and peered at where I was pointing. Then she looked at me, eyes widening. "How did you know?"

"Just what the Moon offered," I answered, as confused as her as to why the Moon would offer such a trivial vision. The woman went and retrieved a broom and used it to shake the tree branches until the doll fell to the ground.

Next to the other house.

"How did you know, really?" Goon A asked.

"I was scrying last night," I told him waspishly. "I told you. I'll prove my innocence!"

The next house was easy to find as well. I immediately circled around to the back door. No note. But my antics quickly drew the interest of the mated pair that lived there.

"What are you doing?" he asked.

"Has your brother been by today?"

"No."

"He'll bring you half the money he owes you, the rest when he can. I don't know if I'd believe that second part, but that's what he'll tell you. So you were both right. He's half good for it, which is an improvement, I guess."

They looked at me like I was absolutely off my rocker. Were they not used to Oracles telling them things?

Goon A asked, as we went back to the house before anyone got their panties in a bunch about me being within the fence-line, "How did you *really* know?"

I stopped walking and turned around to face him. "Lulu thought whatever she thought, but she had it all wrong. Gabel might have believed her over me, and that's his business but—" I choked up throwing Gabel under the bus. Playing along with that hurt, and the Bond writhed against its lashings. I held my belly, aching, for a long moment before I recovered. "But he'll regret that too!"

Goon A's expression made me sneer around my pain. Did these stupid SableFur really think I had done wrong? With everything laid before them?!

"So you really thought I had violated my vows? Bullshit. And I'm halfway to proving I didn't. So anytime you want to stop acting like I'm beneath your contempt, you do that. The only reason I'm here is because of Magnes' little pet spy Lulu. Alpha Marcus was a traitor to IronMoon, and he admitted it. Maybe he knew all about Lulu. I'm only here because of her, and who she answers to, so maybe you should think about how and why that happened!"

Once I was back in my room, and the shaking and pain had stopped, and the RedWater wolves sat across from me, ghostly eyes boring into me that I realized I had made a terrible mistake.

DEATH PHASE

What had I done?

I buried my face in my bandaged hands and whimpered.

Hix had been the one to accuse Magnes of having a spy, and implying that he had been in league with Alpha Marcus, and that he'd manipulated his Oracles, or let his Oracles manipulate him. That was one thing.

Me saying those things? Letting on that I knew—or believed—that Magnes, not Anita, was the reason I was here?

And I had stood there out in the cold open like a raving moron shouting for everyone to hear.

The RedWater wolves sat at the foot of my bed, watching me, patient.

"Hix," I said to the one on the left. "Did you see him?"

The ghost stood, padded over to me, his legs passing through my flesh. He was a spectre. He wasn't there. Just like a cold breeze going through my skin, which made me shiver, and he pushed his face right up to mine.

It was so cold. Not cold like winter or cold water or even the Moon's silvery light.

He was cold like death.

Part of me phased out into the dead wolf's soul, or part of him phased into me. I couldn't tell, but instinct told me everything, even if I didn't understand it.

His eyes phased over mine, merged with mine, and I saw what he had seen.

The dungeon smelled of old death. Generations of death and pain and blood and everything dungeons were meant for. Bleach and scrubbing couldn't erase the generations of purpose.

Hix still curled in the center of the center cage, on a pile of straw and under the blanket. His back was to me, but the collar's buckle laid against his neck, and the chains linked to his ankles and wrists still hung from their rings. The top of his shoulders and neck were exposed, haloed in stripe-like bruises.

Silver toxicity destroying his blood vessels and causing bruising as they leaked.

He smelled of pain. Deep, intense pain. Fresh pain and new pain. And a sort of resolved not-caring. Acceptance. Acceptance that this was his lot, that the pain would only be temporary, that the pain was the price.

I wanted to race down there, open the cage, wash his wounds, help him, *do something*, but if I dared... I had already flashed my cards at Magnes, I might have already ruined everything, but if I went down there it was more damning.

"I'm sorry. I'm sorry. I'm sorry," I sobbed. I was horrible. I was a horrible, horrible, horrible packmate, a horrible Luna, leaving my First Beta to rot just a few stories below me.

I had to get control of myself, and see this through.

"Can you both do that?" I lowered my voice to a whisper.

The wolves wagged their tails in unison.

"How far can you go?" I asked. Did they have a range? Could I send them anywhere?

One wolf jumped off the bed and walked halfway to the

door. He wagged his tail, walked the rest of the way to the door, and fell over, feigning death.

How ironic.

"So..." I struggled. "Not far from me."

More wags.

"Can you go outside the house? To the fenceline?"

They seemed to confer between themselves and gave me a doubtful affirmative. Maybe that far.

But I had spies. Spies. What did I want to know? What could I use them for? They couldn't speak, they couldn't touch or move anything, they could only be my eyes and maybe my ears. They were like little portable scrying bowls! That's how I'd use them. I'd think of them like bowls.

"Go out to the houses," I told the wolf on the left. "Just watch and listen. Prowl around."

The wolf hopped off the bed and disappeared through the door.

The other wolf sat up, waiting for his assignment. I licked my lips. Who did I want to watch? Magnes? Kiery? The First Beta? Luna Adrianna? Or just have him prowl around the house listening for anything useful? Strategy wasn't my strong suit. Who would Donovan spy on if he didn't know what he was looking for? Or Lulu... Lulu had been in MarchMoon longer than I had been in IronMoon, just waiting for... what? Exactly. She had just been waiting and watching.

That's what I had to do. Observe and look for a hole. But to dismantle Magnes, I'd have to prove to SableFur what he really was. So I needed to know what the SableFur believed, not what Magnes knew or when he knew it.

All must believe.

What better key than the First Beta? If somehow I could get Lucas to start questioning Magnes, he could be a useful crowbar. It was like a vision: the actual answer was best understood by the person asking the question.

"The First Beta," I told my spectral companion. "Observe. Listen."

Magnes knew I was up to something—and that I did not like him. Like a constrictor snake, he'd start to squeeze me soon.

There was no time to waste.

Bandaged hands or not, back to the mirror.

THE MOON SHOWED me nothing but trivial visions much like the previous set. Perhaps anything further on the Tides was too dangerous with the mirror.

I stared at the mirror, a little nauseated from the roiling Tides, trying to figure out what the point was. There had to be a point, but I was too exhausted and hurting too much to figure it out. My hands hurt so badly, and my skin was flushed but clammy, like when I had first emerged from the agony of the Bond's being bound off.

I took a handful of visions to their respective owners. There were three this time. Nothing important or special, two lost items and a prediction that the phonecall someone was expecting would come by dusk the next day. Goon B accompanied me, but didn't interfere or even glare.

As I plodded towards the house, Lucas came down the lane towards me, face angry. Goon B jerked to attention.

"You were told," Lucas growled at me, "not to wander around. I put up with it once, Gianna, but you're making a habit of pestering the SableFur."

"Pestering!" I sputtered. "I'm not pestering!"

"You were told not to wander around." Lucas raised his voice. "You are not a guest! You are being humored."

"I am not being humored! I am an Oracle, and it is my right to clear my name and vindicate myself. The Moon gave me visions to give to the people I'm seeing, so I'm just doing what She told me to do! Unless," I growled, "*you* want to obstruct that, First Beta."

Shit. I really need to get my temper under control.

The smart part of my mind hollered at me from across a hot wall of anger.

Was I going insane? Was the tied-off Bond making me feverish and crazy? I didn't feel insane, but that might mean I was the craziest wolf in the area.

"That is not part of vindication." Lucas didn't budge. He was so tall. He towered over me, and he probably could have broken off each of my legs and used them as toothpicks. "You haven't reported these visions to Oracle Kiery, so they're not part of the Secrets Test."

Spouting off about Hix having already passed that test for me stayed behind my teeth. Lucas was right. I hadn't reported any of this to Kiery, so I technically hadn't passed. Did I dare report Lulu to Kiery as the secret?

The Bond spasmed in pain.

And none of what I was doing here were secrets. They were just lost items or things people fretted over. Could I say they were the Moon's indulgence? That was the hardest test to pass. The test that required the Oracle to prove she had the Moon's favor.

Tears sprang up, and I screamed at myself for showing even a little gleam of weakness.

I was a mess. A hot mess, crumbling, and falling down like some burned out building.

Had I already screwed up and all was lost, and the Moon was just punishing me by letting me scramble around?

"I am doing what the Moon has asked of me," I stated, stubborn. "And it's not the Secret Test, it's the Favor Test, and stay out of it. I'll report it when I'm damn good and ready, but some of the things I've said here won't come to pass for a bit. Nosy Beta, if I didn't know better, I'd think you were trying to prevent me from passing!"

"Why the hell would I do that?" Lucas asked, reminding me of Hix in his dry sarcasm.

"I can think of a couple of reasons," I flung back at him. *What are you doing? You're being an idiot!*

Lucas stunned me by laughing. "If you think I care about protecting that old bat Anita's ego, you're wrong. You being here was her call, not mine, and I told Alpha Magnes not to humor the old bag. I don't care how this turns out. I just want it done with."

He thought this was about Anita! I flung up my hands and moaned in despair. This wasn't about Anita! It had never been about Anita! Oh this Beta... oh, by the Moon! There was a First Beta in the dungeon who knew what this was about, and this oaf stood there blind and dumb? Did Magnes have everyone in his thrall?

"I have to say one thing about Gabel," I told Lucas, crazy with despair and my insides twisted violently on his name. "I never had to explain everything to him in miserable tiny detail."

I pushed past him before I said anything else stupid, and oh man, I was going to go off on some feverish, crazed rant. My bandaged hands were like two crab claws for all the good they did opening the front door (thanks, Goon B) and dangling off my wrists. I stumbled into the foyer, drew in a sobbing breath, and—

a scent yanked my spine tight.

I froze, yes, I smelled it! I smelled—

I went down the hallway to the right towards the dining room. Goon B didn't try to stop me. He was watching to see what crazy thing I did next. Two male voices from the dining room, and the scent of lunch. I stepped into the room.

Magnes glared at me with the eyes he had given Gabel.

The other male turned around.

"Aaron," I gasped.

COURTSHIP MASQUERADE

"Gianna," Aaron greeted me, ignoring Magnes' cold stare.

Big surprise. Aaron in league with the SableFur. "So you'll never call any Alpha your King, but you're here with your lips planted on Magnes' ass."

Aaron smiled. "It has more to do with your ex burning the countryside to the ground. I told you, Gianna, Gabel had no idea what he had, and even less idea how to hold onto it. You being here should be proof of that."

"I never betrayed my Oracle vows," I snapped. "Gabel never made me do anything I didn't want to do."

"Are you sure about that?" Aaron asked. "He Marked you without your consent. Everything that's happened from here is the direct result of him making you do something you didn't want to do."

"That's none of your business. You have no idea what was said between us!"

"Exactly. And you're here as a result," Aaron said.

No. I was here because the Moon sent me here. Not because Gabel had manipulated me into saying anything. And if I had betrayed anything, it was only because mates couldn't keep secrets. He could have read my reactions, made his guesses, already had his suspicions. "MarchMoon was in your pocket, Aaron, and they did a lousy job of hiding it. If there's any reason I'm here, it's because you chose stupid allies. I'll prove I'm not guilty, and I'll make Gabel regret not believing me, and I'll make you regret setting me up."

I managed to not say make *Magnes regret moving against me.* But only just barely.

"I didn't set you up, Gianna," Aaron said. "I asked Marcus to send a wolf to IronMoon as a test of Gabel. It really had nothing to do with you, and it didn't have anything to do with SableFur either."

"It doesn't matter now, does it?" I growled, even though I couldn't believe Aaron was Magnes' toady.

Aaron said, "If it's any consolation to you, Gianna, I believe you'll vindicate yourself. When you're done here, perhaps you will come to IceMaw and we can discuss this revenge you want on Gabel."

I gasped. "You opportunistic—"

"Predator? You're done with Gabel. He gave you up on the word of what... some half-formed evidence from the mouth of... who was the wolf anyway? I don't even know." Aaron gestured in a dismissive fashion. "Anita bought it, and Gabel let it happen. What did you do to anger Anita so badly?"

"I don't like your implication, IceMaw," Magnes growled at Aaron.

"Oh come on, Magnes." Aaron gestured with his hands open. "*I'm* the one that sent that wolf to IronMoon to rattle Gabel's cage. Gabel smelled the rat because it was right there in front of him. Now how did you find out about it? Your own little spy. But why would you even care? Your Elder Oracle has it in for Gianna, you're just supporting her as Alphas are supposed to, am I right? Nothing more?"

Aaron's tone made it clear he didn't believe anything of what he'd just said.

I glanced warily at Magnes, then back at Aaron.

"So, Gianna, what did you do to piss off Anita?" Aaron asked.

"You're on thin ice, IceMaw," Magnes growled.

I couldn't say the Comet and Balance and all that. But there was another option that was a neat half-truth, and would muddy the water, and hopefully confuse Magnes about what I knew, believed, and suspected. "Anita didn't approve of me being a Luna. She brought me to SableFur a month before the final vows to tell me to leave Gabel."

"And when you didn't she trumped up some bullshit to prove her point and make you obey." Aaron rolled his eyes and looked at Magnes.

"You have made it very clear you want her for yourself, Aaron," Magnes said in a tone like rocks grinding against each other. "Obviously you will try to hold her as high above stain as possible."

"Of course I will." Aaron grinned. "It just so happens your doddering Elder Oracle is making it very easy. Gianna, when you are done with this farce, do send word to the IceMaw. I am a most charming host."

The remains of the Bond lurched.

Magnes sighed. "Shall I leave you two alone, or do you like the audience, Aaron?"

What the hell is happening.

Aaron chuckled. "I am torn between what is more important. Our business, or charming Gianna."

"Keep your lips on Magnes' ass," I told Aaron. "I only want one thing right now, and that's to clear my name. And maybe when I'm done, I'll go finish what I started with Anita. You aren't in there anywhere, Aaron."

"What did you start with Anita?"

"I sliced her breasts half off." I grinned ferally.

Magnes sighed a little, but Aaron seemed intrigued. "Then I will not distract you from your mission, she-wolf. But when you are done, I plan on provoking you to turn those claws on me."

The Bond flailed.

Then, for a terrifying second, sank out of my awareness completely.

I turned and walked out, and started to tremble so badly Goon B had to steady me and pull me up the stairs.

In my room I collapsed onto my bed and tried to figure out what just happened, and what *was* happening. Because suddenly the world spun and heaved like I was trapped on the Tides.

A knock, then the door cracked open, and a large shape slid through.

"What the—" I gasped. I plastered myself against the far wall. "I don't know what Magnes told you, but I'm not yours!"

Aaron snaked across the floor with a speed that terrified me, and in a breath he had me by both arms and pressed up against the wall.

"Shhh," he whispered. "He doesn't know I'm here."

"You idiot, my goons will tell him!" I hissed back.

"I told the ugly one to take a walk," Aaron whispered.

"I'm not yours." My voice quivered.

He pressed his face into my neck and inhaled. I tried to shove him off me.

"The night-blooming cereus," he whispered.

"My Bond is dead, of course I have a lure-scent!" I whispered, shoving against him. Pain snaked through my stitched fingers. "What are you doing, Aaron?! I swear I will go war-form and tear you to shreds!"

"This isn't what it looks like. Play along, Gianna." He leaned close to my ear and whispered, "Gabel knows I am here."

"What?"

"I know Magnes is Gabel's father."

I stared at him. "How—"

"He told me."

"W-why—"

"Magnes wants the crown for himself. He's just letting Gabel do the dirty work until he can play hero. I will kneel before no Alpha. Gabel and I will work it out between us later."

"Why are you telling me this?"

"So you don't fight me when I try to help you. I know what you're trying to do. Magnes is wary of you, knows he is on fragile ground, and knows his control of the IronMoon situation is crumbling. He just hasn't figured out where the weak point is. I also heard about Lulu. And I know about Hix."

I choked on a sob.

"Warriors fight, and we die," Aaron said with sympathy. "Better to die in service to your Luna than die like cheap pawns between greedy would-be Kings who want power for its own sake. I wish we could all be so lucky."

"Lucky! There's nothing lucky! He's down there right now—"

"He chose the manner and terms of his death."

"He's not dead!" I shoved at Aaron. "He's not dead yet! None of us are dead yet! There's still hope!"

"Fair enough."

I sobbed once. "And you've made Magnes more suspicious!"

"I've confused things in his mind. Do you have an agenda, or is your anger about Anita being a miffed old bitch? He is very wary of you, but if he believes you know nothing of value, and won't return to Gabel, he'll let you go. Hix exposing Lulu and the very questionable series of events that brought you here means he wants you gone as quickly, and quietly, as possible."

I pressed my lips together.

"And because I'm so interested in you, even if he is wary of what you might know or suspect, he won't be quick to make you disappear. I've told him I'd hunt you to the Moon and back, and it's not a lie; you reek of being my partner."

I opened my mouth to tell him he could sniff my ulcered neck all he wanted, but I was still Bound to Gabel and he should respect that.

"Play along, Gianna," he whispered.

"Why did you come here at all?"

"You, mostly. I have dealings with Magnes from time to time. I came to ask about you, which led to talking about Gabel and how I have no intention of letting him be King, and Magnes better get off his ass. Magnes played it like it was beneath him." He leaned closer. "Gabel has agreed to let me take three southern territories. He'll put up just enough of a fight for it to be convincing, so Magnes thinks he and I are fighting. Magnes does not think I will be able to marshal my allies against the IronMoon."

"But you will, because the IronMoon will take a fall."

"I've given Gabel the proof against Anders. I suspect Anders is already on his knees."

"So he was a traitor."

"He was the worst kind of traitor. The one trying to obey a thousand masters. But Anders was in bed with the SableFur too. Tell Magnes that I will succeed in pushing the IronMoon northward out of the south."

"And perhaps let him think I find you interesting?"

"You mean I'm not interesting? I think I am very interesting."

I scowled and shoved. He didn't move. "Get off me, Aaron. I'm still Bound to Gabel."

"If you are, where is your Mark, and why can I smell a scent that speaks to my blood?" He lifted the sleeve of my too-large shirt to admire my bare arm. "I can feel the Mark I would give you, I can see the pattern decorating the lines of your flesh."

"Because the Moon has made it so!" I shook my sleeve back down.

"Gianna, he took you by force and without your consent. You don't have to go back to him."

"That's between him and I." I did not want to have this conversation with anyone, especially Aaron.

"So you're going to make excuses for him? He had a rough childhood, he's a lupine, he didn't mean it, he's not really a bad person?"

"Get out," I hissed, shaking.

"What are you going to do if the Moon doesn't re-open your Bond to him? What if this is permanent?"

"Get out!" I shoved. Hard. My hands protested, and the stitches tore at the skin's frayed edges.

Aaron left without another word.

CATCH A LUNA BY THE TAIL

I'd ripped out some stitches fighting with Aaron.
Everything crushed down on me and pressed me into the bed. Goon A brought me my breakfast, I didn't even turn over to look at it. Oatmeal and some fruit from the smell.

Aaron had apparently slipped out without complication, which was impressive.

Or Magnes knew and didn't care.

Or Magnes was going to let Aaron hang himself.

It had snowed that night, everything coated in fresh powder. Footprints along the usual paths as people moved to and fro. The bloody snow from Hix's capture (or his surrender, or whatever we wanted to call it) covered once more.

I didn't have much time. I still had three tests to pass: the test of favor, the test of prediction, and discovering a secret. Did I declare that Hix had discovered the secret on my behalf? Did I declare that the small, meaningless dreams about toys and notes were the test of favor?

If I said Hix had found the secret, I'd have to tell Kiery about Magnes. Kiery wouldn't be required to tell anyone how I'd passed the test, as the secret would pass to her to safekeep as well. But would she tell Magnes some other way that I knew *his* secret? That the secret Hix had discovered was not just Magnes trading in casual matters of dishonor and low-brow war tactics?

I unwrapped my hands with my teeth.

Swollen, gnarly, flushed. Tender as well. Multiple torn stitches. I cleaned and rewrapped everything as best I could manage, choosing to wrap each finger individually, so I actually had the use of my fingers. Sort of. Instead of giant mittens.

The RedWater wolves were both gone. I fretted that I might have needed to specify they had to come back by a certain time, but that seemed silly. They clearly still had their intelligence. They would be back when they felt like they had something interesting to share.

Gabel and Aaron working together meant I had to sit down to digest all of it. Aaron's "victory" in the south would make Aaron and his allies "contain" Gabel. It would drive more refugees into SableFur, and put more pressure on Magnes. But Magnes would still resist moving while Gabel built his kingdom. Aaron gave Magnes the perfect reason to do nothing, but the perfect reason for SableFur to get restless.

How ironic, though. Aaron would call no one King-Alpha, but his southern allies seemed to take their marching orders from him. He was styling himself a Lord-Alpha if nothing else.

I knelt in my little workspace and sorted my runes, running my thumb along the edge and carvings of each one, hoping for some guidance on my next move.

A knock on my door. I ignored it. Another. I ignored it again. The door handle twisted. I folded my hands in my lap and closed my eyes, feigning meditation. No idea who peeked their head in looking for me. Probably one of the Goons, because I heard the ignored breakfast tray rattle as they picked it up and removed it, then the door was closed.

I fretted away a few hours while I tried to figure out my next move. The mirror kept calling to me. I wasn't eager to go for another ride.

A few hours later I told Goon B, "I need to talk to Alpha Magnes or First Beta Lucas."

"No," Goon B said automatically.

"I've seen something they'll be interested in." I wanted to be around Magnes like I wanted another fifteen stitches, but I needed to tell one of them before Aaron and Gabel got on with their end of things. Knowing Gabel, he was halfway to GleamingFang.

Goon B grumbled, "Go back to your room. I'll see about it."

"Quickly. It's very urgent."

Another forty minutes or so until Goon B returned, this time with Oracle Kiery.

"I don't want to talk to you," I told her. "This is for Alpha Magnes or First Beta Lucas."

"I'll decide that," Kiery said. "By the Moon, Gianna, you are difficult. First the scene with Aaron yesterday, well, that wasn't the first thing." She paused. "Are you well?"

"I'm fine." I didn't feel fine. I felt like I had a high fever, but stress, and riding the Tides constantly and having hands sliced open would do that. Oh, and carrying the weight of an aching, constricted Bond. This couldn't be healthy. And now Aaron and his noise about my scent.

Hix. I had to save him somehow too.

"So what's this about?" Kiery asked.

This would give me a chance to gauge Kiery's opinion of Magnes. "The Moon showed me that Alpha Aaron of IceMaw will attack the southern border of IronMoon, and he will succeed in pushing them back. Gabel, however, is going to attack GleamingFang. Somehow he got the evidence he needed of Anders' betrayal and he's going to do to GleamingFang what he did to MarchMoon."

"Why are you telling me this?" Kiery asked.

"That's why I asked for Magnes or Lucas," I said. "I don't really care if you tell anyone or not. I just figured I'd share what the Moon has told me. Unless you're afraid of telling Anita she was wrong, and I still have the Moon's favor."

"I'm not any more afraid of Anita than you are. Or Aaron is." Kiery added that last sentence with a sly twist of her tongue.

"I don't need Aaron's support to stand up for myself," I snapped, disgusted at her insinuation.

Kiery permitted herself a smirk. "No, but it must be nice to know you've got an Alpha on a lead."

"No, it's not. If you don't want to tell Magnes, fine. I don't care. The Moon shared it with me; if you don't think it's worth sharing with your Alpha, not my problem. I've done my part."

Kiery took a deep breath. She gestured for me to follow her.

"Where are we going?" I asked.

She led me to the other side of the house to Magnes' office, where he sat talking with Luna Adrianna, Lucas, and several other senior wolves. There was a large map on the far left wall, and books lining the wall behind me, but instead of the ancient decor Gabel favored, everything was minimalistic and pale woods, metals, illuminated, airy...

Severe.

Magnes looked so much like Gabel it caught me off guard.

Luna Adrianna gave me a withering look, then turned it on Kiery. The conversation stopped. They had been discussing Gabel's ransacking of the north, and the refugees flooding in, and the voices had been angry.

The map was much fancier and larger than Gabel's, very

detailed, covered in pins and little notes, pieces of string. For
some reason I stared at it intently, trying to memorize all of it
as quickly as possible.

The RedWater ghost I'd assigned to Lucas sat behind the
First Beta, and wagged his tail once to acknowledge me.

"I'm sorry about this," Kiery was saying, "but Gianna has
something that might contribute to this conversation."

"What could she have?" a wolf I didn't know asked.

"She's got a lot of little tidbits of information it seems," Lucas
said dryly. He addressed me, "What do you have, Gianna?"

I tore my attention away from the map. "Alpha Aaron is
going to attack the southern IronMoon border—"

"We know that. He's already moving his warriors into position. And he's already told us he will," Lucas interrupted me,
bored already.

"He'll succeed," I said, annoyed. "Probably because Gabel
is more distracted by the GleamingFang. He's finally gotten the
piece of evidence he needs to rip off Alpha Anders' head. His
suspicion on Anders' duplicity predates him Marking me, and
now it would seem he got what he needed to prove it. He's
probably already on his way to GleamingFang, where he'll do
to that pack what he did to the MarchMoon."

I licked my lips, and sidestepped over to the map. No one
stopped me. I studied the GleamingFang, and remembered
some of where Gabel's own markers had been. I touched one
point. "Here. This is where it will happen."

"But the heart of GleamingFang is a hundred miles to the
south."

I glared at him. "Think what you want, First Beta, but I
shared Gabel's bed, life, and soul for a year. He is not the
mindless, violent cur you want to think he is. It's easier to
imagine a creature so violent and ruthless is also a mindless

beast. It must scare the hell out of all of you to consider he is, in addition to everything else, brilliant."

"Gianna," Kiery warned me.

"I have no love for him," I snapped at her. "This is how he wins. When he's underestimated. Everyone misunderstands his nature. He's not an idiot. He's a lupine."

The First Beta and the other wolves exchanged glances. Even Magnes and Adrianna exchanged surprised looks, but it was hard to tell if this was news to them (it couldn't possibly have been), feigned, or they were just shocked I had dared to reveal it.

Kiery put her hands on her hips and looked at Lucas as if to say *I told you so*.

I kept talking to the First Beta. "The thousands of books in his office aren't decoration. He's read every single one twice. Ask him where one is, he'll tell you. Ask him what it's about, he'll tell you. That is why he has been so successful. It's not just his violence and strength and resolve. It's his mind. Meet him on those terms, or else he will eventually come for this pack. And when he does, it is because he has decided he is ready to win, and you are ready to die."

Magnes shot out of his chair. Adrianna's voice was quicker and sharper, "Be silent!"

Oh, that had gotten her. I tossed my hair, wild and careless, as pain throbbed in every part of me. "Gabel threw me away on some pathetic accusation founded on nothing. He'll win on your hubris. If you think you're prepared because you are SableFur, you are facing the Comet, the Destroyer. I do not intend to be here when he comes. I feel sorry for all the wolves in SableFur who have no say in how you ready yourself for him because you think the name SableFur is preparation enough."

The Bond flip-flopped and flailed in protest to my declarations.

Adrianna didn't take that lightly. "The SableFur name is the SableFur name because we are always prepared for any threat. You were a Luna once, Gianna, but for what a week? Two? Do not come in here speaking like one. You were thrown away quickly enough."

I refused to back down, which was stupid faced with the SableFur Luna herself. "I know what I've said to be true. Ignore me if you want, it doesn't matter. I'll have what I came for soon enough."

"And what is it you came here for?" Adrianna hissed. She advanced on me, and it was then I realized just how big the SableFur Luna was. She was at least a hand taller than me, and strong framed, and moved like a cross between a ballet dancer and a juggernaut. She was beautiful, and she was fearsome.

Not just a Luna in name only. Not like Platinum would have been.

She *knew*.

She *knew* what Magnes had done.

Nobody moved to get between us, and I didn't think Flint had taught me nearly enough to hold off an angry SableFur Luna. No, she'd kick my ass and then tie it up in a little bow before shipping the pieces back to Gabel. In a little box.

A very little box.

The Moon had set all this into motion, I was here because the Moon told me to be. "I am here to clear my name. I never betrayed my vows, and still have the Moon's favor. Ignore me at your peril, arrogant Luna!"

Adrianna grinned and licked her lips, like my heart would be delicious eating.

As she grinned at me, her teeth elongated slightly, just enough to reveal fangs.

I blanched.

Lucas grunted. "Anita *is* wrong, and the sooner Gianna is gone, the happier I will be."

"Don't get involved in the business of Oracles," Kiery told Lucas. "It's not for you to judge."

"Any idiot can see she's still got the Gift, even if the Moon only uses it to tell us about lost dolls and to expect phone calls," Lucas said sarcastically. "Or is that what scares you, Kiery? That you let Anita run your show for you? *Again*?"

"I'm not afraid of Anita," Kiery said as if she had said it for the thousandth time. "And if Gianna proves herself, then it's the last mistake Anita gets to make on my watch."

"*You* also made a mistake," Lucas retorted.

Kiery barred her teeth at him. "And I'm not afraid to say so. I trained Gianna, so I'll be happy to know my student didn't betray her vows. It's always frightening to think our training doesn't weed out the girls who can be bought and sold. Last I checked, warrior training doesn't do that."

Lucas snarled at her. She folded her arms across her breasts and gave him a frosty, scathing stare. Adrianna hissed at them both to knock it off, and slid back into her chair. A delicate hand on Magnes' wrist to guide him back into his own seat.

I almost breathed a sigh of relief.

But what was this with Kiery and Lucas on my side? That was too reasonable. Magnes and Adrianna made no move to silence them.

Lucas and Kiery seemed cute together, though. There might have been some history there.

A lot of history, actually.

"Then is this one of the Tests?" Lucas asked Kiery. "Has she passed another one?"

"She has to declare it."

Tempting as it was, this wasn't one of the tests. This was

just good old-fashioned spy-work. "This isn't one of the tests. Just something the Moon shared with me."

Lies upon lies. Went with the crowd.

Kiery tapped her foot at Lucas. "There. You see? I don't know why she doesn't want to declare this one, but that's between her and the Moon."

It was getting hard to think. A headache formed, pounding into my head with the same rhythm as my aching hands. "I've said what I had to say. I won't overstay my welcome."

Kiery heaved a sigh and gestured to the door. Goon B waited for me outside, and ushered me back to my room. The RedWater wolf attached to Lucas could tell me what happened from there.

Shaking Magnes' cage didn't involve shaking him directly. Lucas already believed I was untarnished, and he clearly didn't like Anita. This was useful. Now what could I do to keep rattling Lucas?

Because if I rattled Lucas, it'd percolate down to the other wolves under his command, and create more doubt.

If Adrianna really knew that I knew... how could she know? How could she even suspect I knew?

Did she have the Gift?

A sudden, terrifying thought gripped my brain.

Did Adrianna have the Seer's Gift?

It wasn't especially rare, just rare to be powerful enough to have the unnaturally pale skin and train to become an Oracle. Adrianna was pale and lovely, but... the terrifying thought curled around my spine. If Adrianna was a weak Seer... if she'd ever received any of the early training...

She had two sons to protect. She'd fight me to the death, and if what Flint had said was true... I wasn't a mother. I'd been focused on destroying Magnes, but could I defeat Adrianna?

GABEL: BURN IT

Gabel stomped through the rubble, claws ripping up chunks of asphalt and stone. Bloody spittle dripped from his fangs, the taste of the dead on his tongue, the scent of their terror still in his snout.

But there was one more thing to do.

He growled with satisfaction.

Anders' Luna stood over her pups in war-form, snarling. Anders, forced back into his human form by a silver spike through his thigh, did not seem nearly so courageous.

The face of a male who knew something worse than death awaited him.

Anders looked Gabel's leathery, nightmare war-form up and down, eyes widening in horror, but his mate snarled even louder, lips rippling back over fangs. She was no match for Gabel, but it didn't matter. Her pups, too young to shift, clung to her in terror and couldn't look upon the Alpha of IronMoon.

"Annnddeerrrsss," Gabel growled, forcing human speech through the dark, murderous rage and thrill of victory.

Anders trembled as if Gabel's voice struck him, and the

children shrieked, but the GleamingFang Luna snarled louder and snapped her jaws at him.

"Lord-Alpha Gabel."

Gabel swung his head around to the warrior that addressed him. The male panted, having run a distance with news. Gabel's eyelids dropped a degree, hooded with satisfaction. He clenched his claws, digging through ruined cement and the *crunch* pushed it through his system even more.

"We just got word," the warrior said, "but—" he looked at Anders, uncertain.

"*Ssspeakk.*"

The warrior gulped. The IronMoon Alpha's eyes were almost entirely black, like a void without stars, and only when the light hit the orbs in the right way did the faint perimeter of a pupil emerge from the blackness, like the faintest ring of light from an eclipsed moon. "Alpha Aaron—"

"*Yesssss?*" Gabel's claws sank deeper into the concrete as he shifted his weight.

"He and his allies have attacked the southern border and taken SpringHide. They're moving to SaltPaw now."

Gabel growled, bristling from instinct, but the memory of the strategy (and his noxious alliance with Aaron) floated to the surface of his mind.

"We're done here," Eroth said immediately. "I'll take warriors and we'll chase them out. His victory will be short lived."

"*No. Ssstay. Emil will take a dozen to meet them.*"

"Emil?" Eroth said, bewildered. Emil was a warrior of only some prestige, not one Eroth trusted to lead more than a hunting party.

Gabel growled his affirmative. "*We areee tooo close to Sssablefur.*"

"But Aaron has dealings with the SableFur. This could be a pincer move."

"Exacccctly, leeet him tthinnk he has won." Gabel grinned. *"It willl makke him sssloppy."*

Eroth grinned in return, unfazed by the nightmare Alpha in front of him. "Yes, Lord-Alpha."

"You will givvvve theee order when we are donnne heeere." Gabel swung his grinning head back towards the GleamingFang. He swung a claw towards the messenger. The warrior wisely left.

With effort, Gabel suppressed the darkness bubbling within him, forcing his body back into the containment of human form. The fury and rage protested, wanting to be free, to destroy *everything*, because he was going to build that damn tower and claw the Moon's Own Eye out. Pain twisted within him, goading his fury even further and burning at the edges of his mind.

The GleamingFang Luna hesitated in her snarls, disarmed momentarily by the way the IronMoon Alpha shifted from nightmare beast to handsome man.

"Anders," Gabel said. "I always suspected you were less than loyal. But to find out you don't even have the courage to be *disloyal?* Who would have thought it was Marcus of March-Moon with the actual courage."

"I will not apologize for protecting my pack," Anders gasped.

"But you didn't. You wore too many collars. Served too many masters." Gabel smirked, cruel and cold. "I finally have the proof I need. I am here to discipline my disobedient vassal."

"You have nothing."

"Oh, but I *do*." Gabel gestured for Eroth to drag Anders out of range of his Luna's claws. The silver spike twisted and jarred in Anders' thigh, blood dripping.

Gabel bent down, grabbed a handful of Anders' hair and whispered in his ear, "Aaron has no further use for you."

Anders yanked back, a patch of hair remaining with Gabel, and he said, "No. He didn't."

"Oh yes, he did." He yanked Anders back to him, and low and sweet by his ear, whispered, "He knows all about you, Anders. That you played him, Marcus, Holden, even Magnes. You made too many deals, Anders. None of your allies will come to save you."

Gabel clutched the back of Anders neck and pressed their foreheads together. "The Moon broke Her vow to me. I made promises in Her name, in good faith, and She took Gianna from me. I am going to add your corpse to that tower. But first, I am going to kill your Luna. And you will live with that agony for however long you endure it. I am going to let your children watch their mother die, and their father destroyed from the inside."

Anders breathed out something. It sounded like a plea.

Gabel dropped him. "Do you know what it feels like when the Bond snaps? It is pain beyond any imagining. It drives you mad. It destroys you from the inside, and you *feel* her ghost, she's *just* beyond the next wall, or the next door, you hear her *whispering* your name. Oh, Anders, you have no idea what it is like. If we only *knew* we would never open the Bond again. But you will know. Soon. I will let you experience what the Moon has done. She sees fit to punish us all for our sins."

"You're insane," Anders whispered.

"Your sins heaped on my father's sins heaped on everyone else's sins. *You* broke the vows you made to me. You said cheap words to defend your pack, not realizing you condemned them. If you had had the courage to honor your promise, you would not have stood alone. Instead, I am not here because you called upon my aid, but because your deceit has summoned me from the shadows of the Moon."

Gabel weighed him a moment. Then, "Restrain him, Eroth."

The GleamingFang Luna resumed her snarling as Gabel shifted back into his war-form.

She lunged at him with a scream.

The impact was enough to send Gabel onto his back through the dirt. He growled, amused as she slashed at his face, and peeled off a few layers of fur, and hooked her claws of her feet into his thigh, stabbing into his leathery hide. She howled and snapped her jaw down.

A pity Anders had not fought with the same ferocity.

Regrettable he had to kill her when she fought so fiercely to save her pups.

Flint was right: the courage of a female was beyond any male.

Gianna would have fought this hard. Gianna would have fought harder.

He slashed at the Luna's face, hooked his claws around her open jaw, and wretched once, snapping the mandible. She yelped, jerked back, bones dangling, then surged forward again with her claws, raking at his eyes while blood and spittle dripped from her broken maw.

Gabel's blood surged with dark admiration. What a pity. She couldn't possibly beat him. She wasn't large enough, strong enough, skilled enough, her claws not sharp enough to penetrate his hide, and he had already shattered her jaw and affected her breathing, and she did not care.

He was going to kill her pups, and she would go to death and beyond to stop him.

He snapped his right claw up into her exposed belly and punched into her insides. She choked, stiffened. He reached deep, grabbed a handful, and yanked back.

She pathetically kept clawing at him.

"Tooo the last, bravvee Lllluna. He issss not worrtthy of you." Gabel
gently pushed her off him and lowered her onto the ground. She made one
more feeble swipe at him. *"Iii musssttt killl you quiccklly, but I willl
sppparrre youurr puppssss. He is worthlessss, but youuu are magggnife-
ceeent. Theyyy may livveee to honnorrr yoou. Yoouuuu have bought thieeer
lives. Nooo hhharrmmm willl come to theeemm."*

Some of the fight left her, the crazed look in her eyes.
Disarmed with the promise that her children would survive,
some of the fight faded.

Gabel raised his claw again, and this time drove it into her
throat.

He stood, and melted back into human form, dark rage
balanced with admiration. He watched, unmoved, as her pups
scrambled to her body, alone in their screaming and tears. The
agony of the dying Bond had incapacitated their father.

Gabel ran his fingers over the slices in his face. Not serious.
Her claws had also left bruises on his thighs.

Gianna had fought him with much of the same courage.
Gianna called on that courage now, from within the depths of
SableFur.

Gabel told Eroth, "When he is dead, Anders' body is to be
burned without ceremony. The Luna is to be honored for her
courage. Make sure the GleamingFang are able to pay their
respects. She bought the lives of her children. A worthless sire,
but a noble mother. Send the children north to IronMoon. We
will find someone to foster them."

Eroth nodded.

Gabel looked towards the west. Now he had complete
control of the mountain pass into SableFur. Regrettable he had
to send warriors to die at the hands of Aaron, but it was in
service to a greater cause. He could deal with Aaron later. It
was much easier working with another Alpha who understood
the rules of honor and war.

It would be much more satisfying to war with Aaron than these cowards or the ambitious scavenger that was his father.

I will set fire to everything before I let you have it, Magnes.

Behind him Eroth issued orders to have Anders supervised, then went to send Emil on his death-quest.

"This is a whole lot of fuck."

Ana reached towards him with an alcohol soaked pad. It stung as she patted his cheek. He said, "You are only bothered because you are not bothered."

"What's it say about me that I'm not bothered you just ripped someone's guts out and her kids are crying over her?"

"You say that as if being human is more noble than being wolf."

"Humans do tend to think they're a little more evolved than beasts," Ana muttered.

"You're just hairless beasts."

"Hey. I get pretty hairy if I don't keep the lawn trimmed. I don't mow, but I keep it groomed. Fancy topiary style."

"Then humans are deluded." Gabel pushed her hand away.

"Are we going after Gianna?" Ana followed him as he walked away.

Gabel hesitated as his blood spiked in his veins. It always caught him, that surge of agony at the reminder she was gone. He'd forbidden the IronMoon from saying her name. Invoking her name sent a surge of anguish so intense through him it could bring him to his knees.

"Not yet," he admitted with difficulty. "It is not time yet. Soon. But I will only get one attempt at the SableFur. I must not waste it, or I will never be with her again."

PEEPING WOLF

They wouldn't let me see Hix again.

I was safe and comfortable in my room, and he was suffering in a dungeon, and they would not let me see him. I smothered my weeping with my blankets. I could send one of the RedWater wolves, but it wasn't about seeing Hix, but being there, so he knew I hadn't abandoned him. I hadn't stopped thinking about how to get him out of there.

Stubborn Beta probably wouldn't want me down there. Probably would give me some bullshit about it didn't matter, he was comfortable with the choices he had made, that his death served a purpose.

But I wasn't going to let him die. I wasn't just going to abandon him down there!

The RedWater wolf I had assigned to prowl around the SableFur compound came back, but had very little to show me that was interesting. As expected, the SableFur were restless about what was happening outside their borders, but not nearly as restless as I would have expected. They did murmur amongst themselves about the little visions I had brought them. Most of them agreed that I was probably wrongly accused.

They were angry with Anita, and very uncomfortable with Lulu.

But nobody wanted to play connect-the-dots between the two.

Spies planted in other packs was sort of an uncomfortable reality. Nobody appreciated having been exposed, but these wolves were higher ranked SableFur that had earned the privilege of living at the heart, and were realists. They didn't approve of Magnes being slippery with Lulu. But it was Anita they were mad at. Anita's reputation for being a petty old bitch had sunk so deep into SableFur it had developed its own gravitational pull, drawing all the potential grime off Magnes.

There were also plenty of rumors about Aaron and I. *Plenty* of those. Holy crap, there were so many of those. They had sprung up like mushrooms! I guess with all the terrible things to gossip about that was what everyone had fun with. That I was finally free of Gabel's clutches (it was no secret how he had taken me), and Aaron had put forth his argument, and if I had half a brain, I'd take his offer.

And rumors he had snuck into my room before he left and stayed for a while.

Maybe it would work to my advantage if everyone was too busy snickering over me honestly having a chance at being the IceMaw Luna. One person even said *the Moon will take care of a Luna.*

Piecing all of that together from the hours (and *hours*) of memories that the RedWater wolf brought left me exhausted and my eyes burning as if I had been crying for all those hours.

The RedWater wolf I had assigned to Lucas came back just as I finished with the first. It was night, and I was exhausted, but it couldn't wait. "Just what you think is most important," I told the ghost.

The two ghosts seemed to confer on that, then the Lucas-one approached me. The cold touch as he phased into me burned, and my eyes *burned*.

~*~ *The Wolf's Eyes* ~*~

Lucas slouched down on the old leather couch in his front room, teacup on his thigh, and stared at the old sitcom re-run on the television. Orange-jasmine tea from the smell. Lucas rubbed the back of his neck and cricked his spine into place. He only had on sweatpants, revealing an expectantly toned torso and body, criss-crossed with white scars in various places. His body had the marks of years of service as a SableFur warrior.

From the sound his shoulders made, it wasn't just cosmetic.

He laughed at one of the jokes on the show. The joke was not funny.

The door opened, and Kiery stepped in.

Lucas gave her a withering look. "Well, come on in."

Kiery flipped him the finger and went to the little fridge tucked under the desk. She kicked it open, surveyed the options, and pulled out a bottle. She flicked the cap off with her thumb and took long swallows.

"There's beer in the kitchen. You don't have to drink my beer."

"Shut up, Lucas. I hate to drink alone." *She sat down next to him and put her feet up on the table.*

"Long day, Oracle?"

"Shut up, Lucas. You've heard the news."

"Of course I've heard the news," *he grumbled and set his tea aside.* "Magnes is forcing me to sit on my ass. The IronMoon are right there at our border! Refugees flooding in from the north, the IronMoon crushed the GleamingFang, and Magnes thinks that Aaron nibbling at the SaltPaw is going to distract Gabel? Aaron's an idiot."

"Aaron's not an idiot. The IronMoon just sawed through Gleaming-Fang. They took losses, and Gabel's been using them hard. We have his First Beta, and his Second Beta is inexperienced. He's so strapped for wolves he can trust he's left his Master of Arms in command at the heart."

"*The way I hear it, Oracle, that Master of Arms isn't anyone to be fucked with.*"

Kiery ignored him and went on, "Doesn't change my point, Beta. Aaron's forces are fresh. He's got his own warriors, plus warriors from his allies. Gabel isn't going to let Aaron have the RedWater. So he's probably going to take his tired forces down there, Aaron will beat him, get RedWater and take a big bite out of IronMoon."

"*Yes, and why let Aaron have all the glory for squashing Gabel? Nobody else has been able to slow the IronMoon down, but Aaron has taken back two territories. The IronMoon are making SableFur look weak and lazy.*"

"*Magnes won't even let you take a token force?*" *She put a hand on his bicep.*

"*No,*" *Lucas snarled. "He won't. Forcing me to sit here on my ass and watch television. He says SableFur doesn't need to get involved. That's not the damn point! The damn point is we are involved! We're the ones who caused Gabel's rampage!*"

Kiery sipped her beer.

"*Have you talked to him?*" *Lucas asked.*

"*I try. He's only listening to Anita right now. The Moon has Her Eye closed to me. The future is too much in flux, but Gianna can still See, and Anita claims she can as well.*"

"*Maybe you are the one She's angry with.*"

Kiery sipped her beer and pondered it. "Maybe. Or maybe Magnes should get off his duff and take control of the future that's changing around him."

"*By the Moon, I love you,*" *Lucas said with thick admiration, reaching towards her.*

She pushed him away. "Don't say that when you don't mean it."

"*I do mean it.*"

"*Then you'd accept I'm an Oracle. I accept you're First Beta and what goes with that. It's not like if I was your mate suddenly you'd be able*

*to tell me everything. I'd still be left in the dark on some things. Discretion
and all that. So what's the difference if I leave you in the dark?"*

"Kiery —"

*"Drink your tea. We were talking about why you have to sit on your
ass."*

Lucas obliged her. "So what did Magnes say?"

*"What does he ever say? I told Adrianna, got a bit farther with her,
but she's like Magnes. They see it as weakness if we lower ourselves to
deal with the rabble."*

"Why am I not surprised Gianna was right about Gabel."

*Another long pause from the Oracle. "I'm sorry she got accused. But
I'm not sure I'm sorry all this happened. Gabel just took her. Then instead
of standing up for her, he dumped her on some of the shoddiest evidence
I've ever heard drummed up against an Oracle. But ultimately I'm not
convinced it's the greatest injustice in the world, even if she won't see it that
way."*

"When I heard Lulu was her main witness, I figured we were in for
it," Lucas said.

"I didn't even know Lulu was a spy for us. Did Anita?"

"Does it matter now?"

Another long swig of the beer. "I guess not."

"What aren't you telling me, Kiery? You know I hate your secrets."

Kiery sighed. "I have a terrible feeling about all this. The Moon has
me shut out, and Magnes won't listen. Gianna did not declare those little
visions she was passing out as proof of the Moon's favor. She's been using
a damn mirror, she refuses to wait for her bowls. I feel like I am locked in
a storm cellar while a tornado approaches."

"Gianna is not showing all her cards," Lucas said.

*Kiery finished her beer, got up and retrieved two more. She shoved one
at Lucas. "Drop the tea and drink with me."*

"You know what happens when we drink together. We end up fucking
each other and waking up with hangovers and regrets."

She shoved it into his bicep. "Drink it."

Lucas sighed. "Why don't we just have a normal relationship, Kiery?"

"Didn't we just talk about this? Here's your reminder, you ox: we've tried. Didn't work. You're the one who can't handle being with an Oracle. So since neither one of us is going to step down, beer and forlorn, drunken, ill-advised sex it is."

"And you still see no conflict carrying around the secrets of wolves and being with a First Beta."

"Oh by the Moon, we've had this conversation a million times, Lucas, including five minutes ago!" She groaned and flopped over backwards over the arm of the couch. "Uggggggggggggggg, Luccccccassssss. We've argued that into the damn grounddddd. Weren't we talking about Gianna instead? And her cards?"

"You mean the one she's hiding?"

"That's more like it. Sobering conversation. None of this mopey why-can't-we-be-together-Kiery bullshit." Kiery sat back up, elbows braced on the sofa arm. "Gianna knows more than she's letting on. Why wouldn't she declare those little visions the Test of Favor?"

"You tell me."

"She's made it perfectly clear she wants to get in and out, to the point she's willing to risk her sanity using a mirror. She could have two tests passed by now, but she's only claimed one."

Lucas frowned.

"Exactly. Now you see why I'm drinking."

"Have you told Magnes?"

"What's there to tell Magnes? It's Oracle business, and she's not spying for IronMoon. I also don't believe her when she spits on Gabel's name."

"You don't? She seems pretty sincere to me."

"And Gabel's been burning down the countryside talking about how he made promises in the Moon's name as Gianna's mate, but the Moon betrayed him and he's going to build a tower to crawl up to the heavens and claw out Her Eye. Seriously, Lucas. Think about this for a minute." She reached over and rapped her knuckles against his skull. "If Gabel willingly *gave up Gianna because Gianna violated her Oracle vows, then why the hell is he ranting about the Moon betraying him?"*

Lucas sagged back against the couch and stared at the television.

Kiery shrugged. "To be fair, I didn't think about it either until the newest report came in and Gianna's predictions about what he'd do were spot on."

"You think we're getting played?" Lucas asked her.

"That Mark is gone, Lucas. She suffered the sickness, she's still not quite right. Aaron is all over her saying he can't smell anything but her. So either Gabel is completely insane—"

"Possible."

"Or there's something way much, much, much bigger than all of us going on here." She shrugged and finished her beer and went to retrieve more.

"Unless Gabel's blaming the Gift itself. I know how he feels."

"Now you're just grasping at straws and being a baby." Kiery shoved a fresh beer at him. "I will bet never fucking you again that Gianna knows exactly what Gabel is on about."

Lucas said, "I won't take that bet."

"Smart Beta." She ruffled his hair.

"So do we tell Magnes?"

"I've already tried. He won't listen. Maybe you don't sense it, Lucas, but I do. The world feels like it's partially in a dream, and I can sense the Moon moving, but can't hear Her. I've been locked in a storm shelter and am forced to wait while things play out around me. But maybe you can figure this out."

Lucas downed his beer. He then took hers and downed it. "Come on."

"Oh, are we still sober enough to walk to the bedroom?" She slid off the couch. "That's new."

"Shut up and take your clothes off already."

Kiery laughed...

I SNAPPED BACK.

"There are things I don't need to see," I told the ghost.

He gave me a wolfish grin.

I would have thought more on it, but my brain crumpled into exhaustion, and I collapsed into the blankets.

A DANGEROUS MEETING OF MINDS

Beta Lucas opened the door to my room. He looked hung over. "Come with me."

I obeyed. Goon A wandered behind us. "Leave," Lucas told A. "I'm capable of handling a sick little she-wolf and don't need supervision."

"You wish," I growled. Sick or not, I'd still bite him.

Lucas took me to an office on the far end of the house, near his own rooms. His office, I realized. In it were Kiery, and two other wolves I didn't know. Lucas introduced them as Bernhard and Matthew, and I guessed from their bearing they were a hunter-type and a senior warrior. Lucas' office was as cluttered as Magnes' and Gabel's were neat, and it was plastered with detailed maps of the entire SableFur territory, and over them, a newer map like the one hanging in Magnes' office, crossed and dotted and pinned and lined.

"Gabel executed the GleamingFang Luna and destroyed GleamingFang three days ago," Lucas told me. "Aaron took some southern territories. Just like you predicted."

"That sounds like an accusation," I said. "Want to get some garden hoses and nylon ropes before we go any farther?"

Lucas sighed.

Kiery came over to me. She yanked my shirt down to expose my bicep. She rubbed the spot where the Mark had been. "Completely gone."

"If you think I'm some kind of spy, why the super secret meeting? Shouldn't you guys just tell Magnes?" I asked, amused in a dark way.

"*Alpha* Magnes," Matthew corrected.

"What does Gabel want?" Lucas asked me.

"To be King-Alpha. Everyone's figured that out by now."

"No. Why is he saying he's building a tower to the Moon to claw Her Eye out because *She* took you from him?" Kiery said. "I was there, and it looked to me like Gabel gave you up. Nothing said he had to. He was expressly told he didn't have to. Why is he howling about the Moon betraying him, when this is, presumably, the result of your failings?"

I shrugged. "How do I know? I haven't spoken with him since that day."

"Because you're *lying*." Kiery shoved her face in mine.

"Gabel probably expected the Oracles to behave decently," I shot back. "The charges against me were trumped up at best. He's probably angry the Moon hasn't punished Anita."

"But he's the one who repudiated you, and if he knew it was bullshit, he's got nobody else but himself to blame. Why not just wait for you to vindicate yourself?"

"Coward? Idiot? Suddenly realized what a mistake he made?"

"But you said Gabel is clever and doesn't make stupid mistakes like that."

The little fractures between my stories and the known facts began to widen, and Kiery pursued them like a hungry shark going for blood. I hadn't expected them to drag me into their conversation, and I hadn't prepared a song and dance to keep

my head above water. Kiery was right: why was Gabel howling
his rage at the Moon and blaming Her, when he was the one
who had put the Oracles over me?

*Dammit, Gabel. Did you not realize you had to keep up your end of
the song?! Letting everyone think you had gone a little mad from your
Luna's betrayal would have been fine, but just outright telling everyone you
hate the Moon... that's not helping!*

Kiery expected an answer, so I went with one that was
close to the truth. "Perhaps the *appearance* of impropriety was
more than he could stand, especially considering what he did
to Alpha Marcus at our wedding. My Mark is gone. You can
see that for yourself. Gabel's reasons are his own."

"Why haven't you declared passing two more tests?" Kiery
demanded.

"Because I don't think those are the tests the Moon means
for me to notch on my headboard," I retorted.

"You're *so* eager to get out of here you're using a goddamn
mirror but you aren't shoving passed tests in my face?"

Dammit, she was relentless. "If you're going to accuse me
of something, get to it."

Kiery stared at me intently. She was listening for a cue from
the Moon, but didn't get one. I knew the din of restless sound
well. The pressure of knowing *something* was going on. Her
analogy of being locked in a basement while a tornado was
outside was absolutely right.

They weren't telling me everything they knew. I looked at
the maps, and the room, trying to figure out my next move, but
the lack of sleep, and the pain in my hands, and the general
malaise had worn down my mind. I had already made a few
mistakes, and I couldn't risk anymore. I might get Hix killed, or
fail in my mission.

But they were already on the scent. I knew from the
RedWater wolf that there was a little spark of doubt, and the

wet pile of leaves called SableFur was starting to smoke. Right now they were undecided, but if I kept stonewalling them, they might think me a spy, and turn me over to Magnes and Adrianna.

Gabel would let Aaron take RedWater for the same reasons he let him have SaltPaw and SpringHide. It would prevent Magnes from striking if the SableFur saw that the IceMaw were having success. That was good. I couldn't let Lucas goad Magnes to move, or rally the rest of the senior SableFur to lean on Magnes. Not yet, anyway.

But I had to keep playing Lucas. His doubt was about to topple over and outweigh his loyalty.

Time for a risk. A huge one.

I pushed hair behind my shoulders. "Aaron is going to attack the RedWater next. He'll succeed. Gabel, instead, is going to go north. To Shadowless. I will declare this as my Test of Prediction."

Bernhard said, "Shadowless is your birthpack, isn't it?"

"Yes."

"Why would Gabel attack Shadowless? Especially if Aaron is about to take the RedWater and be able to liberate the remains of GleamingFang. It makes no sense, Gianna," Matthew said.

Because I'm going to tell him to.

I shoved the heavy feeling aside. It was necessary. It was the only card I had to play against Lucas. Gabel couldn't stand by and *let* Aaron take the RedWater. He needed an excuse to let it happen, and that meant he had to be occupied elsewhere.

"Because Shadowless betrayed him." I looked right at Lucas, trying to see if the First Beta already knew the deal that had been struck.

Instead, nothing but confusion.

Magnes had never intended to honor that promise.

"Before Gabel went to Shadowless, Kiery had a vision that Gabel chose one of the Shadowless females as a mate. It wasn't me, it was my packmate Amber. Magnes told Jermain to let Gabel have her, as a spy, and Magnes would help Jermain get her back. Magnes did not keep that promise, and at my wedding the Shadowless tried to get me to leave with them while Gabel was on the Moonlight Run. Jermain pledged loyalty to Gabel when he was actually spying for Magnes. Gabel has known since our wedding. He's let Jermain live. Now that he's dealt with Anders, he'll go to Shadowless."

I swallowed. Hard. Shadowless was still my birthpack. Still my family.

Gabel was going to gut them eventually. I *knew* that. And I was disgusted that they had sold me for their safety. They had just given away a female on some vague promise Magnes would help get them back. It hadn't been right. It hadn't been okay.

And nothing would ever make it those things.

I knew what Gabel did to the packs that betrayed him. I had been there. I had *helped*.

Had Gabel turned me into a monster?

Or had I always been this?

"Is that true? Is that what you saw? Is that what Magnes did?" Lucas asked Kiery harshly.

"I can't answer that," Kiery retorted.

"Is it *true*, Kiery? Any of it? All of it?"

"I can't tell you. Back off!"

My heart ached for them. It ached for Shadowless. I realized I was crying and pulled at the tears. My father would probably die a good First Beta's death. The sort of death Hix wanted, and Lucas wanted. He'd get that, at least. I'd tell Gabel my father had to have that.

Lucas pounded his fist into the map. "Dammit, Kiery!"

"I can't tell you," Kiery said in a frosty tone.

"Magnes wouldn't have done that," Bernhard said like the words were unfamiliar.

"Why would she make it up?" Lucas demanded hotly. "This whole thing is shit! The entire thing! Someone is lying and playing games, and I know it's not me, so who the hell is it?!"

"Those are dangerous words, Lucas," Matthew said in a low tone.

"Dangerous! Who cares?! Everything about this is dangerous! The world is on fire and nobody is paying attention!" Lucas ranted. "Did our Alpha strike that deal with Shadowless? Because if he did, he didn't tell me about it, and I would need to know!"

Bernhard and Matthew shifted and exchanged very uncomfortable glances.

"Lucas," Kiery said. "Choose your words carefully here. Gianna's prediction hasn't come to pass."

Indeed. If I couldn't reach Gabel through the tourmaline spear in time, I'd fail the test.

But I was out of time. Adrianna was on my scent, I couldn't let Magnes stonewall, I couldn't let Lucas back away. My story was crumbling, the cracks were showing. I had to save Hix, I had to get back to Gabel before he destroyed everything. He'd run out of justifiable targets soon, and then what would he do?

He'd come to SableFur.

The Bond twisted. I'd see him again soon. Would I reign at his side then, as a blood-soaked Lady-Luna, let him put a crown of shattered obsidian on my head as Anita had foreseen?

Lucas spun around and faced me.

I stared back. I wasn't afraid or intimidated by the SableFur Beta. Not when I had been in Gabel's bed.

"Are you pregnant?" Lucas asked.

"What?" I asked blankly.

"Are you pregnant."

"No."

"Are you sure?"

"Yes."

Lucas shook his head once. "Kiery, I want that checked. I want to *know* she's not pregnant."

The RedWater wolf hadn't shown me this. Why would they care if I was pregnant or not? Distressed by the sudden question I didn't understand, I asked, "Why? What does it matter if I am? I'll be gone from here."

"You don't think Gabel's going to come find you?" Matthew asked sarcastically.

"I think when he repudiated me he gave up any claim to anything in my belly."

"Make it happen. Now," Lucas ordered.

Kiery shrugged, unimpressed with his authority. "Fine. Not difficult."

I dared not protest. Why did this suddenly matter so much to Lucas? Kiery, however, took my arm and pulled me out of the office.

FLINT'S SONG REDUX

"Why did he want to know if I was pregnant?" I asked Kiery.

"I don't know."

Lucas held back secrets from her too. That street went both ways, even if Lucas didn't want to accept it. He probably felt it wasn't equal: Lucas dealt with the safety of SableFur, and Kiery didn't... at least not directly.

Pregnancy tests were easy, and I, of course, wasn't. I had been exposed to so much silver that if I *had* been pregnant, I would have miscarried. Assuming the Moon hadn't had a plan for *that*.

Kiery shoved me back into my room. She slammed the door behind her and advanced on me, smelling of anger. "You hear the storm, don't you. You know what all this is about."

"All of *what*?" I wasn't exactly lying. I wasn't sure what was happening anymore either. I had just signed my family's death warrant and reeled from the fact I wasn't reeling at all. I *knew* what Gabel would do to them. Oh, by the Moon, I *knew*. I'd beg him to give my father a warrior's death. The same death

Hix wanted. Not that he really deserved it, because he had
gone along with it all.

Oh, who was I anymore!

"*This*," Kiery hissed.

"Ask Anita." I wasn't lying there either. Anita knew every-
thing. Kiery could take her suspicions to her. Fat chance of
Anita telling her anything. "I'm here because of Anita, so if
Anita tells you, you let me know!"

Kiery snorted angrily. "I can only hear the storm, you're
standing out in it. Give me the weather report, Gianna."

The storm pressed down on me too, the vastness of it, and
for a moment it paused, like the eye of a hurricane passing by.

I couldn't tell her.

Kiery needed to play her part in this as much as I did, and
Magnes... no, the *SableFur*, having absolute faith in their Oracle
and her loyalty was the most important thing. Kiery couldn't
betray what she didn't know.

"I'm only here to vindicate myself and clear my name," I
said. "Ask Anita why it's come to this. I don't know."

How this secret had been buried so deep, or why Anita kept
it at all, or what had happened to Gabel's mother, who she had
really been. Hell, I'd like to know.

Kiery's face pinched and her scent, for a moment, seemed
like salt, water, and dead blood. The taste of a memory.

An ally in SableFur was something I wanted, but couldn't
risk. Kiery and Lucas needed to be exactly as they were, frustrated with me, angry with me, believing I was hiding a secret
and lying to them, that Magnes had done something, that
Anita reeked of a private agenda, that I was done with Gabel,
actively entertaining going to IceMaw. If they wanted to know
more they'd have to claw it from the Moon and the dirt.

Kiery growled at me, then turned to go.

"I want to see Hix," I demanded.

"I don't get a say in that."

Kiery closed the door behind her. Time to deal with the tourmaline. I knelt, picked it up, and grimaced. I didn't want to do this, but there was no choice. Gabel had to know, *now,* what he needed to do. It was still daylight. I might have a long time to wait in the spear if he only could access it when he was sleeping. Assuming that's how it worked.

Assuming Gabel slept at all.

Time to try. If I had to wait, I had to wait. Better to wait in the void than not be there when he showed up.

I stared into its blue depths, half-believing it would take me somewhere else, that it wouldn't take me anywhere at all—

The blue roared up around my mind and yanked me into the tunnel.

~*~ *Through The Stone* ~*~

It wasn't the grove. It was a marble box.

A box? An urn? I was in an urn?

No. A small, rectangular room, with three torches on each of the walls. There was no wind, so the light was steady and a cheery yellow, and the room was warm, but the back of the room from where I emerged was pitch, inky blackness. I stepped forward into the yellow-red light, and the blackness slid off my shoulders like tatters of silk.

At the end of the room was a raised stone dais. At first I thought it was a sarcophagus, then I realized it was just a simple block of solid marble.

On the platform were the shattered pieces of my obsidian bowls, arranged in a swirling pattern of many arms in the shape of an extravagant but unfinished necklace.

I touched one piece. The power was still intact. That shouldn't be right. They should be dead and broken.

A gap appeared in the wall, rectangular and tall, like a window. Light punched its way into the room, and a gust of fresh, humid air. I moved to the window and saw I was once again in a jungle, almost level with the green tree tops, and facing west. It was the pyramid from the first vision, complete with Flint's song calling a Queen to war, echoing across the air.

The sun set low over the lush tree tops, bathing everything angry red and orange.

As I listened the song faded.

I needed to be in the void-grove. I needed to find Gabel.

I hefted myself onto the wide window sill and leaned out. It wasn't exactly a pyramid, but looked like a step pyramid built as part of an ancient temple complex, covered in lush jungle growth and flowers, with a few lazy afternoon birds sailing about overhead. No bugs, curiously, and the air was hot and thick and pungent with the scent of green things, and rotting things that would one day become green things once more.

"Gabel!" I shouted. "Gabel!"

I looked back at the carefully arranged necklace. I hadn't noticed it before, but there were other shards on the dais. Not all my bowls had been obsidian. Like most Oracles, I preferred the dark, reflective surface of obsidian, which was most like the night sky. But a few of the smaller ones had been clear quartz. I had used them mostly for purification and rarely for scrying, but Gardenia had shattered those too.

I didn't remember Gabel taking those shards. There weren't so many of them, but they were lined up separate from the necklace, wrought with platinum wire into a brooch or hair comb (I couldn't tell) in the shape of the Balance rune.

Where the hell was I? What did the Moon want?

My hands were still bandaged and hurt, but I retrieved one of the torches from the wall and wriggled out the window, and dropped onto the ledge below.

"I'll probably set myself on fire," I muttered about the fire flickering perilously close to my head.

It was very, very quiet. The echo of Flint's song had faded, and there wasn't any noise from the jungle below. The sun didn't seem to be getting any lower in the sky.

The next ledge up was over my head, and probably more than I could manage with my wrecked hands.

"Oh, hello," I said when I inched around a corner to the next side. That face had, right in the middle, stone stairs overlaid onto the steps.

The top of the structure was flat, like before. In the center, on an ancient, raised altar, were the runes from my first vision, and tangled around it the string-of-fangs necklace, and set to the eastern side of the altar was a circlet of bleached, polished white wood, and from the upraised tangles of branches it clutched pieces of obsidian, blue tourmaline, and clear quartz. It was carved with deep, but narrow grooves all over, very fine and intricate, and the grooves were stained carmine red. I picked it up to examine it.

It wasn't bleached wood. It was bleached bone, and those little grooves weren't stained red, they were tiny channels of blood.

Blood trickled out of the grooves and down my hands, staining my bandages.

It was not a large crown. I did not think it was intended for a male's head.

Trembling harder, I set it back down.

The tangle of fangs caught my eye again. A simple piece of black thread, looped around the widest part of the fangs. The fangs had been cracked off, like Gabel had de-fanged the RedWater wolves. There seemed to be so many! Fang, fang, fang, fang. I tried to count them all but by the fiftieth I couldn't see anymore from the tears and had to stop.

Had Gabel done it? Were these the souls Gabel had desecrated?

The runes were different this time. There were three sets: one made of obsidian, one made of quartz, one made of blue tourmaline, and there were one for each rune: Balance, Courage, Love. They were arranged in a neat, tight line, with the tourmaline sitting between its obsidian and quartz companions. Nine stones.

The sun still hadn't set.

In the east, the full moon peered just over the horizon, and the sky was red, melting to violet, to darkness.

"I get it," I said to the sky. "Balance. I think. I just don't understand what it means."

And if the crown was out here on the altar, why was the necklace still down below in the little antechamber?

"A crown." I picked back up the crown again, shuddering at the bone and blood. "A crown for a female head. But where is Gabel's?"

No answer.

Was Gabel going to die?

What was the fate of comets that slammed into the Earth? They incinerated.

"No," I said, shaking. "No. How can I wear that crown if he's not here to win it for me?"

Being King-Alpha was Gabel's wish. If he died, then I would never be a Queen Luna. He had to triumph and survive long enough to crown me. It couldn't be the right answer. It couldn't be my crown.

"No. You didn't send Gabel here as your Comet to die once he served your purpose."

A large enough comet, a heavy enough one, one made of metal, might not blow apart. It might embed itself into the Earth.

Gabel. I had to find my way to the grove, and tell Gabel about what he needed to do.

I left my torch burning on the altar and hurried down the ancient stairs. I scrambled over the side down to the third ledge, and slipped around the corner, and I half-expected the window to not be there, but it was. I hauled myself up through the window, flopped over onto the stone floor and smashed my shoulder and hip falling into the room.

"Ouch," I whimpered.

At least it hadn't been my skull.

The unfinished necklace was still there, along with the inky darkness. I got up and walked to it, and it engulfed me.

THE GROVE: SING OF LOVE

Battered and exhausted, I woke to the scent of flowers.

"Buttercup."

"Gabel!" I opened my eyes, realized I was cradled against him, in the dark, silent grove.

He looked equally battered. Gaunt, drawn, scratches healing on his face, and bruises, and his knuckles were like raw meat, and he was missing two fingernails, the nail beds bloody. He was naked, sliced across the hip and burned with silver on his left chest, the burns and bruises blooming like flowers across his skin.

"Anders put up a fight," I said with understanding.

"His Luna put up a better one. Buttercup, what's happened to you?" he gripped me with his hands and peered at me.

"Ow." I flinched as his hand closed over my shoulder. He brushed my hair away, revealing a huge blue contusion where I had hit the temple floor.

"Your neck isn't healed. Your hands." He lifted one and examined the blood-soaked wraps. "Buttercup, what have they done to you?"

"Nothing. I haven't been harmed but they have Hix and —" I choked.

"I know. Aaron told me." He kissed each of my hands, then turned his attention to the necklace of still-healing wounds around my neck.

I needed to tell him before it was too late. Before the Moon sucked us back into the world. "Gabel. You need to attack Shadowless."

"Why?"

"Because I told First Beta Lucas that would be your next move. The SableFur think you'll attack Aaron over RedWater, and will get suspicious when you don't."

"Shadowless is your birthpack. I was going to hold off."

"Hold off?" I laughed miserably. "I know you're going to go for them eventually! Just give my father a warrior's death."

"He doesn't deserve one. He should have demanded his Alpha act like an Alpha, and not like a belly-crawling coward."

"*Please.*"

"No," Gabel said coldly. "I will *not* give him the death you want for Hix. He doesn't deserve it. Hix deserves it. I'll give your father a *quick* death. I'll kill him before I confront Jermain."

I wept. "Don't talk about Hix dying! I won't let it happen!"

"How will you stop it?" Gabel asked. "He is a warrior, Gianna. Warriors die. It is an inevitable truth."

"I won't let it happen"

Gabel glared at me. "Foolish. You'd ruin everything to save the life of one wolf who had already agreed to die, but you want a warrior's death for a wolf who wasn't willing to die?"

I shoved at him. He didn't move. "Shut up, Gabel! Shut up!"

"Your father's soul will know he didn't die a warrior. Be grateful I don't dishonor him further. He gets a clean death, and I'm being generous. They betrayed me, they *lied* to me, and they *sold* you. I would *never* sell one of our daughters."

"And if they had fought you how many would have died?!" I lashed out.

"That's the point of warriors. To fight and die. Jermain is a warrior, and his choices were fight or surrender. He chose dishonor. You want me to give your father a warrior's death, but he is a warrior who let his Alpha give away his own honor. He should have bled in your name. That's what honor costs. It costs blood."

I shuddered.

He lifted my hands in his. "Is this your blood, buttercup?"

"Some of it," I whispered, shuddering over the bleeding crown's memory.

A smile. "Buttercup, have you been bloodying up Sable-Fur? What have I told you about your temper?"

I managed a watery smile. "They haven't let me train. I get no indulgences there."

"That I approve of. Flint humoring you is not going to continue."

"We've argued about this."

"A King needs his Queen, and they need their heirs."

"Don't get too hasty," I said automatically, not wanting to talk about pups. Not after I had already been exposed to silver, pregnancy tested, wandered around a jungle temple, and handled a crown of bleeding bones.

"Yes, yes. I have other things to do. Like attack Shadowless while being conveniently elsewhere so Aaron can strut around like a bird of paradise."

Aaron.

"I've seen him," I told Gabel. "He was at SableFur."

"Yes, I know. Not that I trust him, but I can deal with him later."

"That's what he plans to do with you."

"I am not surprised. You were able to speak to him in private?"

"Ah... he ah..." I fumbled. "He made it clear to Magnes and I that he... he wants me to come to IceMaw. You... will probably hear rumors on how he came to my room."

Gabel gripped my chin between his thumb and forefinger, and forced me to look up at him. "So he still wants you, and without my Mark, he thinks he can have you. What happened in your room?"

"Not that! He told me what his agreement with you is."

"But everyone thinks he was taking what is *mine*. That perhaps he laid you down on your bed and made sweet, tender love to you?" Gabel leaned close to me, growling his words. "Is that what happened?"

"How can you even say that!" I shoved him back. He didn't release me and his grip wrenched my neck. "First Hix, now Aaron? Are you jealous of every male who talks to me?!"

"Yes," he growled. "I enjoy having what everyone else wants."

"Hix doesn't want me."

"You are blind if that's what you think, Gianna. Don't insult the man. He's going to die for you."

"Not if I can help it!" I flailed, but Gabel held me firm. He yanked me to him, the pressure a dull ache on my face. "I won't let him die, Gabel. I won't, I swear I will find a way to save him!"

"You are naïve. They are just playing with their prey."

"And that's what I'm doing with Aaron! To everyone, I am not yours. Aaron says I smell of the night-blooming cereus as loudly as you talk of punching Her Eye!"

Gabel snarled, "You are *mine*, buttercup."

"It is safer if Magnes thinks that I will have somewhere to go after I leave SableFur," I whispered.

"You are *mine* and you will return to me."

"It's just part of the plan!" I pleaded.

"Curse the plan! He seems to think because I permit him take my territories that it means he takes my mate?!"

"My Mark is gone. My scent has returned," I whispered.

"And you're defending him?"

"I'm defending the situation! If Magnes thinks that I will become the IceMaw Luna then he won't be so quick to kill me!"

Gabel's dark fury multiplied. "She takes the Mark, but then gives you back your scent and now I must suffer mongrels sniffing you like they *matter*?! The Bond still *lives*, Gianna. How dare the Moon-Bitch, I swear I am going to gouge out Her damned Eye! And then, I am going to kill Aaron for daring to touch what is mine!"

He wasn't listening, and I was sick of this nonsense. I shoved him off me. "Are you afraid now that I have a choice I might choose him? That maybe I won't want you back?"

Gabel snarled, "So we're back to that, are we?"

"You always do this! You always focus on the small thing instead of the big thing. Let Aaron make all the noise he damn well pleases if it gets us what we want!"

"And how much dishonor must I suffer to know my Luna fucked the IceMaw Alpha?"

"I am *not* your Luna and I haven't done anything! I haven't even kissed him! You repudiated me, remember?! I have no pack, I have no Mark, I have no mate!"

"Haven't *even*! So you thought about it, you just haven't gotten around to it?!"

"No!"

"I am going to rip that Moon's Eye out with both hands

and piss in the socket!" He surged to his feet, the petals a storm around us and the void hot and burning with his rage. "I am not doing this to not have you back, Gianna! I *will* get you back, or I will rip the cosmos apart!"

"Speaking of that," I interjected, wanting to *not* talk about Aaron and remembering we had actual *things* to talk about and I didn't want to argue in the grove with the little time we had left. "You need to stop telling people you're going to punch the Moon in the Eye."

"Why? That is *exactly* what I'm going to do. Now more than before! Now I am going to plunge both claws in at once!"

"Because it doesn't make any sense. To everyone but you, me, Flint, and Hix *you're* the one who repudiated me because I betrayed my Oracle vows. Why are you mad at the Moon? Kiery and Lucas are on to me, they just can't prove anything because my Mark is gone, but it's stirring up questions."

"Good." Gabel glowered. "It *should*."

"Adrianna is going to go for my throat. The instant she decides that I'm less trouble dead than alive, she'll kill me."

Gabel shrugged, dismissing this new threat with terrifying disregard. "The bell's been rung, buttercup. I can't stop now. I'm sure you're a match for Adrianna."

"And if I'm not I was never worthy of being your Luna at all?"

He ignored me. "After Shadowless, there is nothing left to distract me. I *will* come for SableFur because there is no where left for me to waste my time." He curled his lips at me, exposing teeth that extended into hungry fangs. "I will rip Magnes into pieces and put a crown of his bones on my head."

"Ready or not, here you come?" I didn't want to think about crowns or bones. There seemed to be only a crown for *me*.

"Unless you have something else to distract me." He lifted

my hands in his. "Who did this to you, buttercup? I'll start with them."

"Nobody. I cut myself holding a mirror."

"The Moon once more. I will start with Her," Gabel growled. "You do look unwell, buttercup."

"You look like shit yourself."

"Do I? I think I look the part of the King-Alpha setting his kingdom in order for the return of his Queen. Marked with the glory of pain, and savoring it. I am alive to feel the pain. I am alive to know pain when my enemies only know coldness and death, parted from their broken bodies." Gabel kissed the bloody bandages.

I lunged forward and kissed him, holding onto him with my battered hands and trying to push the memory of the crown on the altar out of my mind. Gabel *couldn't* be dead. No, that's not what it meant. I *knew* that.

Then what did it mean? I didn't care about being a Queen!

"I doubt the Moon-Bitch will give us enough time." He told me as he pressed me into the soft ground.

"Maybe if you didn't insult Her," I chided him.

He kissed my throat, his tongue moving in a quick swirl around the hollow of my throat, then moved lower. "Have you missed me, buttercup?"

"Less talking."

"We are short on time, aren't we?" he lifted his gaze to the rotating heavens. "And I want you to remember my name when Aaron takes you to bed."

He pulled me back into the pile of petals. For a few moments his eyes reflected the stars and they circled his pupils, points of light orbiting a black hole. His hands gripped my thighs and pulled me astride him while he kissed me hungrily.

"I'll forgive your curiosity," he whispered as he slid my body higher on his, and guided his cock into me. I arched my back and shuddered. His hands grasped my breasts, his thumbs rubbed my nipples, and I braced my bandaged hands on his strong chest. Blood smeared his skin. Traced the rivulets and patterns of scars on his chest. Like blood flowing through veins.

"I'm not curious about him," I gasped as I sank down his full length. My spine drew into a tight bow, and I cried out, the Bond surging and alive again. I opened my eyes. The heavens rotated above us. "I don't want to talk about him. Fuck me until I can't see straight."

Laughter. "The mouth on you. Look at me, buttercup. Not at Her."

I obeyed, breathing hard. His fingers dug into my hips, roughly guiding my motion on his cock. Petals rained around us in an unseen breeze. Drifted and stuck to the blood smeared on his chest. Hot starlight coiled inside me, tightening and tightening like a serpent about to strike.

"Don't hold back," he groaned. One of his hands raked my breasts, twisted a nipple, sent a shock of pain/pleasure through both of us.

The serpent struck both of us, blinding and aching, I opened my mouth to scream, everything fractured—

I woke in a bed that wasn't mine. In a room that wasn't mine. Naked, except for changed wraps on my hands.

With a throbbing bruise on my shoulder, and a matching one on my hip, and my thighs sticky.

And First Beta Lucas looking at me from the foot of his bed.

BACK OF BEYOND

In my memory, I had been with Gabel, in the grove, and it was his seed on my thighs.

But I was in Lucas' bed?

Terror lashed my heart to a crazy rhythm that left me faint and struggling to breathe. Had I done something with Lucas believing he had been Gabel?

Lucas, right ankle perched on left knee, sat in a chair at the foot of his bed.

Paralyzed and confused, I didn't dare say anything. My brain sloshed and throbbed against the inside of my skull, and I felt feverish, like I had been in the sun too long. The sticky, dried feeling on my thighs needled me. What had I done? Who had done it? How? Had it been Gabel?

It had to have been Gabel.

Had I been... writhing about moaning in the flesh and they had come in and found me like that? How mortifying.

Did they think I was sleeping with a SableFur? That a SableFur had had his way with me?

And if I could have sex with Gabel in the grove... how would I explain if I got pregnant?

Oh shit.

Could I get pregnant? If Gabel had me in the grove, could I get pregnant in the real world? What would that mean if we conceived a child? Would the baby be normal?

Well, I'd be gone from SableFur by then, one problem solved, and Gabel would know how, even if nobody believed us. Who cared about that. I wasn't Gabel's mate right now, so if I conceived a child outside of the matebond and he claimed it... big deal. People might actually be soothed if they thought Gabel claimed my offspring but it wasn't biologically his.

Why, though, was I in the middle of Lucas' bed?

The RedWater wolves slept on the floor. Could they tell me what had happened?

Lucas did have very soft sheets. They were bleach-white, but didn't smell freshly washed, and he had a rather plain quilt that his grandma had probably made for him as a kid stretched over top. The rest of the room was the sort of messy-clean I'd have expected from a confirmed (if reluctant) bachelor.

We stared at each other.

No way. I was not talking first. I knew this tactic, and I felt shitty enough that talking was an effort. He observed how I looked about, pale, stricken, confused, my reactions told him a ton of stuff. He was the one who needed to start explaining. How, why, when... and had it been Gabel I had been with, or someone else.

"Nice bruises," he said.

I stayed quiet.

He glared at me. It was not feigned.

"What day is it?" I decided to ask. Speaking made me swoon into the pillows.

"You've been gone for three days." His voice reached me across the roar in my ears.

Three days.

Three days. If I had been gone for three days, then Magnes and Adrianna had to know. Oh, passing these tests had become elementary now. They probably wanted me gone. Why had the Moon wasted so much time taking me to the temple?!

Lucas stood up. He retrieved something from the top drawer of a small table and walked over to me.

He dropped the small bag of items and leaned down, arms on either side of me and shoved his face in mine.

I shoved myself back against the pillows. He leaned closer, staring at something on my face. He placed his hand over my left eye and pulled the lids apart. I screeched and tried to yank away, he grabbed my neck and shoved me down, pinning me by my throat. My eye dried and started to water.

"What the hell is that!" Lucas snarled.

I couldn't breathe. What the hell was *what*?! My ears hummed and I gagged. Romero had tried to strangle me. I clawed at Lucas with my bandaged hands and tried to kick him. "Get off me!"

He yanked his hands away. He snatched the bag off my lap, upended it and shook the items out. The runestones and the shard of mirror. He grabbed the mirror and shoved it at me. "Look."

Shaking, I picked up the mirror, the prickle of its power intact, and raised it to my face. In the pitted, rust-marked surface I immediately saw what he was talking about. The bottom of my left eye's iris was pocked with a white-grey crescent moon. The tips of the moon pointed upwards to cup my pupil, while the fat curve dipped downward, and it floated in a field of hazel.

What is happening to me?
Is this the price I pay for using the tourmaline?

I looked at Lucas, shaken and trying to hide it, but it's hard to hide how shaken you are when you're actually shaking.

He pointed at the items. "Tell me what they mean."

"You know what they mean." He had been at dinner. His beloved Kiery had translated them, even if she had spared him the purest translation.

"Tell me the *secret*," he snarled. "Tell me why a war is about to break out, and no one but me seems to recognize it. Gabel did *exactly* what you said he'd do. Yesterday evening he took his forces out of GleamingFang, *all* his forces, and *right now* is razing Shadowless. Aaron is in RedWater. GleamingFang is undefended but Aaron's not taking it. And you, in deep meditation clutching a tourmaline with bruises forming on your body as it happened, and then reeking of sex, and now your eye."

Reeking of sex? Awkward. Verrrry awkward. So Lucas had brought me down to his bed to watch me, and while he had been watching me—

Oh my.

Oh my.

Was there wet spot on his sheets?

Maybe one day we'd look back at this and laugh... but probably not.

Ana would laugh. She'd laugh at this, funny or not, no matter what. Because on some level, this was sort of cosmically, horribly, hilarious.

"Ask Anita." I touched my eyelashes and looked again at my marked eye. What was the Moon *doing*? One of the RedWater wolves got up onto the bed and curled up next to me. The frigid, icy tips of his fur made me shiver.

"Oh, I'm going to ask Anita." He took the mirror, and the stones back. "I'm going up there today to ask her."

He leaned close again, sniffing my neck, my shoulders. He looked me full in the face, his features having taken on a darkness that bespoke a coming shift. He yanked the blankets off me and shoved my thighs apart. I kicked. He slammed my legs to the mattress.

The thing about... that stuff... is that it doesn't dry clear. It sort of looks like dried toothpaste. And my thighs were still streaked.

Lucas needed absolutely no more confirmation at all something completely fucked up was going on his pack, and the scent of his prestige, authority and fury erupted into my nose. He snarled, looking between my eye and my thighs, teeth elongating into fangs as he tried to sort out who the threat was, what it was, and what he had to protect his pack.

Oh shit.

Oh shit shit shit shit.

"Do not move," he growled.

Lucas wasn't nearly as fearsome as Gabel, but that made him even more dangerous. Gabel's rage ran deep, his violence intense, but it didn't lash out into all directions like a panicked, angry ocean. Gabel was always in control. Gabel delighted in being the master of fear and pain.

Lucas was spooked and all his male instincts—and probably the ones that told him Kiery was his mate, even though she rejected the terms—were on high alert. I was the outsider. I was the harbinger.

Lucas hadn't decided *who* needed to die.

I didn't think he'd be willing to hear *Magnes*.

Lucas stormed out of his rooms. He was gone long enough I debated if I wanted to get out of bed, but he *had* told me to not move, and he had *meant* it, and I didn't really want to end up with a claw in my gut. But I decided that I was going to get up and get the stuff off my thighs. *Moving* probably meant *leave my rooms*, not literally *stay on the bed*.

My head swam as I stood up. I caught myself and stumbled towards the bathroom. My hip had a huge lump on it, all black-red from dried blood and it hurt like hell, and my shoulder matched, sending throbbing pain through my fevered body.

"I do look like shit," I told my reflection. I looked like I had been sick for weeks, and now my eye. I found a washcloth and dabbed at my thighs.

Just a little while longer. Soon it would be over. Now things were moving on their own, and I just needed to catch up and steer.

Maybe sex with Gabel had been a bad idea.

If it had been Gabel at all. Well, if Lucas had been *staring at me* and there wasn't anyone on me... then it either had to have been Lucas or Gabel, and I didn't think it was Lucas, which brought me back to the same question of where was the grove, and what happened if I conceived a pup in there?

One of the RedWater wolves followed me.

"He didn't... you know... did he?" I asked the wolf. "I mean, Lucas."

The wolf shook his head.

Okay, not that that had seemed remotely possible. Lucas was in love with Kiery. Maybe he occasionally kept someone else's company, but he wasn't the sort of sleezeball who preyed on incapacitated women.

Romero had been that kind of sleezeball.

The door to the rooms opened and Lucas came in carrying some of my clothing. "What are you doing?"

"Cleaning up," I retorted. I tossed the washcloth into the bathtub and carefully stood. "Or do you think I want to walk around with gunk on my legs?"

"I'd like to know who your spirit-lover is." Lucas threw the wad of clothing on the bed. "Get dressed."

"Where am I going?"

"We're going to go see Anita."

"How have you explained a naked me in your bed to Kiery?"

"I don't have to explain who I sleep with to Kiery," Lucas growled.

"I think you do," I needled him. "Does she know where we're going, or are you keeping that from her? It's Oracle business, isn't it?"

"Get dressed."

"What is Magnes going to say when you disappear with me?" Anita lived hours away. Lucas couldn't just disappear without tipping his hand to Magnes.

"I think he's busier summoning Aaron here for an explanation on why Aaron hasn't attacked GleamingFang."

"Aaron isn't empire building."

"He took Gabel's southern holdings, but he won't take GleamingFang when it's undefended?"

"You aren't there. You don't know what the situation on the ground is."

"Get dressed." He sat down in his chair to watch. "We'll leave when you're ready. Oh, and be ready in ten minutes."

LUCAS WASN'T one for conversation. I put my feet on the dashboard and stared out the window as he drove us to Anita's. Talk about a place I never wanted to be again.

Ever.

"You aren't acting like a Queen Luna." Lucas observed about two hours into the drive.

"I'm *not* a Queen Luna."

"Are you sure?"

"Damn sure." I rubbed my lips with my index finger and tried not to think about the bone crown with its veins of blood.

Bones had a blood supply. The crown had been a living thing, now that I had had a few uninterrupted hours to think about it.

Which made me more convinced (and terrified) than ever that it was *my* crown.

But where was Gabel's crown? And there had been no bowls. There had been the set of runestones: three by three, three runes, three sets of stones. Obsidian, tourmaline, clear quartz.

I pondered the selection of clear quartz over milky white quartz. I didn't understand the symbolism. Clear quartz meant that to use the stone you usually had to tilt it towards the light to see the carving to indicate what the stone's rune was. Why not just use milky quartz? Most of the quartz runestones I had seen had been the milky variety.

Flint would know.

Lucas snorted.

"Do you *see* a Mark? Do I *look* like a Queen to you?" I growled at him. "I give exactly no shits about being a Queen. The only reason I got dragged into that conversation was because of Gabel."

"So what is Anita going to tell me?"

"Like hell I know. I'll be interested to hear it myself."

"You *know* what all this is about." He pounded his fist on the steering wheel. "You *know*, Gianna! You know why all this is happening."

"I only know part of it. I haven't figured out the rest. But aren't you a smart First Beta, figuring out that Anita is the key to it. Probably." I was so not in the mood, I had a headache, and the Moon showing me a crown meant for my head but not Gabel's was *not* cool. I did not want to be a Queen Luna, or a Lady Luna or even a Luna.

Oracle suited me fine.

I had been born with the Gift, I had mastered it, I had

earned the title of Oracle, and I would earn it again. I would rip it from Anita's hands and make it my own. She wasn't allowed to take it from me.

Now I sounded like Gabel.

"So tell me the part you know," Lucas said.

"No." There was no point in bullshitting him. "You wouldn't believe me, and even if you did, you wouldn't do anything about it."

I knew those two things to be true. Lucas would not believe me. And he would *not* go against Magnes. Not on my word alone.

Not yet, anyway. Maybe never. Not because *I* told him anything.

Kiery, on the other hand...

He slammed on the brakes. "Who do you think you are saying that?"

I winced as my body jostled. "The person you were just accusing of being a Queen Luna? I *know* you won't do anything with what I'd tell you, just like I know Kiery won't let you Mark her because you can't accept she's an Oracle. And no, she didn't tell me that."

Lucas stared at me, furious. "How did you know that?"

"Because I'm not stupid, and I recognize your type. Anita isn't going to tell you anything either. Mark my words. I don't know *why* she's protecting the secrets she's carrying, but I know she'll protect them to her death. She'll stonewall you, and we'll go back to SableFur, and you won't have your answers, but you can *bet* Magnes will want to know where you've been and why you've been there. So stop thinking about Anita, and start thinking about what you're going to say to your Alpha."

THERE AND BACK... AGAIN

Anita was pleased to see Lucas, and she looked at me like I was a fat suckling pig led back to her for slaughter.

"Are you returning her to me, Lucas?" Anita asked, not nearly as skeptical as she should have been of having a rabid she-wolf back in her little house. The two acolytes cowering behind her seemed properly terrified at the possibility of my return.

You want me back, don't you. So you can make me disappear for your precious pet Magnes.

Lucas said, "No. I have some questions, Elder Oracle. I figured I'd bring Gianna along for the ride."

Anita frowned, her craggy brow wrinkling even further. "Why?"

"Because the Oracles have started a war, and I want to know why." Lucas pushed past Anita into the house, and pointed at an acolyte. "Tea."

He snapped his fingers when she didn't move right away. That sent her scurrying.

"This is *my* domain, First Beta," Anita told him. But the old she-wolf sidled to the side, eyeing Lucas with sharp eyes as she moved to her favorite chair. "What question do you have for me?"

Lucas pulled me into the sitting room. He pushed me down onto the couch, then sat down himself. The unoccupied acolyte knelt in a corner.

"What Oracle in the past fifty years has used a mirror?" Lucas produced the small bag holding Gabel's mother's tools. He shook them out onto the coffee table. The mirror gleamed like a dirty accusation.

"Kiery has already asked me this," Anita said, eyes on the mirror. "I have no answer for her. I have no answer for you."

"You have to know. No Oracle could pass through SableFur without you knowing their tools. This is very rare. What Oracle used a mirror in living memory?"

Anita shook her head. "I have no answer for you, First Beta."

I poked Lucas in the bicep. "That is how Oracles say they don't want to tell you. She knows. She just has no answer she wants to tell *you*."

Anita snarled at me.

I snarled back and stood. I was *not* going to be nice to this bitch any longer. *Kiery* was the one who mattered, not this withered old hag.

Lucas grabbed my wrist and yanked me down onto the sofa. "*Sit.* And *you*, Anita. Answer my question directly. War is about to break out and you're the one who started it!"

"Me? I've started nothing. This is Oracle business, not the business of Alphas and Betas."

"I am sick of Oracles dancing around behind the veil of the Moon going nyah nyah, *Oracle's business!*" Lucas growled. "*You* sold Gianna out and convinced Magnes to listen to you, and not Kiery. I don't believe the bullshit story about Gianna not being able to be Luna and Oracle. This is about something else, and I want to know what it is."

Anita scoffed, "Why should Alpha Magnes care what some IronMoon dog says about his honor? And what do I care what an IronMoon mongrel does?"

"You'll care when they come through the mountain passage and turn you into a scarecrow. Gabel executed the GleamingFang Luna and swears he'll gouge out the Moon's Eye. I think Oracles will be tasty targets, considering you're the Moon's favorite pets." Lucas smirked at her.

Anita recoiled, and the acolyte in the corner turned gray-pale. Anita's fingers curled into the arms of her chair.

"Right now Gabel is off razing Shadowless for betraying him. Apparently they had struck a deal with Magnes before Gabel claimed Gianna, because Kiery had a vision of him claiming a Shadowless female," Lucas went on. "All of this, Anita, points right back at the Oracles. So you've started this war. You tell me why."

"Don't question the Moon, pup," Anita hissed. "I've only done my duty!"

"Your duty!" Lucas shouted. He got to his feet and grabbed me by my hair. I screeched and scratched at his wrist. He hauled me up and shoved me straight at Anita. "Look at her eye and tell me about *your* duty, you old hag!"

Lucas shoved my face right into Anita's, eye for eye.

She stank. Yuck.

Anita breathed hard and rough, and Lucas' hand tore at my scalp as he trembled with fury. Anita's failing old eyes focused on my eye, and all the color drained from her face, and a huge amount of the fight—

And most of her faith.

Her face transformed into that of a damned woman. A woman who realized that her sins had been noted, that she would not escape, and that she had chosen the wrong thing to defend, the wrong cause, the wrong man. And now, years later, she had her confirmation that she should have sided with Gabel's mother, instead of defending Magnes.

"You could have stopped all of this," I whispered to her cracking facade. "You could have prevented all of this."

She could have protected Gabel's mother, she could have protected Gabel, she could have protected whatever littermates Gabel had had... all this, because Anita, who had been the SableFur Oracle, had sided with a powerful Alpha family instead of a single, vulnerable Oracle with an innocent litter in her belly. She had made the weak choice to protect the powerful.

A very normal choice. A very *wrong* choice.

"No." She shoved me away with shocking strength. Lucas held onto my hair, and as I fell backwards, a clump ripped out of my scalp. I fell onto my rump, caught myself on my ruined hands, and ended up in a heap.

Yeah. Queen Luna. *Right.* I picked myself up.

"No," Anita told me. "You're wrong. You're *wrong*, youngling—"

"Youngling!" I shouted. "Youngling! I am an Oracle, I was a Luna, and you *dare* call me youngling? I'm not the one who set all this into motion! Look at my eye and tell me I'm wrong! Ask Lucas what he saw, and tell him I'm wrong! You *know* what I am, and no matter how hard you try, you won't stop what's happening!"

I trembled with rage and weakness. "Why did you do it, Anita? All of this is because of you. *You* were the last one who could stop it. Who was she? What was the name of the Oracle who used mirrors?"

"I will never speak that name," Anita rasped. "I swear I will never speak that name!"

Horrified, I believed her. Her refusal struck me dumb. "Why not? It's going to come out. It will be revealed."

"Not by me, it won't! I can't stop *you* from being vindicated, but I won't vindicate the Comet! I am not going to just let it smash into the Earth and destroy everything I love! What do you *think* is going to happen if I speak what I know? I will never do it! Never! I will *never* give you the last piece you need!"

"Even into damnation?" I asked.

"If you're right then I'm already damned," she said with narrowed, sharp eyes, "and if you're wrong, then I won't damn myself."

I snarled, "I can tell you what *will* happen if you don't tell me."

"No, you can't. The future is too much in flux." Anita laughed. "If the Moon wanted things to be a certain way, She'd force it to be so. The future isn't set yet, Gianna. Otherwise you'd already have told Lucas, confident it'd all work out."

"I don't know her name. I don't know how this happened. I don't know *why* it happened," I said.

"And I won't tell you." Anita laughed, high and crazy, like a harpy. "Let the war come. It won't matter. Let your precious Gabel come here. He will meet only death. He will *fail*, and yes, there will be death and destruction and ruin, but it won't matter, because SableFur will endure, and grow stronger."

"Have you seen that?" I asked her, thinking of the crown.

She smirked at me. "Have you? You've seen many things, Gianna. The Moon's Eye is burned into your own. You aren't well, and you don't even realize how sick you are, or the price you're paying. Where have you begged the Tides to take you? Foolish, foolish girl."

She was lying. She was just trying to frighten me. I had only gone where the Moon had taken me. Whatever price I had to pay for it didn't matter. Anita was right, though: if

Gabel came to SableFur now, he'd be overwhelmed. Perhaps if he came in force with Aaron, but even then. The plan had never been for Gabel to defeat an intact SableFur, but for me to somehow dismantle Magnes and throw the gates open.

Anita's wild grin told me she had seen something: a future where I had failed, and there was war, but in the end, SableFur triumphed and Magnes remained unblemished.

Just as Aaron predicted he would.

Had Anita seen Magnes crown himself with bones?

There was still a possibility Magnes could triumph. I looked at Lucas in realization. There was no time left. None at all. Anita had seen a version of the future where I failed. So what did I do? Lucas was the key.

But *how*? Lucas couldn't just confront Magnes. He had no proof, and Anita would deny everything.

Lucas grabbed the shard of mirror and waved it at Anita. "You *know* who this belonged to. Answer me plainly, Oracle!"

"I do. And I will not tell you the name. If I do, Lucas, it will endanger all of SableFur. You and I both want the same thing."

"What's that?" Lucas asked.

"SableFur's continued survival," Anita said like it was stupid. "If I tell you who that mirror belonged to, it'd destroy this pack."

"Is that what you told Kiery?"

"I told her I'd have to look at my records," Anita said. "Now I'm telling you. I won't destroy SableFur."

"And what happens when I do it?" I asked her.

"You won't succeed," Anita sneered. "You don't have any proof. You don't have a name. Only a few ever knew the secret. No one is left who might remember."

"Dear Moon, what did you *do*?" I breathed "How did you

accomplish it? There's not even a *rumor* or a whisper. How can an Oracle who uses a mirror just *disappear?*"

Anita was smart enough to say nothing.

"Kiery thinks she knows," Lucas said, as if something from years past had dawned on him. He looked at the mirror clutched in his hand, then back at Anita, biceps trembling as he resisted throwing it against the walls.

"You *will* destroy SableFur if you chase that mirror." Anita ground it a little deeper. "Walk away, Lucas. Gianna can't return to Gabel since she can't prove who that mirror belonged to."

"The Moon showed me, but that isn't enough to make you tell me?!" I asked.

Anita ignored me, walled in with her reasons.

Lucas moved on to another conclusion that horrified him. "You were never going to let her vindicate herself."

"No. I wasn't." Anita glared at me, sourly.

"How are your tits?" I smirked at her. "Oh wait, why am I asking? You haven't needed them for about fifty years."

"How is the hole in your soul?" she growled back.

"Fine," I lied.

Anita turned back to Lucas. "Let it go, Lucas. You'll destroy SableFur. Thousands of wolves' lives changed and ruined. Let Gabel come and smash into the mountain, and wreak havoc that will be suppressed, and heal the damage. The alternative is much, must worse, First Beta. Your duty demands no less!"

"Look at her eye and tell me that *I'm* the one who will destroy SableFur!" Lucas shouted. "What is that, *Oracle?* She has the Moon in her eye! If SableFur is destroyed, it's because *you* set it into motion years ago with whatever bullshit this was!"

Anita didn't respond. She didn't have anything she could tell him. There were old stories of the ancient, great Oracles

who had moons-in-their-eyes, but in the stories their eyes had
turned to blue and the moon had actually been a white ring
around the pupil. Not crescent Moons swinging in a sea of
ordinary hazel.

Did she realize her soul was forfeit, and she was damned?
Was she trying to redeem herself by protecting SableFur? Or
did she really not see that what she had done years ago had
been a grave sin? I could see her believing she had done the
right thing, except she was an Oracle, and the Moon had to
have warned her. The Moon had to have shown her what
would happen if she didn't defend Gabel's mother. The Moon
did not just send Comets and destruction without warning.

Warnings had gone unheeded. Honor not served.

No, all this had been decades, perhaps centuries, in the
making.

We were supposed to be able to turn to other Oracles, especially our elders, for safety, like a pup running to her mother.
Anita had betrayed Gabel's mother, and failed her when she
had gone to Anita for help: that she was carrying a litter of
bastard pups, and had been abandoned and rejected by the
upstart who had impregnated her.

Centuries of bad behavior had rested on Magnes' shoulders, and it had been Anita who had been the last guardian.

And she had ignored whatever warnings or whispers she
had seen or heard.

I *almost* pitied her. Almost.

Almost.

Lucas grabbed me and dragged me back to the car.

ONE THREAD CUT

Lucas was silent on the drive back to SableFur's heart. An hour out he pulled over. He handed me the bag. "Tell me what the runes mean."

"Kiery told you."

"*You* tell me."

"Don't you believe her?"

"I want your version."

I picked out each one in turn. "Pup," I said, holding that one. I picked out the next. "Betrayal." I picked out the third. "Balance. Kiery translated it as Justice, which is how it is normally translated, but it is literally Balance. Justice is its own rune."

I picked out the fourth. "Faith."

And finally, the last one. "Love. Kiery translated it as mates, which is how it is normally translated. But it actually is passionate desire, not the matebond itself. That is a different rune."

"So lust."

"Not exactly. It just means passion, I suppose, but not random passion. There is no rune for wanton lust. This is something like what you and Kiery have. There is no formal bond between you two, but there is that connection, and there's sex."

"How do you know that?"

"You're very transparent." I hadn't needed the RedWater wolves to tell me that. Perverts.

He took them and lined them up on the dashboard.

I waited.

Lucas' expression melted into something very, very sad for a few moments, turned inward. Was he remembering something from his own past? I had seen that reflective expression before. Did he *know*? Had he heard rumors?

Then he picked up the pup rune and said, heavily, "A bastard pup. Passion, betrayal, justice. Pup. But faith? There's no faith in any of that. I don't understand faith."

I put the mirror on the dashboard. "Yes, you do."

His gaze focused on my marked eye, and his thoughts returned fully to the present.

"Gabel," he said as he came to the slow, difficult realization that forced him to consider a whole new realm of dark possibilities. "Gabel's mother. Oh by the Moon, this is all about Gabel's mother!"

Lucas sat back in his seat, ran his hands over his face, stared at the runes and mirror.

I remained quiet while Lucas grappled with the enormity of it. Telling him that Magnes was Gabel's father was more than he could have heard right then. Oracles knew a great deal about the strength required to look on cruel, horrible things, and our faith and belief shattered to be rebuilt anew. It wasn't the time. I sensed Lucas was right on the tip of understanding. That he was right on the cliff, but couldn't bring himself to look down at what lived within it just yet.

Lucas suddenly betraying himself to Magnes (and I figured

he would, just like Hix had never been able to keep his opinions to himself) would blow everything to hell anyway. Best that he not be looking right at his Alpha like he doubted him.

I put the stones and mirror back in their bag and held them on my lap.

Soon.

"I was born in SableFur," Lucas said. "I've lived in SableFur my whole life, and I've never heard even a rumor of one of the Oracles disappearing. The students have come and gone, often quite suddenly, but I've never heard of one going missing."

"Anita could easily have sent Gabel's mother away and no one would have questioned it," I said. "Simply gone."

"Kiery—" he started to say.

"What about her?" I asked.

"When she came here—she's from far away. I'd never heard of her birthpack. Why did she come all this way? She's never said, not really. I think—"

"She was looking for something?" I asked. Had Kiery been tasked with this before me?

"No, not exactly. Like she was haunted by—nevermind. It's probably not important." He put the car back into gear and pulled onto the road. He balked at asking the dangerous questions. The ones like *why* and *who is Anita protecting?*

We had been gone a long time, and it was dark by the time we arrived.

"What the—" the front lights of the main house were on, which wasn't unusual. But in the center of the cluster of buildings was a tall pole, with something silhouetted against it. Something human-shaped was tied to the pole.

A horrible, horrible, horrible feeling slammed into me.

"Oh no, no, no, no," I gabbled. The headlights illuminated everything.

It was a *man*. Lucas stopped the car, and I clawed my way out.

Hix.

I staggered up to the pole. It was a single long pole, about eight feet tall, with a large iron ring at the very top. They had chained him, his wrists stretched over his head and dangling from the chain, feet just above the ground, and he had been bound around his thighs and chest to the pole with leather straps. From the blood and bruising, they had silver bars on the underside.

The blood had frozen on his body. His head sagged on his neck, the one eye he had left open and staring, frozen in the cold.

"No." I flung myself at the pole and clutched my arms around his legs. He was stiff and cold.

"*No!*" I screamed, shaking him, the chains jangling. "*No!*"

His eye stared back at me, dead and empty.

"*No!*"

On his chest was a single strange prick that caught my eye, just a tiny slice. Of all the other abuse, that thing stood out to me. Dazed and stumbling, I went around to the back of the pole.

A war-form had stabbed him in the back.

Not even a warrior's death.

I dropped to my knees in the snow, paralyzed, beyond tears, beyond screaming, beyond even my heart beating.

No.

I had sworn to save him. I had failed.

...he's going to die for you, buttercup...

I screamed.

I couldn't stop screaming. I just screamed, and screamed, and screamed.

No! He can't be dead. It can't be over! It can't be!

The RedWater wolves threw their heads back and howled ghostly, silent howls with me.

...*Gianna*...

The Bond flailed and bucked against the tether, my soul screaming for my mate to come carry this anguish with me.

...*Gianna*...

From the house emerged several forms.

One of them separated themselves from the group, moving with a serpentine grace.

Luna Adrianna bent down by my ear as I shuddered with grief and rage. "He called you his Luna until the end," she whispered in my ear. "I do believe the poor wolf loved you. He seemed quite happy to die in your name."

"You bitch, you horrible, horrible bitch—"

"What would *you* have done, *Luna*?" she whispered. "How many have *you* executed?"

It wasn't zero. It *wasn't* zero.

"What did you think was going to happen to him? He served his purpose, had nothing useful to say, so now he's gone. He was never leaving this place alive, stupid girl, no more than Lucas would have left IronMoon alive. But it was amusing to watch you think he just might. Hix was more practical. There. I remembered his name and spoke it."

"But you didn't give him a warrior's death!" I snarled at her. "You stabbed him in the back!"

"Would your precious Gabel have given my Lucas a warrior's death?" Her eyes pierced mine. "Think about the fangs you carry in that pouch and ask yourself that. Think about how many Gabel has killed and thrown away while you watched. He justifies it as crimes against honor. Well, so do I. The First Beta of another pack does not get to come here and shout about *my* mate's honor and get treated with dignity."

"Even if what he said is true?" I hissed.

"What would you have done to Lucas? We aren't different, Gianna, no matter how much you want to think we are." She patted me on the head and straightened.

I snarled and swiped at her.

She ducked away with easy grace, pivoted on one foot like a ballet dancer, and kicked me in the rib. I rolled backwards in the snow, coughing. Her graceful pivot didn't stop for me, and she completed the neat three-sixty and continued on the walk to the house as if she had been doing a simple twirl.

"Follow her," I choked to the RedWater wolves, "and Lucas."

I crawled to the pole and lay in the snow, weeping and praying the Moon would return him to me.

But the Moon had already set, and there was nothing but winter's brittle silence.

Eventually my two Goons came to carry me back into the house.

LUCAS : END, BEGINNING, MIDDLE... IN THAT ORDER

Lucas faced Magnes, balling up all his feelings and wadding them into a corner. His anger about Hix being executed without him present, and the manner in which it had been done, pissed him off and wasn't feigned. Hix had been his counterpart. It would have been a courtesy to give him the option of executing his counterpart. There had been no *need* for Hix to be executed *in that moment*, he hadn't been gone long, it *could* have waited a few hours.

It was an insult to him that Hix had been thrown out like so much garbage and left to dangle like a morbid scarecrow.

"Where did you take her?" Magnes demanded.

"To Anita," Lucas replied. "I wanted some damn answers. You could have waited to execute Hix until I returned."

"That First Beta was an insult to the title and not your peer," Magnes said.

A day before that might have mollified Lucas slightly. Now it only made him feel more disgusted.

"Anita called me and told me all about your conversation," Magnes said. "Leave this alone, Lucas. It's Oracle business, not ours."

"I think you've made it pack business," Lucas retorted. "Who was the Oracle that used mirrors? Who is Anita protecting?"

Magnes pinched the bridge of his nose between his thumb and forefinger. "I don't know, and I don't care. Alpha Gabel has lost his damn mind and is rampaging around like an idiot. Please do not join him."

"We all know that Anita leveraged Gianna using a spy you planted, and you let her do it," Lucas growled.

Magnes shrugged. "True and fair, and I'll accept responsibility for that much, now leave this alone. We have bigger matters to deal with. Aaron is not inclined to get his claws dirty with Gabel's blood. I've summoned him here. He has some explaining to do."

"I would rather take warriors to the other side of the mountain and explain things to the IronMoon personally."

"No." Magnes waved off the idea. "Not yet."

"Then I'd like to go get a shower," Lucas growled. "Since you won't let me get dirty."

"Betas and their desire for a fight." Magnes snorted. "Fine. Go. And don't meddle with the Oracles again, Lucas. In so much as is possible given your affair with Kiery."

"That's *my* business, not yours, and Kiery's made it damn clear she's not budging," Lucas snapped.

"Consider it a blessing. Look how well it worked out for Gabel," Magnes commented, unruffled by Lucas' anger.

Lucas left the office and stomped down the stairs and halls to his room.

Kiery sat on his couch, heels tucked up against her rump and head bowed against her knees. The television was on a channel doing terrible ancient sitcom reruns.

"What are you doing here?" He shut the door behind him, torn between Kiery being the only person he wanted to see, or the last. Another Oracle. An Oracle who could have stopped this. An Oracle who perhaps knew.

She raised her head. Her eyes were rimmed in red from crying, and she was still blotchy. "Drinking your beer and waiting for you."

Lucas sighed, melting. Kiery never cried. That's one thing he could say about Oracles. They were a tough breed. The weak ones were culled, one way or the other, and the ones who made it, especially those who were powerful and smart enough to rise to any seniority, were the toughest of all.

They had both had shit days.

"I had to watch." Kiery put her hand to her forehead and tugged at her hair. "Had to go watch an execution. I tried to get Danit to at least say wait for Lucas, then *I* said it and got told to shut up. Didn't even give the man a decent death. Just hung him up by his wrists and let the silver burn him. He howled the Luna's Song the whole time. Then some two-shit warrior I don't even know the name of stabbed him in the back."

Lucas stood rigid and still.

"And where were you, First Beta? You let your IronMoon counterpart, who died for his Luna, be cut down by a warrior so worthless I don't even know the little shit's name. If you had been here, you could have at least made his death have some dignity. Instead he had to yank it from the air howling. At least he died happy." Kiery growled, "Oh, that's right. I know where you were. Ranting like an enraged dog at Anita, who called me and crawled up my butt the instant you left."

"He died serving his Luna. No one can take that from him," Lucas said. It was something, at least. "He got to sing. He got to sing and everyone heard him, instead of doing it in the dungeon."

Kiery snorted.

He went to the fridge and pulled out two beers. He popped the top off both and handed her one. She took it and guzzled down a long swig, then dropped her head back onto her knees, shoulders shaking with silent sobs.

"I need a goddamn shower." Lucas drank half his beer. Then he pulled off his shirt, threw it on the couch. Then the belt. Then his jeans. "Go away, Kiery."

She raised her tear-streaked face, and whispered, "Why?"

"Because I don't trust Oracles. You're all in it together."

He had never said anything so harsh, in such a cutting tone. "What are you talking about?"

"You know who the Oracle that used the mirror was."

"No." Kiery shook her head. "I can't be sure. I don't know."

"Who was the Oracle that used the mirror Gianna found?" he shouted over his shoulder from the bedroom.

Kiery slid off the couch and went after him. "I was just a kid back home in NightScent. Thessa didn't know, and Anita said she didn't know either. I just came hunting rumors and stories and I—I don't want to talk about this."

Lucas got into the shower, the cold water slamming into his tired body. "Well, they're lying. Anita knows. Anita just won't tell anyone, and I guess Thessa is her little bitch."

"What? Thessa knows?" Kiery yanked the shower curtain back.

"Don't act like this is news to you." He yanked it closed again. "Go away, Kiery."

"Whoa, fuck you, buddy—"

"Not tonight you won't."

She yanked the curtain rod down and tossed it away. It clattered to the ground and splattered water everywhere. "I am the SableFur Oracle, and don't you dare accuse my Oracles of being corrupt! You tell me what Anita said to you. Now."

"Your Oracles? They're Anita's Oracles, you just apparently haven't realized it! Did Anita tell you about Gianna's eye?"

"No. What's wrong with her eye?"

"I see you are spectacularly well-informed, Oracle. Such a fine job you do. So much respect you command."

"Oracles are not warriors, you prig. Not the same level of mass stupidity and violent tendencies. But I'm starting to feel violent."

"You're not a match for me, Kiery."

"You won't fight back either. So I'll carve you up like a goddamn goose if you don't start talking. You tell me what the hell happened! You tell me what my dreams mean!"

"What dreams?" Lucas asked.

Kiery shook her head and waved her hands. "No, I can't even describe them. Tell me about Gianna."

"She's got a white half-moon where her iris should be." He pointed to his own eye. "She came out of that vision or whatever she was in with white smeared on her thighs and white in her eye and bruises like she'd been beaten."

Kiery drank some of her beer. "What sort of white goop?"

"That sort of white goop."

"You sure she wasn't just having a little alone time under the sheets? Your sheets, weren't they?"

"I know the difference between what a woman smells like and what a man smells like, Kiery. And I didn't touch her except to carry her like you told me to."

Kiery finished off her beer.

Lucas leaned on the shower wall and the water pounded over him. It also splattered Kiery and made puddles on the floor for lack of the shower curtain. "So forgive me if I don't trust Oracles right now. You guys are into some very weird shit, and there's an angry Moon goddess glaring at all of you."

"I'm not one of the cool kids, I guess." Kiery wandered out of the bathroom and back into the front room.

Ten minutes later Lucas, wrapped only in a towel, appeared and said, "And you're still here."

"Yep."

"I am not drinking with you."

"You are. And you're going to tell me all the complaints you have about my Oracles. I can't undo what happened with Hix—"

"Hix was always going to die."

Kiery grabbed the towel. "Lucas, please don't let them defang him. Please make sure he's at least buried well. Please. He died singing the Luna's Song, he died for a Luna who wasn't, and he died so gladly for her. If you never do anything else for me, please make sure they don't defile his corpse and soul."

Lucas gripped her hand and lifted her fingers off the towel. "I would not permit such a thing to happen to a fellow warrior."

"Good. Now tell me about my Oracles."

Lucas sighed, and got more beer. Then he sank down close to her, and told her everything from the moment he had put Gianna in his bed, to the conversation on the way home. That took one beer. It took half of the second before he could say, "Gianna isn't pregnant. I thought that this might be about her. The runestones she found. About the pup. That maybe Gabel... I don't know. Rejected her or something. That she has a now-bastard pup in her belly." He winced and put the beer to his forehead.

"He did repudiate her. That's sort of rejection times five thousand," Kiery said.

"I don't know. Something. Ug."

"But?" Kiery asked.

Lucas looked at her. "You already know."

Kiery said, "I saw a face in the mirror. I saw... tell me, Lucas. Tell me what I think I already know."

"It was Gabel's mother. Gabel is the pup. He's a SableFur bastard, his mother was chased off with a litter in her belly. There may be more, there may not. Nobody seems to know who she is. Anita disappeared her, and Anita says she will not say the name or it will destroy SableFur."

Kiery swallowed hard, stricken.

Lucas peeled at the label on the beer bottle. Then he set it aside and pulled her close to him, gripping her to stop her shaking as much as his. "I'm right, aren't I. You've seen it."

Kiery nodded.

"What are we going to do?" he whispered. "Adrianna has to know."

"I'm certain she does," Kiery whispered. "I'm certain she's always known. But we can't prove it, Lucas."

"It would be your word and mine and Gianna's. The only thing we have is the mark in her eye."

"It's not enough."

"Why wouldn't Magnes confront Gabel? Why is he resisting attacking the IronMoon while they're weak?"

Kiery shook her head. "I dreamt of Magnes wearing a crown carved of Gabel's skull, and wielding a scepter made of his right arm and hand, and a cloak over his shoulders made of Aaron's hide. Row after row of werewolves howled his praises in a dark cave made of burning stone, but thanking him for saving them from the Comet."

"What does it mean?" Lucas asked.

"That Magnes will use Gabel to become King-Alpha," she whispered by his ear. "And Aaron is, I think, working with Gabel."

"Magnes defeats them, he gets all their holdings," Lucas whispered.

"Yes. Quite an incentive to let Anita do whatever she wants, isn't it? Anita buries Gabel so no one ever knows about her sins, Magnes wears his crown."

Lucas pondered this, his entire world view pivoting around.

"Aren't the other senior wolves restless? Don't they want to attack Gabel now?"

"Yes. Magnes has been deflecting our insistences."

"Now you know why."

Lucas hugged her tighter, and searched her eyes with his. "Kiery, the only proof we have is Gianna's eye. Even if we got a name, no one would remember it to care. It would be meaningless. But Magnes' deflection has caused ripples. There's only one thing we can do."

"Are you asking me if I will die at your side?" Kiery asked him.

"If I fail, you and Gianna will die with me. I believe I can defeat Magnes in combat, but Adrianna will still have the support of others, and we will still die unless... unless something unforeseen happens."

She kissed him warmly, hands shaking as she held his jaw tight. "Howl your challenge, First Beta. I will go with you."

"Will you..." he touched her arm.

She asked, "What happens if we survive? Can you live with your Luna being an Oracle?"

He grimaced. He didn't want to be an Alpha. Lucas pressed his fingertips into the skin. Their star-crossed romance was no secret to anyone in SableFur. The rift between them so large everyone had seen it. "We'll need something else in our favor. It's a fool's errand. We'll die just like Hix died."

"One of my sisters was violated. I cannot allow this to happen, and the one who did it must be held accountable. Gianna has sown the seeds, she has the mark in her eye, the pack wonders and doubts, Hix uncovered the secret in his

Luna's name. Now the Moon needs a champion. And I think you just volunteered." She smiled at him and stroked his cheek fondly.

He slid his hands lower and gripped the edges of her shirt. He pulled upwards. She smiled and raised her hands over her head, letting him strip her shirt.

She sighed and turned her head to the side, exposing the length of her neck, and her shoulder to him.

An intense trembling excitement overtook him, like hot lust, but something else. He gripped her arms instinctively, tightly, pushed his face to her neck and inhaled her scent. The scent that was always in his nose, tormenting him, sweet and alive, and her. No matter how hard he had tried to shove her away when they had reached their impasse, she had never heeded him, and he had never had the strength to do more than push.

He inhaled again.

"Yes," she whispered to him.

He pulled back, and released her arm, drew his fingertips down the smooth skin. Bones elongated, nails into claws, and he slid one claw against her pale skin. A trail of redness bloomed, and a burning, exquisite pain echoed on his own bicep.

"Kiery," he whispered her name as the Moon guided his claw and the bloody pattern bloomed through her skin.

She gasped, then relaxed under his hands as the Bond, so long denied, ripped open between them.

He breathed hard, barely daring to believe it, the Bond pulsed between them, a new, living creature, their fates entwined.

"Take me to bed," she whispered. "If we live long enough, we'll take the vows, but consider it all said and sworn, you stupid First Beta."

"We will start on pups right now," Lucas said.

She laughed, soft but wild. "I am not getting any younger."

"Wonders of wonders, you agree with me for once? The Mark has made you docile."

She shoved him away and stood. "I am going to bed. I'm going to have some fun. If you want to have some fun, you can come along. Or you can sit here and drink away your last night on earth with bad sitcoms."

STAND UP

I t hurt so much to move I had to crawl to the bathroom. I sobbed until I couldn't see.

The contusions on my shoulder and hip, and my aching body and my ripped up hands... none of it was anything compared to the furious, scalding pain burning inside me, eating away at me like an ulcer.

Hix.

Hix was dead.

Stabbed in the back and tied to a post and left to bleed to death in the freezing cold. A warning to anyone else the price for challenging the SableFur.

Hix.

I had failed him. I had been too weak to end his life in the dungeon when he had first arrived. I had believed in happy endings. I had believed it couldn't possibly end like this. I, an Oracle, trained to look upon horrors and truths, had ignored the one in front of me because it was too hard.

And I had failed him.

I lay in the tub and the icy water pounded on me while I whimpered.

I hope for a good death because I have not led a good life.

I'd find a way to honor his life. I vowed that to myself. Avenging him would dishonor him. No Luna avenged a fallen warrior that had died in her service. She *sent* warriors to avenge a wrong against the pack. But I'd find a way to honor his life, and make sure it was known the truth of how he had died, and why. And how cowardly, and pathetic and without honor his death had been.

Adrianna was wrong about Gabel. Gabel, the Gabel he was *now*, wouldn't have executed Lucas that way. He'd have tortured him, made him suffer, maybe executed him quietly, maybe tied him outside and left him to die slowly to see if he'd be broken and start begging, but Gabel would never have stabbed him in the back.

Romero would have stabbed a wolf in the back and laughed, thinking it proved something. The only thing it proved was that wolf's cowardice.

The day after, Kiery came into my room. I hadn't moved—I had been too sick, and in too much pain, and grieving and empty.

"Get up."

"Why?" I asked, at this point believing I was the next to be murdered.

"Aaron is almost here."

"Aaron? Who cares?" I did not care about the IceMaw Alpha's arrival.

"You should," Kiery hissed. "Now get dressed. I'll parade you in front of the dining room."

"What—" She had on a short-sleeved shirt despite the cold, and as she moved, the sleeve rode up to expose the scabbed Mark twisting along her bicep in a tangle of harsh angles and crescents.

Kiery tugged on her sleeve.

"Is it a secret?" I asked her. "Lucas. You let Lucas—"

"It's not a secret. Just habit," she said, a little flustered. "Hurry."

Reluctantly, I sat up, aching in every part of me.

"That looks terrible," Kiery said of my contusions. She unwrapped my bandaged hands. I had been neglecting them, and now my hands were swollen and red and a little yellow-crusty. "Damn, Gianna. You are falling apart."

She stopped me again and looked at my eye.

"Is it still there?" I asked her.

"I don't think it's ever going to leave. You *are* falling apart."

Who cared. Hix was dead. My strangled Bond was killing me, and there was a version of the future where I failed. I was so close to failure it almost seemed pointless to keep fighting.

"Did they take down his body?" I asked, tears brimming again.

"Yes."

"His fangs? Who did it?" I pleaded.

"Lucas took care of it. Hix wasn't de-fanged."

"Stupid Beta. Stupid, stupid Beta!" I whimpered.

"Yes, Betas are stupid," Kiery agreed softly. "Stupid and wonderful at the same time. Hix died serving you, and Lucas buried him with admiration for what he did. He said it was the finest death any warrior could hope for. I'm sorry, Gianna. That's all the comfort I can give you. He died in your name, and he did it gladly."

I sobbed. "There's no comfort in that! Would that comfort you if Lucas died that way?"

"No," Kiery admitted. "It wouldn't."

Kiery pressed her cheek to my forehead, then looked around the mess of a room for something halfway clean to wear. My laundry had been brought to me and I had been ignoring it. She fetched some clothes.

"It's Magnes, isn't it?" she whispered as she wrestled a shirt over my head.

I looked at her.

"Magnes is Gabel's father. All of this leads right back to Magnes," she whispered.

"You can't let Magnes know. He'll kill you."

A grim smile. "Adrianna would kill me first. Magnes is trying to make himself the King-Alpha off his bastard's back. I've seen where he succeeds."

"No." I grabbed her. "No, not you too! Have you seen the crown of bones and blood? The bleeding one with obsidian and tourmaline?"

"No. I've seen a crown made of Gabel's skull, and a scepter made from his arm, and a cloak of Aaron's pelt."

I trembled.

"How do we prove any of this, Gianna? Tell me we have something."

"I only have my eye, and nobody seems to remember the mirror except Anita, who won't talk! It's the only proof we have, but nobody will say who it belonged to! Was Thessa here?"

"She was a child," Kiery said. "It was twenty-seven years ago. The memories are long gone, or buried deep. All the adults are silent. Either they don't know, or they know, and they keep the secret to hide their own shame. No one is going to speak."

I wept.

"I've been trying to figure out how to get rid of Anita and shame her, but she's too clever for that. Magnes will protect her."

"For obvious reasons," I said sourly.

"You got more honesty out of her than I did, but she probably thinks Lucas and I are still on bad terms. Publicly I'm telling Lucas to stay out of it, it's Oracle business."

"That works until people see the Mark on your arm."

"Which is why I'm covering it carefully. Nobody has noticed yet." She shook her head once. "Gianna, there isn't much time. Magnes already suspects Aaron's agenda. That's why he's here. You need to put on a good show to get Aaron out of this."

"Oh yeah, because I feel like making out, Kiery. And I look fabulous, don't I."

"For males, it's the scent," Kiery said. "Looks are secondary. It's all about the scent."

"I bet I reek of blood and grief."

"Lucas and I need a little more time," Kiery said.

"What are you planning?"

"The only thing we've got," Kiery whispered. "Gianna, I'm going to march you sternly past the dining room under the pretense you need to be looked at. Which you do, but it can wait while Aaron fusses over you."

I nodded.

"If he offers to take you with him, accept. I'll vindicate you using your eye as the mark of the Moon's favor. I'll say you satisfied the secret test, I won't need to be more specific. Leave. Quickly. Get away from here. In a few days, I won't be alive to protect you anymore. If you escape with Aaron, you still have a chance of setting all this right."

"Lucas is going to challenge Magnes," I whispered.

"Yes."

It won't work.

And looking at Kiery, she had already seen it wouldn't work.

She put her hand on my shoulder. "I'll vindicate you, you leave with Aaron. He'll take you with him, he'll put the Mark on your arm and make you his Luna within three days. Lucas and I will say what needs to be said, and if you're safe, you might still have a chance of helping Aaron and Gabel *not* end up crowning Magnes with bones."

There had only been one crown, and it hadn't been for a male's head.

"Maybe if I shout it loud enough *someone* will remember and whisper the name to you." Kiery's hand trembled a little bit. She would face her death bravely, but it was still her death.

She swallowed, and then said, "Seek out my family in NightScent. My mother may have a story to tell you. It won't be much, but it might be something. Don't tell them how I died, if it comes to that."

"They deserve to know."

"So tell them I died at my mate's side," she said with a bittersweet, teary smile. "Tell them I died with my mate, the First Beta, and he died a warrior's death, and he died so loved I went with him."

"It will be the truth." I blinked back my own tears. "How long until Lucas challenges Magnes?"

"A few days, if things go in his favor. He's stirring the pot right now, stroking the fires of discontent, as it were."

"If he's a First Beta like Hix, he doesn't know how to keep his opinions to himself," I said softly.

"First Betas *never* do." Kiery smiled warmly, then turned serious.

I swallowed. I couldn't leave. But if Kiery *and* Anita were having visions that Magnes would prevail, and kill not just Gabel but Aaron too, then the future might be in flux, and I was perilously close to failure.

And an Oracle couldn't scry for herself. Anita I didn't trust, but Kiery I did. The only way I could scry for myself was to use the tourmaline to go to the place beyond the Tides, and I didn't have three days to do that. I didn't have the strength left.

Had I failed so dramatically that now the only way left to succeed was leave with Aaron?

There had to be an alternative. There had to be *something*. The Moon would not have marked my eye, given me the tourmaline, and, now that I thought on it, planted the mirror and runestones.

Those hadn't been sitting there for nearly thirty years. The five exact runes I needed, and a piece of a broken mirror? In my vision Gabel's mother had been in wolf-form and fled, she hadn't taken anything with her except the pups. She hadn't even taken her human name.

If the Moon had planted those items for me to find, those *exact* items, then that had to mean there was no evidence left in this world.

And *when* Lucas failed it would make Magnes that much stronger.

My hope flickered. This wasn't going like I had thought it would, although I wasn't sure how I thought *any* of it would go except just... not like this. I had thought the Moon would offer more help, *something*, not just cryptic messages and strange, tiny, ordinary visions mixed with the bizarreness of the place beyond the Tides that I could tell to no one.

I looked at Kiery, focused on her face. "You and I have had different visions."

"For our sake, I hope yours is the right one."

"You know as well as I do there's no such thing. Fine." I sighed to myself. "Parade me in front of the Alphas."

THE BLOOD OF AN ALPHA

"Gianna," Aaron said before he even saw me. "Wait a moment, Oracle Kiery."

"We are expected somewhere," Kiery told him, coldly, from the hallway.

I dredged up the energy to peek around the doorway and look curious about Aaron's presence in the dining room.

"Gianna." Aaron smiled. "You look drawn, beautiful one."

Beautiful? I was so far away from beautiful he shouldn't even have tried. "I told you flattery wouldn't get you anywhere."

Still, I had to flirt with him... sort of. At least that's what Kiery said, and something about it rang true.

"Gah." Kiery threw up her hands. "Fine. I'll be back in ten minutes. Males and their scents."

"We have business to attend to," Magnes told Aaron.

"What business?" Aaron gestured for me to come into the dining room, more interested in me than whatever Magnes was rattled about. Magnes glared at me, but the power of his presence was diluted by Aaron's own prestige.

Aaron stood up very well to Magnes. He had given a good

account of himself against Gabel, and probably would have
fared a little better if he hadn't underestimated him. He could
partially shift, and he had done enough damage to Gabel we
had had to get it treated sooner than later.

Had Aaron really underestimated Gabel, or had he just
wanted to see what Gabel was about?

I didn't believe physically Aaron was any match for Gabel
in war-form, perhaps only Flint was (Flint was beyond terrifying and literally ripped other war-forms into two pieces), but
Aaron was cunning, clever, and ruthless in his own way.

I believed when Aaron said he would never kneel before
another anyone. I wasn't sure Gabel could make himself a
King, but I knew for certain Aaron would never kneel.

Magnes, hands folded on his lap, narrowed his eyes at
Aaron. "The matter of why you didn't attack GleamingFang
when Gabel left it unattended."

"Because it'd be too easy." Aaron gestured with his broad
hands as if it were not even worth discussing. "I have my eyes
on what was MarchMoon. Then I can squeeze GleamingFang
like a boil. I'm not empire-building, Magnes. I'm proving a
point to all of Gabel's thralls: he can be beaten."

Aaron stood and gestured for me to take his chair. I did so,
aware of Magnes studying my altered eye. Aaron leaned back
against the table, hands braced on the edge. "Your eye. What is
that?"

"The Mark of the Moon's Favor." I hadn't been prepared
to answer and just coughed it up. Crap.

"Ah, so you are almost done here? And then you will have
your Oracle title back? Time to move on to your revenge?"

My mouth went dry. "Kiery gets the final say in that."

"Perhaps Magnes summoning me here is most fortuitous.
Regrettably, I am going back to RedWater, which is no place

for you. But I'm certain the wolves of IceMaw's heart will treat you well in my absence."

"Aaron," Magnes lost his patience, "enough. I am not going to sit here and watch you dance and yip around with the scent of a female in your nose. Why haven't you taken March-Moon if GleamingFang isn't to your tastes?"

Aaron smirked like Magnes was an idiot. "Are you *accusing* me of something, Magnes?"

Magnes' eyes hardened, and I quailed inwardly at the brutal cast his features took. Aaron grinned a little wider, *daring* Magnes to come at him, he'd welcome it. Magnes growled, "Should I be?"

"I told you, *I* am not empire-building. Gabel is off exhausting his army on personal vendettas and imagined slights. I'm not going to whip my forces into a froth just to grab at things because they're there. Gabel will come back from Shadowless, be furious I am within earshot, and attack. *My* forces will be fresh, his will be exhausted, and I will run them back to IronMoon's heart."

Magnes' expression twisted into something between a frown and reluctant nod, being forced to accept the validity of Aaron's plan, but he didn't trust Aaron. Nor should he, but the SableFur didn't accept Alphas acting on impulse and instinct.

A critical flaw that Aaron now gleefully exploited.

Aaron continued, "Perhaps I will even kill him, so I can rip off his head and present it to Gianna." He reached out and tilted my chin up to face him, his touch very gentle, but his expression sharp and cruel, thrilled at the prospect of such a violent victory. "The Alpha who, in fact, had no idea what he had, and even less idea how to keep it. Up to and including his very own head."

My skin prickled, and for another terrifying second, the

Bond dropped out of my awareness completely before resurfacing. I whispered, shaken, "You're just as twisted as Gabel."

"No, I am an Alpha, and I *intend* to stay an Alpha. But I notice your first response isn't that you'll refuse my gift, just an observation that I am similar to your previous mate." His grin grew a little brighter. "I did not lie to you, Gianna, but you are lying to yourself if you ignore your nature. How many executions did you watch? How many offerings of blood did you accept from Gabel's hand? How many did you order he bring you?"

I couldn't answer that. The answer wasn't *zero*.

"You are a Luna who knows and appreciates violence, and I, despite my civilized exterior, am an Alpha."

"She is not a Luna," Magnes corrected in a brittle tone.

"Temporary. I will make her one again." Aaron all but purred at Magnes. His fingers left my chin and caressed my exposed arm, which was purple and blue from the spreading bruises. His fingertips found where his Mark would go, pressing in just slightly. "A palette for the future, hmm? I can see the design I will give you, and it is glorious."

I forced myself to not flinch away.

He pulled my shirt's neckline over my battered shoulder. "Such bruising. What happened to you, Gianna?"

"I fell."

"You *fell*."

"No, really. I fell," I said. That was true, and he could tell, which terrified me that he could read me so well. He tried to figure out how I had honestly fallen without being shoved.

"You have only one thing on your mind," Magnes said, irate.

"Of course. Don't you remember what it was like when you caught Adrianna's scent, and she sat and spoke to you, giving you the time of her day?"

"All I smell on Gianna is blood, bruising, pain, and grief."

"I smell those things too. And the Moon, and that she will be mine."

Aaron said that with absolute conviction. He wasn't playing around or saying pretty words. He meant it.

"Aaron. I want you to take GleamingFang or March-Moon," Magnes directed.

Aaron laughed. "I *cooperate* with you when it pleases me to do so, SableFur. I've explained my plan. Do you want Gabel dead or not?"

"I want to know my associates can be trusted."

"Associate. The great SableFur can't utter the word *ally*? What you want of me is what allies do for each other. A favor. A huge one, at that. What will I gain from it? I don't need SableFur. I am dealing with IronMoon myself," Aaron taunted. "I want Gabel dead and his IronMoon de-fanged. If you don't like the manner in which I do it, do it yourself."

Aaron touched my cheek again, fingers trailing over my neck to where the necklace of healed ulcers lay. "Would it please you, pretty wolf, if I brought you the head of the wolf who marked you without consent, humiliated you in every way he could, and threw you away on the words of an oppor-tunistic little SableFur spy?"

When he said it like that... the tears so close to the surface escaped and I closed my eyes, trying to recover my dignity.

It wasn't like that. It wasn't like that.

Even if it sort of was.

My mind showed me again Gabel presenting Gardenia to Anders at dinner, kissing her hand, her arm, flirting with her as he forced me to sit with the dregs of the pack in utter humilia-tion. The agony he had sent through both of us just because he could.

It still hurt *so* much.

And I saw in my mind again Hix carrying her away from my wedding, her screaming and pounding on him.

I choked on a sob.

Hix.

Magnes did not care. Aaron, however, caressed my cheek with his fingertips, a gentle, comforting touch I didn't have the presence of mind to flinch from.

"I'm sorry, Gianna," Aaron said softly.

"Don't be sorry." I rejected his gentleness. "I'm not."

The only thing I was sorry for was I hadn't been able to save Hix. I wasn't sorry about anything else. I wasn't even sorry for sending Gabel to Shadowless. I wasn't sorry for Platinum, I wasn't sorry for Anders, or Marcus, or Holden, or any of them. I pitied the warriors who had died in their service, and I pitied the pups, but I wasn't sorry.

And I wasn't going to be sorry when I exposed Magnes for what he was.

Aaron withdrew his hand. "You do know why Gabel razed Shadowless, don't you?"

"Yes. They came to my wedding and told me. How do *you* know?"

"Gabel shouts his reasons for everything, so of course I've heard. I was just thinking how it's funny everything is a circle." Aaron drew a circle in the air. "The entire reason you're even here at all is that deal Magnes struck with Jermain."

Magnes shot out of his chair and snarled at Aaron.

Aaron shoved off the table and deftly placed himself between Magnes and I. Magnes' face twisted into fury, his scent darkening and burning. "What did you say, IceMaw?"

Aaron gave him a baleful look, but his own body was tense and alert, ready. "Before you start accusing *me* of playing *you*, *you* should think about how you're going to answer to your pack for the games *you're* playing."

"As if you do not have spies of your own, IceMaw," Magnes snarled.

"Of course I do, but unlike you, I don't deny it. And I don't tell packs to let the likes of *Gabel* take one of their daughters as a spy, but don't worry, I'll help get her back—and then *not help them get her back.* You never raised a damned finger to help Shadowless. She was here in SableFur before their final vows. You could have protected her. Shed some damn blood, broken some damn bones, but you didn't. You never intended to."

Blood is what it costs.

Magnes lunged at him with a roar. I scrambled out of the way as Magnes impacted Aaron, and the two smashed into the dining room table.

Aaron's war-form was silvery ice-white, the hair a little longer and giving him a sort of shaggy appearance, and as he moved, the white hairs reminded me of a dusting of snow skimming snowpack in the breeze. Magnes' was smoky grey, and his coat was long in places, but patchy in others, his tough hide revealed.

Like Gabel, but Gabel was a fully-formed, undiluted, nightmare.

Magnes swiped down with a huge, sharp claw, Aaron dodged, ducked, Magnes shattered the dining room table. Splinters flew. I tried to press myself towards the exit. Aaron roared and lunged at Magnes, and the two tumbled into the nearest wall. Clawed feet met the wood and tore up huge planks, and Aaron snapped his jaws. Magnes jerked out of the way, and Aaron got his target: Magnes' upper arm. He bit down, deep, blood squirting and splattering. Magnes punched him, loosening Aaron's jaws enough that he ripped away.

A chunk of his arm came with him. Aaron spit it out. Magnes slashed at his neck, missed, raked Aaron's chest open in large strips. Blood bloomed over his white fur.

I ducked a flying piece of furniture.

More war-forms suddenly burst into the dining room as the SableFur descended onto the scene. They mauled Aaron. Then more warriors appeared and attacked *those* warriors.

"Stop!" I screamed over the din. "Stop it!"

Nobody heard me.

Magnes snaked his claws forward again, then leapt backwards, barking a command for his warriors to break off. Aaron's warriors pursued until a barked command from the IceMaw froze them.

Magnes snorted, still in his hulking war-form. He was huge, and like his son, cared nothing for the blood and injuries. Aaron shook off the brawl, and straightened, seemingly uncaring about his own injuries, and curled his lips back over his fangs.

He melted back into human form, his human body strong and laced with scars.

Aaron snorted once, but also melted back into his own human form. He was carved, chiseled, and I caught myself looking in a way I shouldn't have, so I averted my gaze, which he noticed. "Don't be bashful, I'm not."

"Your arrogance is astounding," Magnes snarled.

Aaron touched the bleeding gashes on his chest, then pointed at the large piece of meat missing from Magnes' arm. "Losing some speed, Magnes?"

Magnes shoved his finger into it, felt around and said, "Not bone deep."

"Alpha?" One of the SableFur warriors asked.

The dining room had been ruined and now lay entirely in shattered pieces and splinters.

"Leave," Magnes told them. "The IceMaw Alpha needed a lesson in manners."

"Is that what I needed." Aaron grinned. "Shall we keep

going then, Magnes? I'm not sure I learned a damn thing, and I don't think you're in a position to make demands."

One of the SableFur, still in war-form, shoved him. Another IceMaw shoved back.

"Enough," Magnes commanded. "Aaron, I want GleamingFang, MarchMoon, or Gabel's hide by the close of the week."

"So you won't leave SableFur to squash Gabel, but you'll come at the IceMaw for *not* doing it? Magnes, if I didn't know better, I'd think you were afraid of IronMoon."

Magnes snarled at him.

Aaron smirked right back. "You won't do a damn thing to do me."

"Consider yourself unwelcome at SableFur until you do what you've been told."

Aaron bristled. "I kneel before no Alpha."

"But I have Gianna," Magnes reminded him, "and if you want her to make it safely to IceMaw, you'll do what I want."

"You wouldn't dare hold her prisoner."

"Of course not. I'm just saying it is a very long trip from SableFur's heart to IceMaw," Magnes said. "Show yourself out."

NO SAND REMAINS

Magnes left the dining room with his warriors. The blood on Aaron's chest trickled down his abdomen, groin, and then his thighs. He didn't seem to care. "Are you hurt?"

"No."

"Well, that got out of control." Aaron gestured to one of the warriors, who left on a missive.

"What did you think was going to happen?" I asked bitterly.

"Oh, I don't know. A shouting match. SableFur warriors don't tend to punch first and ask questions later. They're like rattlesnakes. They give plenty of warning before they strike."

Now Magnes had threatened me and all but put a price on my head, he was on high alert, I had perhaps days. Maybe hours. Maybe not even that. Aaron was right: Magnes couldn't attack IceMaw and not attack IronMoon.

Damn, Aaron was sort of a genius.

Not that it would matter. Lucas and Kiery would move before Magnes... unless Magnes did something to throw Lucas off whatever it was he was going to do.

Aaron took my upper arm. Blood wept out of his chest, but he smelled of triumph, arrogance, and prestige.

It was actually intoxicating, but I was already such a mess that even a whiff of booze probably would have set me flat.

He asked, "Do I get a reward, hmm?"

"What kind of reward do you want?" I asked blankly.

He bent and whispered in my ear. "Invite me to your room."

What?

Confused, it took a moment for it to register.

"We should talk about your upcoming trip to IceMaw," he prompted.

Like hell I was going to IceMaw but... "Perhaps we should."

The IceMaw warrior returned with a bag. Aaron took it. The blood now had met his feet, and he left bloody footprints.

"Don't you want to put on some clothes?" I asked.

"Why? They'll just get bloody."

"You're also naked."

"I know. I will march through the SableFur house in all my naked glory. But I'll bleed on it. Fair trade." He looked down at himself. "Unless you think I'm not worth beholding?"

"Ah..." I had to look him up and down just because he was insane. "Ah... no, well, you're not deformed..."

Complimenting a naked Aaron on his manbits (which was exactly what he wanted me to do) or his strong body (he really was looking for a compliment on the manbits) was *not* what I wanted Gabel to ever hear about me having done. But he was worth being complimented. He was leaner than Gabel, but not by much, just as strong and chiseled, and—

"Not deformed!" he laughed.

I took him up to my room, and he did indeed leave bloody

footprints the whole way, parading himself through the house like he owned it.

He also left footprints on *my* floor. I pointed at my bathroom.

"Talk to me," he said.

I leaned against the door frame while he stood in front of the mirror. He opened the bag and inside was a well-stocked first aid kit, and a few changes of clothes. He examined the slashes while bleeding onto the ugly blue tile floor.

His back was strong, the muscles moving as he worked, and mid-back, right across his spine, were four slash marks. The injury ran from left to right—I could see where the initial strike had carved four trenches into the softness of his torso—and spanned almost the width of his back. Very, very deep, and the scar still pink and angry against his skin. The skin had filled in, and the scar was four raised ridges against the rest of his back. The edges were ragged and torn, burning away from whatever had caused the slash.

It reminded me, in a way, of my old Mark.

Without thinking, I brushed my fingertips along it.

He froze.

"What caused this?" I asked. The cocky Aaron with his cunning fox-like genius had a wound I would have expected on Flint. I examined him up and down, there were more marks on his thighs and shoulders and arms, but nothing like this. On second inspection, the IceMaw Alpha was speckled with scars. But the one across his back held my attention. It was a spectacular testament to something.

His reflection stared at me, unblinking. "My fight to become Alpha."

"It wasn't easy?" Often fights to be named Alpha weren't violent and brutal in established packs like IceMaw. It was more inheritance. An aging Alpha abdicated, or died, and the heir-apparent simply took his spot. There was sometimes some growling and snarling, or a trial by combat, but in an old pack like IceMaw, murderous brutality wasn't one of them. It was ceremonial, perfunctory, nothing more.

Usually.

"My uncle was incompetent," Aaron said with an edge to his voice. "I had to get rid of him. And his two Betas."

I lifted my hand away.

"Silver claw-tips. He did not dig deep enough to get my spine."

"Are you sure about that?" It looked like he had been carved deep.

"He nicked my vertebrae. I feel cold mornings. Why, Gianna, are you asking about my soundness? My fitness to be your mate? Did I not just prove that taking on Magnes?"

"Magnes is at least ten years your senior," I said, rejecting his other questions.

"I sometimes think I may have used up at least twenty years of my life freeing IceMaw from them. Life well spent."

"Why did you overthrow the Alpha?" I asked, voice hushed.

"Not ambition, if that's what you're implying. Incompetence, depravity, and stupidity. No one wanted to deal with him. So I did."

"How long ago? To prove to me you know how to keep what you have."

"Eight years. You do not look well, Gianna. Are they treating you well?"

"I'm just exhausted." Anita had hinted I was paying a price for going beyond the Tides.

"Those bruises are impressive. How did you fall?"

"I was beyond the Tides and fell through a window onto a stone floor."

"And your eye?"

"I have no idea."

He examined the slashes on his chest. He took a small lipstick tube from the bag, twisted it, and ran the pale, clear stick over the gashes. There was the brief scent of burning flesh, and a sizzle. The edges of the wounds curled slightly, but the bleeding began to stop.

"Silver nitrate. A very weak compounding of it. Cauterizes wounds."

"You don't bleed more from it?" I asked.

"Not for use on anything more than superficial wounds, and not a good idea for wolves who are especially sensitive to silver because it will make things worse."

"Sounds useful." I had never heard of it.

"Usually it's more dangerous than useful. But I'm not in my own territory, and don't have time for this bleeding to stop on its own."

He tapped the wounds, then helped himself to my shower. He didn't bother to draw the curtain. I couldn't decide if he was just being the usual Alpha-cares-not-who-sees-I'm-busy-with-important-matters or if he was giving me a peep show. I had other things to worry about besides what water looked like sluicing off his body.

The Moon had lined everything up, I had hit all my marks, survived this long. But now I was out of time. I had passed all the tests, Kiery just had to say so. Silly me for thinking that the tests would point a finger at Magnes. Instead they just sort of waved hands in his general direction.

We'd only get one shot at Magnes, and it had to be the right one, and it had to drop him. It couldn't wound him. He had Luna Adrianna. Magnes had to be *destroyed*, and he had to be hit hard enough the collateral damage would mortally wound his mate.

The surest way for Magnes to defuse this situation would be for him to simply *admit* his past indiscretion, acknowledge Gabel as his son, and take the dishonor. It didn't have to be like this. The admission would knock Gabel back, *hard*. But it would bring the SableFur back to Magnes' hand. Maybe Adrianna would have to repudiate him, but maybe not. SableFur would probably unite under Magnes, and then it would be plain old war for Gabel, and Gabel would have a harder time getting the SableFur throne.

I sighed. "Magnes could make this very easy on himself."

"How so?" Aaron toweled himself off.

"It doesn't matter. He won't."

"No, he won't. He stands to lose too much, and he is making the reasonable gamble he will prevail." Aaron stepped out of the tub, retrieved a change of clothes from his bag and dressed.

Magnes could just make it go away by doing the right thing. Oh, the irony.

Blood is what it costs.

Aaron wasn't quite as tall as Gabel, but was just as solid, the strength radiating off his body, his prestige almost as thick, but without the dark, cruel undercurrent. Where Gabel was a dark, cruel storm, Aaron was cold and spartan, resolute and relentless.

"Leave with me," he said in a hushed voice. "It's over here. Kiery knows it. You've vindicated yourself. Magnes *will* kill you. I saw it, I smelled it. He will take you as he takes a rabbit, even if the kill is messy."

"I know."

"Then leave with me."

"I can't. Things aren't finished here. I haven't come this far to fail."

Aaron gently drew his knuckles along my cheek, caressing

me from temple to chin in slow, tender strokes. "This is over, Gianna, it's not safe to remain."

Aaron's fingers slid under my chin. For a second, his touch tried to pull me to him. I gasped as the Bond slid out of my awareness again, a dead silence, and instinctively flinched away.

He dropped his hand, breaking the connection. "I'm sorry. You're unwell and overwhelmed. Your scent howls to me to— nevermind. It's not an acceptable excuse. I apologize for touching you."

I hugged myself, suddenly cold.

"But say the word," he whispered to me, low by my ear, thrilling my skin and torturing my soul, "and I will make you my Luna."

"I'm not yours," I whispered back.

"You're not Gabel's either. Who is to say you aren't *mine*?"

My whisper shook in my throat, "I say so."

"I could grab you and force the Mark on you, and it wouldn't fester. No one would stop me. Gabel did the same thing, and now you're free, but you'll invite him to put it back on your arm?"

"I'm not yours."

"You're not his either. He repudiated you," Aaron said.

"Our Bond is tied, not severed," I whispered. "The Moon did that Herself so everyone would believe."

"Then that makes it true on some level, doesn't it?" Aaron pressed. "Ask yourself this: if *you* have to invoke the Bond again, will you? Will you make him a King?"

"A King? That has nothing to do with me." I backed up a step to get distance between myself and the strength of his presence.

There had only been a crown for a female.

I trembled.

Aaron shook his head once. "One doesn't chop the head off a serpent without blood spraying everywhere as the corpse thrashes. If you succeed and remove Magnes, you will surely be the one pointing which way that blood sprays. So I am asking you again. Will you make Gabel King?"

"If I tell you I will, will you kill me right here?" I asked.

A sad smile. "You know I won't do that. But I will kill Gabel, and I would spare you going through this pain again, and my having to spend years proving I'm worthy of you."

There had only been the one crown. The crown for a female's head.

"Leave with me. I will take you to IceMaw myself. Let whatever happens here happen. Wash your hands of this. You've set it all into motion, the planets will move through the cosmos without you."

"Gabel will come for me. He will always come for me. He will rip apart the cosmos to find me."

"I'm sure he will, but it doesn't change his mind is gone, and he clings to his sanity by threads. IronMoon will be defeated within a year with or without you."

"Then I won't destroy what's left of him." I was still Gabel's mate by promise, if not by Bond or mortal fact. "Anita and Kiery have both seen a version of the future where I fail, and I know if I leave with you, I *will* fail."

He bent and looked me full in the face, hungering to kiss me and restraining himself with a trembling effort. "You and I will meet again. Forgive me in advance for what I will do to the wolf who has his unworthy claws so deep into your soul. He destroys everything he touches, and I will not let him destroy you."

Deep in my mind, I sensed the Moon turning and moving, sly and almost mocking, but not cruel, as if clouds had finally passed before Her and now the forest before me was better lit.

Fat lot of good that did: I had no comprehension of what I was seeing.

"I am still mated, in my own mind," I whispered.

"But in your heart?"

"Get away from me. Get out! I'm done humoring this! Get out!" I hissed, shaking all over.

He obeyed.

Will you make him king?

ALL MUST BELIEVE

"What have you *done*?" Kiery grabbed me, shoved her face in mine, and hissed, tears brimming high. "I told you to leave with him!"

"I can't," I whispered back. "I can't leave, Kiery. I have to stay."

"You will *die*, you stupid bitch!"

"Have you seen that?"

"The Moon won't show me," Kiery said. "I can barely see, Gianna. It is so dark. Lucas and I are going to die, I can accept that. But *you* have to live. If you stay here you'll die! You are the Balance-Keeper!"

"If I leave, I fail."

"What are you going to do?"

"I don't know," I confessed.

"Gianna, you *aren't* well. You're sick, weak, messed up. You don't know what you're saying. Let me summon Aaron back here."

"No. I have to stay here. The answer is *here*, Kiery! I just have to find it."

"You don't have time," Kiery whispered. "Lucas is going to

call Magnes out in front of the pack for why he refuses to move against Gabel."

I gasped. "He has no proof!"

"Do we have a choice? That's why you have to survive!"

"But I can't leave!"

Kiery rubbed her eyes with her hands. She composed herself, then grabbed my wrist. "Come on."

"Where?" I pulled back.

"To the doctor to get your hands looked at. And then I'm vindicating you."

"What?! No!" I tried to yank away, but her grip was too strong.

"*Yes,*" she snarled. "Whatever is going to happen is going to happen fast. I'm probably not going to be alive much longer, and if you somehow manage to *not* get yourself killed, I want you vindicated."

"Don't say that, Kiery, you aren't going to die." I couldn't handle another death. I couldn't let Kiery die.

"If it makes you feel better, I'd rather not die either." She yanked me after her.

I couldn't let her and Lucas die. I *had* to find a way to save all of us.

Kiery dragged me to the clinic and bullied the unwilling doctor (who didn't like me) into looking at my hands.

I had to look away as he unwrapped them. My hands were still swollen, flushed, the cuts crusty and dry around the edges and some of the stitches had popped again. I hadn't been caring for them properly. Laying in snow and bathtubs and shoving grabby males off me and all. Bad patient I was.

The doctor said, "You have to let them heal. You also have a fever. You have an infection brewing."

Well, that explained why I felt like garbage. Aside from everything else. What had Anita meant about the *hole in my soul?* Did she mean the Bond? Something else? She had implied she knew I was going beyond the Tides, and that I was paying a price for it.

"Do you need to keep her?" Kiery asked the doctor.

"No, you can take her."

The doctor wouldn't have kept me even if I had been dying right in front of him. He gave me a sideways look, wary, noting my altered eye.

"Does it make you nervous?" I asked him.

"No."

Liar.

After that, Kiery took me to Magnes' office.

"Will he even be there?" I whispered to her. "Aaron ripped his arm up."

"Yes. He's seething. We'll have an audience."

"Shit," I muttered. "Kiery—"

"Shut up."

Magnes' office wasn't empty, and it wasn't just him. A seething Luna Adrianna was there, along with Bernhard, and several other SableFur I didn't know. Lucas wasn't present. Was it a good or bad sign that Bernhard was? Bernhard was one of Lucas' allies... unless he wasn't.

Kiery didn't seem shocked Bernhard was there. Bernhard must be the inside man in Lucas' impromptu rebellion.

"Oracle," Magnes didn't hide his annoyance at Kiery's intrusion, or seeing me again that day.

Luna Adrianna gave me a withering look.

I glared right back. That bitch had ordered Hix's execution. I suppressed the urge to growl at her.

I'd be a Luna again soon, and then I'd grind her face into paste.

"We are busy, Oracle," Magnes said. Although his arm was bandaged under his shirt, he didn't move like it bothered him at all. If Gabel was anything like his father, Magnes didn't care about missing flesh, and possibly got off on it.

"This won't take but a moment, Alpha," Kiery said, "and it will be one less thing for you to worry about."

Magnes gestured for her to speak. "Then the floor is yours, Oracle."

Kiery said, matter-of-factly, "Gianna has passed the final test of revealing a secret to me. She told me her intention is to send word to Aaron. She has accepted his offer to visit IceMaw."

What?! No, I hadn't!

It took every shred of my Oracle training to not whip around and throttle her. That and I didn't feel well, and my reactions were dulled.

"How *droll.*" Luna Adrianna clicked her fingernails together.

Magnes cricked his neck one way and eyed Kiery. "So you will swear before the Moon, Oracle?"

"Of course. She has found something hidden, her eye is proof of the Moon's favor, she has predicted events that came to pass, and she has revealed a secret to me. I cannot mention the secret, however."

"So you will never tell anyone the secret?" Adrianna asked.

"It would be a violation of my vows to do so," Kiery said.

Except that's exactly what we were going to do, because it was the Moon's secret, and She had told us we could.

Adrianna clicked her nails together a few more times. She sat on the edge of Magnes' desk, he within reach of her. He glanced at her, then touched her thigh with gentle fondness.

Kiery added, "To be clear, Magnes, I don't need your validation of this, nor Anita's. I've informed you as a matter of courtesy. I have restored Gianna's title and honor as an Oracle.

She will not remain in SableFur longer than is absolutely necessary."

I closed my eyes. It was a profound relief even if it wasn't over yet.

"Aaron is not welcome here at the moment. She will have to travel to him," Magnes said. Adrianna gave me a look of pure venom.

Kiery nodded. "The Oracles will make arrangements for one of our own. I will also see her bowls are supplied to her when they are done."

Afterwards, back in my room, I hissed at her, "What were you doing? I'm not going to IceMaw!"

"Stupid! You can't stay here, and it backs them off you if they think you're leaving sooner than later. Or did you not see that Adrianna wants to eat your liver?!"

"I saw," I said sourly.

"You're an Oracle, Gianna, you've reclaimed your title."

"I want to see Anita's face when she finds out."

"You and I will both have to just imagine the old hag twisting like an rag."

I laughed.

"If we live long enough," Kiery whispered, "one of us will have to do her in, and strip *her* of her title. She's no Oracle."

"She is if she still Sees."

"I don't think she's had a vision in years," Kiery said dryly. "Whatever you are going to do, Gianna, do it quickly. Lucas is pushing to have Magnes held to account *tonight*."

I reached out and clutched Kiery's wrist.

"If we don't meet again," Kiery said, "remember. *You* are the Balance-Keeper. Make this right. Somehow."

She left.

One word, one phone call, one messenger, and I could be

the IronMoon Luna again, or the IceMaw Luna. I could leave this place.

But that wasn't the answer. This had never been about vindicating myself.

I knelt before my tools and picked up my bag of runes. I ran my hands over the lumpy shapes. There had to be an answer. Something I had missed. Some small detail.

I poured out all the stones and examined each one. A few were blank, still the little tourmaline chips that I had brought back from the Rock Warden, not yet carved but had spoken.

Using a nail file, I carved a rune on one of the blank chips: *comet*.

I couldn't scry for myself, but I could pray, and I could meditate, and see what the Tides offered me.

I was back at the grotto at the border of the Tides and the Place Beyond. The RedWater wolves flanked me on either side. I turned around, absorbing it all again. I knew this place. Through the tunnel was the destroyed ancient house, with the pup-ring in the box. Now that made sense: the ramshackle house was Gabel's mother. Her life had been destroyed, burned out, used. The pup-ring had been—or should have been —hers.

Overhead the Moon sailed on, watching with a slitted eye, a waning crescent, just the thinnest sliver before She went dark. The ocean was calm, and the air suspiciously still and thick. Waiting. Darkness, darker than the night around me, waited on the horizon.

The water was so still and quiet it seemed like I could walk on it.

I walked towards the water, seeing the little island curve left and right in a rough arc. A scent caught my nose.

I walked up a tiny bit of rock, and three figures stood on top of the grotto, facing east.

I hurried up the hill towards them.

I approached the three figures: one was me, wearing the necklace of fangs from my first vision for Gabel. In her (my?) left hand was the crown of blood and bone, in the other the still unfinished necklace of obsidian and white quartz. Standing just behind Other Me was Gabel, standing by the arm with the necklace, and Aaron stood on the crown-side.

Gabel had the Comet rune carved into his chest, the skin peeled down to muscle and blood weeping black and thick onto the ground, the rivulet staining my toes as it flowed to the ocean. Aaron had tattoos like Flint's, but they were carved in blood as well, his right arm and upper body entangled with ancient symbols, half of which I did not recognize. On his right arm was a large tattoo gripping the curve of his bicep, an ancient rune I did not know, but that burned at the edges, smoldering and lava-like, while dark blood wept from it. Like Gabel, his blood flowed towards the ocean.

Then they looked at me.

I gasped. They knew I was there!

This was not...

"All must believe," my other self told me. "Even you must doubt. Even you must question. But all must believe."

"Stop saying that!" I yelled at myself.

"All must believe," Gabel told me.

"All must believe," Aaron told me.

"Stop it!" I screamed. "They believe! They believe, dammit! They believe!"

"Do they?" Gabel asked me.

"You know they do," I told him.

"Do you know what they believe?" Aaron asked me.

"All must believe." The other me told me. "Or else it doesn't matter."

"Believe what?" I asked.

"Exactly," Aaron said.

"But—"

Gabel pointed to the horizon. The sliver of the Moon sank towards it, like the downward blade of a scythe. The horizon churned with darkness, punctuated with glimmers of fetid yellow-green-orange lightening.

It brought damnation with it.

I uttered a tiny, terrified mewl, then wretched my gaze away from it.

"All must believe," Aaron said.

I FELL FORWARD onto the little mat, gasping.

The RedWater wolves stared at me.

"All must believe," I whispered to them, heart still thumping from the sudden shove back into the waking world. "How long was I gone? More than an hour?"

A shake of the head.

All must believe. Or else it doesn't matter.

What had they been talking about? It was important. Desperately important. I felt around for my runes and found the one for the comet. I looked at it, frowning. I didn't have much time.

Believe what?

Exactly.

Believe. Faith. Believe.

Everyone had to believe. Believe what? Everyone *did* believe that my Bond had been broken. Even I questioned if it would ever be the same again. I doubted. Mission accomplished.

Believe.

I stared at the ceiling, rubbing the comet rune. The Moon had sent Her Comet to punish us for the collective sins of our kind. She was angry about Alphas like Magnes playing games, wolves who didn't behave the way the Moon had ordained, and Oracles letting themselves be used and not honoring their—

Oh.

I stared at the rune. *Believe.*

I sat up. The Moon wasn't just talking about the *Bond.*

The Moon was talking about *Herself.*

"But if the Moon sent the Comet, why even bother with a Balance-Keeper?" Because it was kind of pointless to just destroy *everything* and punish everyone without explaining why because then nothing would change. If She had intended to destroy the werewolves for their sins why not just let Gabel ravage the countryside? Why involve *me?*

No, there was a point to it. She *wanted* everyone to know about their sins. But if I was the Balance-Keeper, I was in the middle, between light and dark. Gabel was darkness... I couldn't figure out where the light would come. Lucas, perhaps.

But Kiery and I had both foreseen Lucas *failing* to overthrow Magnes. It couldn't be Lucas, and it wasn't me.

The rune on Aaron's bicep. What had it been? Why had he been marked up like a Moon's Servant? Why had he been in my vision at all?

I clutched the rune in my wrapped fingers. I didn't have *time* to puzzle over that. My problem was more immediate.

All must *believe.*

"Oh, by the Moon," I whispered. "If I'm wrong, I'm going to die. Then again... I'm going to die anyway. So does it matter?"

I couldn't let Lucas challenge Magnes. He'd fail, I'd fail, I'd die. Kiery would die. No one would believe. We'd all fail.

I looked at the RedWater wolves, shaking all over, feeling every strand of weakness and pain in my body, how I was threadbare and tired and terrified and grieving. They sat shoulder to shoulder, calm but alert, betraying nothing except that they would go with me.

I set the rune down. I took a breath, then another, then a third.

"An Oracle," I whispered the old, familiar words to myself, "looks at the difficult and terrible. She rides the Tides. She listens to the things that whisper from shadows. She sees the Moon's glory, and the Moon's wrath. She will lay down her soul in her duty."

I was an Oracle, and with that came the risk to my soul, that I would be lost on the Tides.

The Moon called me, and the price I'd pay would be my life, and perhaps my soul.

What I was about to do was within that purview.

I had only the mark in my eye.

It would have to be enough.

STARLIGHT FALLS

That night, Lucas got his way: Magnes needed to explain why he refused to move against Gabel, when it was obvious Gabel needed to be dealt with, and why he had shed blood with Aaron when he had ordered Aaron to deliver Gabel's head. The matter was considered so grave that there was no pack meal that evening.

Word came to my ear that Luna Adrianna, citing the youth of her children, refused to attend, but sent her disdain.

The SableFur had a very large hall at the edge of their heart, like something out of an old saga, complete with carved wolves adorning the walls, and iron chandeliers burning over-head, suspended on long chains from the vaulted ceiling. Tapestries hung on the polished oak walls, and at the end of a long blue runner rug, was a raised dais with two antique wooden chairs.

The SableFur were quite serious when they said their rulers held court. This hadn't changed for centuries.

I squeezed and pressed my way through the crowds. The RedWater wolves sat out on the middle of the carpet, getting a prime view, tails slowly wagging back and forth, ears perked.

The SableFur instantly recognized me as I inched forward, and pressed back to make room for me, more astonished I was present than anything else, and not sure what to do about it, but reluctant to make a scene. The hall smelled of warm metal, tallow, oil, wolf, and extreme anxiety.

Alpha Magnes was in one chair, alert but composed, waiting as the crowd milled about and sorted itself, and everyone settled into position. I managed to secure a spot one person deep, able to peek between the shoulders of the she-wolves in front of me. Magnes' eyes swept over me, his gaze hard, but he otherwise didn't acknowledge me.

My skin twitched, my blood hummed, and spinning in the back of my mind was the Moon, the *knowing* that the Tides pulled us out to sea, and we would either drown, or survive.

Lined up along the runner rug were the ranked members of SableFur able to be present. Lucas and Kiery were already there, Lucas directly at the foot of the dais, and Kiery on the opposite row, standing next to Second Beta Bernhard. She was ghost-pale in the yellow light, her face seeming gaunt with stress, but her resolve wouldn't falter, and her courage wouldn't fail.

She was an Oracle. Lucas was a warrior.

Magnes' blue eyes swept over me again.

If you're scared... good. You should be.

Then Magnes turned his attention to Lucas. He did not stand. "I am here, First Beta. You will excuse Luna Adrianna for not humoring this matter with her presence. You may speak what concerns you."

Lucas separated from the line, entering the empty space on the rug, right in Magnes' line of sight. "Why have you not attacked IronMoon? This morning you shed blood with Alpha Aaron of IceMaw, demanding the IceMaw bring you Gabel's head, but you will not let *me* take our warriors across the border? Why does the IceMaw get this honor?"

Murmurs and nods and growls of agreement. A few warriors howled their desire for battle.

Magnes was unmoved. "As I told you, Lucas, it is not time yet. I do not trust Aaron. We have a fox in the henhouse, and he is a greater threat than that cur Gabel. This is not about Gabel, or the courage of SableFur warriors, this is about forcing the IceMaw to ultimately expose himself."

Magnes had dodged one volley. Lucas clenched his fists and plunged onward, his resolve not wavering. "Who is the Oracle that used mirrors?"

Magnes pulled back, face bewildered, shocked, annoyed. "Are you still on that? I do not know. Anita does not know. No matter how much you shout at her, Lucas, you won't force an old woman to remember something she never knew."

"She *knew*," Lucas snarled, "and she's protecting you!"

There was no gasp. There was just silence as if all the air had been sucked out of the room at once.

Magnes surged to his feet. "What did you say, *Beta*?"

Kiery stepped out of the line and spun to face Magnes. "Anita knows who the mirror and stones belonged to, so do you, and she's protecting you. She confessed that much to Lucas and said she would never reveal the name."

The silence was so complete not even the candles dared to flicker.

Bernhard and the others in Lucas' little group didn't move to intervene or add their voices. Had this always been Lucas and Kiery's plan? To ring the bell, to die for it, and their hope fell to *me*?

I couldn't let them die. I gulped. Stupid, stupid wolves!

Magnes' shoulders clenched under his shirt. "I do not know what you think Anita is protecting me from, but I have never asked her to protect me. I do not get involved with the business of Oracles, Kiery."

"This is SableFur business!" Lucas pointed at Magnes. "Get down here, Magnes! I will not let you destroy this pack!"

The silence shattered as SableFur shouted and howled and stamped their feet, but the howls were shock, or screaming for Lucas to be killed. There were no voices of support.

My heartbeat slowed as my heart pounded, like there was a fist clenching it over and over again.

"Betrayal!" Magnes' roar rose over all of them. "Ambitious, aren't you, Lucas? Did you promise Kiery she'd be a Luna if she'd take your Mark? Is that the only thing worth her giving up being an Oracle?!"

"I have seen your sin, Magnes!" Kiery shouted. "You cannot hide from the Eye of the Moon!"

"You have seen nothing!" Magnes shouted back. "Nothing but what your Lucas *wants* you to see!"

Nobody shouted support for Lucas and Kiery, not even Bernhard moved, *no one* spoke in favor of them. The crowd pressed forward. The senior members pushed back, restraining the furious tide. For now. Kiery glanced back at me, gaunt, pale, terrified, but resolved.

Her lips mouthed one word: *run.*

There might also have been a *you stupid bitch* in there, but that was probably implied.

Magnes raised his hand for quiet, and the crowd settled like snorting, stamping horses, the scent of blood-lust drowning everything else. "So this is how it ends for you, Lucas. You were such a fine First Beta. Until you weren't. There will be no challenge, stupid wolf. Only your death, and that of your beautiful mate. How tragic. You finally convince her to wear your Mark, and she will die by your side. It's sickening."

All must believe.

If I was going to do anything, it had to be now.

Believe.

There was no chance I was going to get out of that hallway alive once Kiery was killed as a traitor. And even if I did, there was no way I'd make it to IronMoon or IceMaw before I was hunted down. Better to just die quick, ripped apart by an angry SableFur mob.

I shoved past the wolves in front of me and onto the carpet. The RedWater wolves padded alongside me, one just under each hand. They were a comforting, if ghostly, presence. Perhaps once I was dead I would run with them.

The crowd quieted, curious, humming with violent intent.

"*Oracle* Gianna," Magnes said. "You didn't take Aaron's offer, hmm?"

"I wanted to see this through," I replied, walking up the runner, shaking inside, but somehow my voice didn't tremble. "I am here in SableFur because the Moon made it so. I have been beyond the Tides, Magnes of SableFur, and the Moon has shown me your sins. I have seen the secret Anita keeps. The reason you won't attack IronMoon. The reason no one remembers the Oracle of Mirrors."

The crowd snarled like a single, large beast.

"Have I not proven myself?" I asked them. "Have I not found your lost items? Did I not predict when debts would be paid, or not? Did I not find that which had been lost, and do I not have the Moon's Mark within my eye? Did First Beta Hix not prove to you your Alpha deals in cheap spies and even cheaper pettiness to disgrace Lunas and Oracles?"

Snarls.

I nudged Lucas and Kiery aside, so that I was ten feet from Magnes, which was, honestly, *way* too close. He could spring on me and have me dead within seconds. "I was sent to SableFur by the Moon to destroy you, Magnes. I have seen what you have done. You know who that mirror belonged to, and so does Anita, and so does Luna Adrianna."

"You have seen *nothing*, Gianna."

"Look at my eye and tell me I have seen nothing! Tell me the Moon has not marked me!"

Magnes snarled at me, an Alpha's threat. A threat that meant death for one of us.

But it had no effect on me. None.

Instead, I snarled back.

A ripple went through the crowd.

"Be silent and speak no more," Magnes commanded.

"I claim the right to speak as an Oracle and reveal what I have been shown!" I shouted. "You cannot take that from me, Magnes!"

Bernhard spoke for the first time, calm in the storm, "She must be allowed to speak."

"She will speak nothing of consequence!"

"Then it does no harm to let her speak," Bernhard replied. "You cannot deny an Oracle the right to reveal what the Moon has shown her. She has vindicated herself, and even if Oracle Kiery's honor is in doubt, there is no arguing with Gianna's eye. Gianna is an Oracle. She will speak."

"Are you afraid, Magnes?" I smirked at him.

"No," he said coldly. "I am *impatient*."

I judged the distance between Magnes and I again. I took a breath, then plunged forward. "You are Gabel's father."

The crowd, once again, went dead silent.

"You lured his mother to the grove where I found the mirror. You coerced her, had your fun, and when she came up with a litter of your bastards in her belly, you drove her away. Anita hid your secret, as did Adrianna, and hid your unsavory tryst from the pack. You are Gabel of IronMoon's father, and the father of an unknown number of other pups who perished in the forest where he was born.

"You feel no paternal devotion to your bastard pup. You merely are waiting for him to conquer the east and the south, then you will swoop in, defeat him, and crown yourself King-Alpha with his and Aaron's bones. Why be the conquering monster when you can be the conquering hero?"

I took a step forward, the silence bent entirely towards me, everyone listening, horrified, stunned, not believing, terrified. "The Moon has seen. Aaron saw right through you. Oh, you're right about him. He's been playing you like a cheap, pathetic pawn, and I've been using the Moon's gifts to relay to Gabel your every move. I never predicted where Gabel would be. He *told* me, or I told him where he needed to be. And now, Magnes, I am here to send you to the Hounds. You just made things so much easier by foolishly letting Anita take the bait Lulu offered. You brought me right to your heart."

Magnes laughed, "Is that a *challenge*, little Oracle? You, challenging me? What makes you think you have a chance in a trial by combat?"

I didn't have a chance, but that wasn't the point. "You are unworthy to lead, Magnes, and the Moon has sent me to remove you."

"And why not just blight me Herself? This is all very amusing, Gianna, but obnoxious. You will never beat me, little Oracle, and even if you did, SableFur will never follow you. Adrianna is their Luna. Not you."

"Adrianna knows your crimes. She is a party to them. She is just as guilty, and your two sons cannot inherit."

"I am guilty of nothing, and if I was, I would never share my guilt with my mate, and risk her or our sons. You come for my *family*, little Oracle?"

"She knew every wolf who was here in SableFur. An

Oracle disappearing suddenly would be noticed. Oh, she knows, Magnes. I *know* she knows. Her claim to the throne is invalid because of her crimes, as is your sons'!"

"I am going to enjoy ripping your eyes out," he snarled at me, "and being done with Gabel's rabid bitch."

"I am your daughter-in-law, and he is your son."

"I am guilty of *nothing*, and he is *not* my son."

He stepped down off the dais, clothing ripping and stretching as he melted into his war-form. I had no choice, I'd have to meet him in war-form. I had challenged him.

"No!" Lucas shouted, "Not her!"

Believe.

The RedWater wolves shimmered brightly, like starlight touched the end of every hair on their bodies as they reshaped into ghostly war-forms made of starlight and ice.

Okay, I was about to sound crazy, but in three more steps, I was going to sound like a gurgling dead corpse, so who cared?

"I name my champions!" I shouted.

The RedWater wolves lunged forward, starlight-white forms solidifying into corporeal bodies, tips of fur glowing like a thousand stars, and they howled a bell-like cry that dropped half the hall to their knees.

The starlight wolves descended upon Magnes, consuming his dark form with snarls and starlight-tipped claws that melted and burned his skin as they pierced him.

Blood splattered the carpet, the dais, me, the wolves, every-one, *everything*, as the wolves tore Magnes into pieces.

Magnes, to his credit, did not surrender, nor howl in pain, but fought, biting and snarling and he succeeded in flinging one off him into the crowd. That one lunged back into the fray as his companion sawed off Magnes' arm and flung it away in revenge.

The second wolf grabbed Magnes' maw, snapped it open,

then twisted. The touch of the starlight claws melted Magnes' fangs, and the liquid tooth dripped from his ruined jaws.

Then, it was over.

Magnes' mangled body lay in pieces on the ground, and in front of me were two starlight war-forms.

The silence in the Hall was complete.

The ghosts stepped forward, blood sliding away, leaving their forms unmarred and untarnished.

I hadn't been able to save all the RedWaters from Gabel's unjust punishment, but these two... these two I had saved, and they had agreed to serve the Moon's purpose, and stay at my side. A little bit of light on that side of the scale. I smiled, knowing I would never see them again, and that when I returned to my room, their fangs would be gone. The Moon would claim them for Herself, and these two wolves would go to their reward, their souls safe forever.

"Thank you," I told them. "Your souls can rest now."

They bowed to me, and transformed into wolf-form, and bolted out of the hall, howling a song of honored farewell and joyful thanks.

I dropped my head and stood, shaking.

It was over.

Magnes was dead. Destroyed. Dismantled. His broken, smoldering, mangled remains strewn in a pile on the runner, everything soaked in black-red blood, the scent of bowels and death and bone thick in the air.

He was worse than dead. His fangs had been taken by the Moon Herself, turned to a strange, foul-smelling yellow-white liquid that burned through the carpet and now, as I watched, burned through the wood floor.

Lucas pointed at Magnes' remains. "Bernhard. Find someone to clean that up."

Kiery broke from Lucas and returned to her place in the line, and Lucas to his.

I raised my head, weary, done.

Lucas, however, gestured to the dais, to Luna Adrianna's chair. "Luna."

BOOK 3: ICE & IRON

WILL YOU MAKE HIM KING?

Adrianna has fled with her two sons to the north of SableFur, vowing to take revenge on those who betrayed her, and secure a future for her sons. Gabel marches on SableFur's heart, sworn to reclaim what belongs to him: his birthright and his mate. Aaron has vowed he will call no wolf King.

With a fresh Mark etched into her arm, and a secret that will be unravelled at Beltane, Gianna must decide who will wear the crown... and who will die.

Available now!

ABOUT THE AUTHOR

Merry is an independent author living in the Napa Valley of California with her husband and two cats. She enjoys coffee, combat sports, casual games, and low budget disaster flicks.

————

www.merryravenell.com
(freebies, festivities, oh my!)

Follow Merry on BookBub

————

ALSO BY MERRY RAVENELL

The Breath of Chaos Series
Breath of Chaos

Bound By Chaos

Chaos Covenant - *2020*

The IronMoon Series
The Alpha's Oracle

Iron Oracle

Ice & Iron

Obsidian Oracle - *2020*

The SnowFang Series
The SnowFang Bride

The SnowFang Storm - *2020*

The NightPiercer Saga
NightPiercer - *2020*

Other Titles
The Nocturne Bride

On The Bit

Mirsaid

APPENDIX

IRONMOON

Gabel, Lord-Alpha
Gianna, former Luna, Oracle
Flint, Master-of-Arms, Moon's Servant
Hix, First Beta
Eroth, Second Beta
Romero, Second Beta (deceased)
Ana, veterinarian (human)
Donovan, Hunter
Gardenia, unranked (deceased)
Violet, unranked
Brian, cook

SABLEFUR

Magnes, Alpha, Gabel's father
Adrianna, Luna
Kiery, Elder Oracle (primary)
Anita, Elder Oracle (retired)
Lucas, First Beta
Bernhard, Second Beta

Lulu, Hunter

ICEMAW
Aaron, Lord-Alpha
Carlos, First Beta

SHADOWLESS
Jermain, Alpha (deceased)
Rogan, First Beta, Gianna's father (deceased)
Amber, warrior

MARCHMOON (destroyed)
Holden, Alpha (deceased)

REDWATER
Marcus, Alpha

GLEAMINGFANG (destroyed)
Anders, Alpha (deceased)

Other Minor Packs
EmeraldPelt
NightScent
SpringHide (destroyed)
SaltPaw (destroyed)
RockTail (destroyed)

Printed in Great Britain
by Amazon

18194380R00192